W9-BWM-117

BEYOND
THE
OUTPOSTS

*Also by Max Brand
in Large Print:*

The Border Bandit
Clung
Dr. Kildare Takes Charge
The Lightning Warrior
Murder Me!
Outlaws All
Rippon Rides Double
The Wolf Strain
The Hair-Trigger Kid
The Longhorn Feud
Fighter Squadron at Guadalcanal
The Black Rider and Other Stories

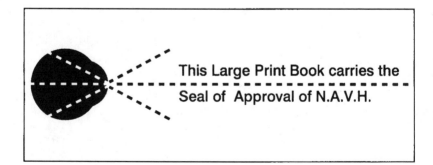

BEYOND
THE
OUTPOSTS

MAX BRAND

Thorndike Press • Thorndike, Maine

The name Max Brand™ is a registered trademark with the
U.S. Patent and Trademark Office and cannot be used for
any purpose without express written permission.

Published in 1998 by arrangement with
Golden West Literary Agency.

Thorndike Large Print® Western Series.

The tree indicium is a trademark of Thorndike Press.

The text of this Large Print edition is unabridged.
Other aspects of the book may vary from the original edition.

Set in 16 pt. Plantin by Al Chase.

Printed in the United States on permanent paper.

Library of Congress Cataloging in Publication Data

Brand, Max, 1892–1944.
    Beyond the outposts / Max Brand.
      p. cm.
    ISBN 0-7862-0768-X (lg. print : hc : alk. paper)
    1. Large type books.   I. Title.
    [PS3511.A87B48 1998]
     813'.52—dc21
                                         98-24822

BEYOND
THE
OUTPOSTS

Prologue

Books are queer things, mostly written by people who want to show how many ways they can tell a lie. Scratch a writer and you'll find a liar every time. As old Chief Standing Bear used to say: "A man cannot work in two ways. He must live by his hands or by his tongue. Talk is for squaws, my son."

But every white man, including me, is half squaw, and that's why I'm writing this book. Partly, too, because a good many things I've done have been misunderstood. Everything that I put down here is fact, and I hope the doubters will come to me for the proofs. That includes you, Chuck Morris. All that I write is the truth and only half the truth, at that, because how can Indians and the prairie be packed into words?

Now that I've said this, I suppose that I'd better start in the usual way.

Chapter One

WILL DORSET'S RETURN

When a man writes of his own life, he generally begins with the house in which he was born and goes back to the list of his ancestors — modestly, of course, and by a sort of inference. For instance, in furnishing the hall he cannot help mentioning that the clock was given to the family by his father's dear friend, the Duke of Abercrombie, or that the basket-hilted sword that hangs from the wall was won by his great-grandfather, Sir Ernest, at Colloden. He goes on in this way until the reader, unless he is a born fool, has to guess that there is the blue blood of an old nobility in the veins of the writer. I confess at once that my family never had a coat of arms. If it had, my grandfather, Tom Dorset, would have traded it for one dram of whiskey, and, for another dram, he would have thrown in the whole family tree. As for the house in which I was born, I cannot remember it, because to celebrate my birth there was such carrying on that the house caught fire and burned to a cinder. They carried me, squalling, I suppose, out of the room where I lay just as the ceiling began to smoke, and so I had my first sight of the open sky that I have loved so much from that day to this. My poor mother was taken out next, and she died the following day of the shock.

My father decided the house must have been set on fire by our old enemies, the Connells. He was a silent man who did most of his talking with his hands, after the way of Standing Bear, the Sioux chief I would come to know. This time he simply took down the rifle from the wall and went out with his dog to find a Connell or two, just as another man might have started out to hunt coons. He was too lucky, you might say, because, when he found one, he found six, and all fighting men. He gave them warning and got behind a tree. Take it all in all, that was about as sizable a little battle as a man would care to mix into on a summer day. My father, Will Dorset, killed Jerry Connell first — then Peter and Jasper. After that the other three shot him to pieces and left him there for dead. The sheriff came along a little later and gathered him up.

Of course, it was taken for granted that he would die, but he had a way of disappointing people. He got well, and then nobody knew what to do with him. He had killed three men, but, when the odds are six to one, you can't call it murder — at least not in Virginia. Everyone was puzzled by the case and, when the case was tried, the judge was no exception.

It was hard to catch a Connell for testimony at that trial because they had three good reasons for wanting to see Will Dorset set free. And those three reasons were their three dead men. They didn't want Virginia law at all. They wanted to use Connell law on him, just as he had used Dorset law on their dead men. Besides, if he were set free, it would open up the entire feud and keep everyone amused for a long time. They could go after Uncle Abner. They could even go after me, because in a real hundred-per-cent feud age doesn't count. I was pretty small, but a life is a life. The Indians feel the same way about scalps, so I suppose that it's human nature. If Father were hanged or put in prison, that ended things.

No one wanted to see Will Dorset hanged, and no jury would have called him guilty if it hadn't been for the judge. He said something had to be done, and he promised the jury that, if they would find Father guilty, he would see that Will Dorset didn't hang. They all said guilty after that, and the judge turned right around and sentenced him to life imprisonment! It was a mighty poor decision, as anybody can see, and that judge was so unpopular in Virginia afterward that he couldn't have been elected dog catcher in our county. However, that didn't prevent Father from going to prison, and it didn't help me, because it gave Uncle Abner Dorset a sort of whip hold over me. He could always tell me that I was bad by nature and bad by inheritance from my father who was rotting in jail. My Uncle Abner could do more harm with his tongue than any other man could do with a blacksnake whip.

Not that I can claim that he was wrong, and that I was good. But I've noticed that there's usually something to be said on both sides of every question — even for Indians, in spite of the bloodthirsty fools who say that the only good Indians are the dead ones. Since I'm limited to the facts, I have to admit that I loved trouble from the time I could walk. I have an idea that most good boys are weaklings. I was strong. I had to be strong or else die young from the life that Uncle Abner made me live, because he started me in at a man's work when the plow handles were as high as my chin. It was rough work and hard work. Perhaps it made me a little smaller than I might have grown, but it kept me compact and tough and limber. From as early as I can remember, I have had more strength in my arms and hands than other boys, or other men.

Let me say right here that strength has nothing to do with bulk. I've never stood more than five feet and ten inches, and I've never weighed more than a hundred and sixty-five pounds, but I've never found a man who could put me down, not even Chuck Morris, of whom I guess you all have heard. I hope this doesn't sound like boasting, but you have to start with this understanding of me in order to appreciate all of the things that happened. And I attribute my strength entirely to the tremendous work that my uncle made me do. It would have killed most boys or wrecked them. But I was too mean to die. In addition to strength I had to have a quick eye and a quick foot because, when anything went wrong, Uncle Abner never asked questions. He simply came to me and threw the first thing that he put his hands on. Once it was an axe that cut a gash across my head. Once it was a big hunting knife that just missed me and clipped a little notch out of my right ear.

Every time I touched that nick in my ear, I couldn't help remembering I led the life of the hunted around my home, and, therefore, it was my right to hunt others just as

I was hunted. That was boy logic, even if it was bad logic. I started after the white boys in the neighborhood, naturally. Sometimes they won, and sometimes I won, until I was about fifteen and had my full weight together with a good deal of my settled strength. After that, things always went my way, and finally the fathers of the white boys called on Uncle Abner and told him that their sons would carry guns from that time on.

I had to turn my attention to the Negroes. This was away back before the war, and perhaps some of you who live in the North and never understood Negroes and never will, might wonder that slaves would stand up to a white boy. They wouldn't, if the white boy was the son of some rich plantation owner. But I was out of blood, only a step or two above white trash. Those slave boys had to work almost as hard as I did, and they were as tough as leather. However, fire will burn through almost anything, and I was fire in those days. Eventually they never went out to play or hunt except in bands of five or six, and I found ways of plaguing even groups like that.

Altogether, I have to admit that I was a thoroughly bad boy. About once a week Uncle Abner cornered me and gave me a hiding with his blacksnake whip. I used to fight back until he knocked me out. He was like my father — a giant of a man — and I still lacked a man's hardened strength.

There were some pleasant times that had nothing to do with fighting. The best were the long winter evenings when Aunt Agnes taught me my lessons. She was a lean, withered woman with a long, skinny neck. Books used to fire her eye, and she managed to get me interested. I worked hard, partly because I felt that one way of getting free from Uncle Abner was to learn enough to fit myself for a better way of living. But I was never meant for a life indoors, and, even when the whole countryside was crusted over with snow, I found enough mischief outdoors to keep me busy.

In the spring of my sixteenth year I felt that I was close to manhood and decided to run away, and I did. Uncle Abner, however, had no mind to give up a strong hand who worked on worse food than a slave could exist on and who never had to be paid. He caught me ten miles from home. We had a grand fight while it lasted, but he finished me with a blow from the butt end of his big whip. Then he tied my hands behind my back, tethered me to the pommel of his saddle, and drove me home like a horse. Every few steps that whip sang behind me and cracked across my shoulders. It was as long a ten miles as I ever walked. But I set my teeth and made up my mind the next time I would get away and leave no trace.

That night I went to bed early, but on my heap of straw in the attic I couldn't sleep. The whip cuts across my back were too sore. I lay there, turning and twisting, until I heard Aunt Agnes go to bed. Uncle Abner was busy repairing a broken yoke, and he was still up when someone knocked at the front door. It opened, and a gust of wind sneaked up into the attic through the open trap door. Then I heard Uncle Abner shout out: "Will!"

I heard a big voice answer: "Well, Abner, here I am!"

"Are they after you?" asked Uncle Abner.

"I suppose they are," said the big voice. "I'm not here for long. Only stopped off to see how the boy is comin' on."

I knew it was my father. I knew he'd escaped from prison. And I was so excited that the cuts across my back stopped burning. I wriggled over on my stomach and looked down through the trap door, and I saw the biggest man I've ever laid eyes on, except Chuck Morris. He wasn't actually any taller than Uncle Abner, and I don't imagine that he weighed many pounds more, but bigness isn't in pounds. He looked like a man chopped out of raw rock. He sat by the fire with his big, ugly head dropped on one fist, and that fist looked strong enough to knock down an ox.

Chapter Two

TROUBLE IN THE SHACK

It was like seeing a ghost turned into flesh and blood. I'd heard so much about Will Dorset and heard him put into the past tense so often I'd almost forgotten that he was still alive. Only at Christmas time Aunt Agnes always made up a package and sent it to him. The rest of the year he was dead. Now that I saw him before me, I could understand everything that I had wondered at before — why he had killed three men out of the six before the last of the six had been able to down him — and why people in that part of the country always used to say of a powerful man: "As strong as Will Dorset." He was the sort of man that one picks out of a thousand — or a million.

"Now where's it to end?" asked Abner, standing up and looking down in a helpless way at my father.

"Get me some food," commanded my father. "I haven't had a bite for forty-eight hours."

One could believe it, too, seeing the

amount of cold pork and cornbread and milk that he swallowed while Uncle Abner told him how things were.

"I've been doing all that a man could do for any son of his own," said Uncle Abner, "but your boy is turning out wild, Will. Mighty wild."

"I'm glad of it," said Father. "I hate a mealy-mouthed mama's boy. I want a man for a son. Is he a man, Abner?"

"Watching him grow up and caring for him has made an old man out of me before my time, Will," said Uncle Abner.

My father raised his head as he finished eating and gave Uncle Abner a queer look, which made me guess that Will Dorset was nobody's fool. "You look able to stand up and take care of yourself," he said. "How big has he grown?"

"Small," said Uncle Abner.

"Small? That's bad."

"But tough, Will. Tough as hickory."

"Well, that's something. I'll have a look at him after a time."

"Are you taking him along with you?" asked Abner, very anxious.

"Not I. Take him along with me? The way I travel and the life I live from now on would kill a dog . . . even if I get away from them."

"Are they close after you?"

"I don't know. Two of them came up with me at Glendon. I knocked their heads together and came on."

"Glendon! Then they'll guess you're heading for home. They'll spread the news. . . ."

My father frowned at him. "Those men are dead," he said.

Uncle Abner coughed like a man half strangled. "Dead," he echoed. "If you're caught here, then. . . ."

"The devil, man," said Will Dorset. "Stop that talk. I know you, Abner, as well as you know me. Let's tell the truth and listen to the devil groan."

Uncle Abner bit his lip. "I have a horse you'd be welcome to, Will, if you want to start right on. . . ."

"Horse? I know your horses. They wouldn't stand up under my weight. It takes a mean man to make one of your horses walk a mile. I've used spurs on your cattle before, and I'd rather walk. Life isn't that dear to me. It's kind of you, Brother, but I'll trust to my own legs. Now tell me how your luck has been. I've had few enough letters from you."

"I've been working day and night like. . . ."

"Don't whine. I hate a whiner, you know. Well, let the letters go. What I want to know about is the money. I suppose you've used it?"

"I had to, Will. I had to. With another mouth to feed in this family. . . ."

"Haven't you been able to get any work out of the boy?"

"Quicker to do things myself," said Uncle Abner. "A lot quicker. Maybe a harder man and a sterner man would have got work out of him, but I never could stop remembering he was your flesh and blood. I was too tender with him, and I started him in lazy habits, I'm afraid."

"He's been useless, then?"

"Worse'n that. Much worse."

My father yawned. The wind cuffed the door and rattled it so that Abner Dorset jumped as though a voice had shouted at him. But my father gave the door not a glance.

"I think that's a lie," he said. "I know your tenderness. I remember it pretty well when *I* was a boy and a younger brother."

"A lie," said Abner with a dark look, "is a pretty dangerous thing to give, even to a brother."

"Now you talk like yourself," said my father, nodding. "You haven't changed much. Well, the thousand dollars is gone, then?"

"Soaked up long ago . . . long ago. Agnes

could know when we had to spend the last of it on clothes and shoes for your son. But I've forgot, it was so long ago."

At that, I laid hold of the rags that clothed me and felt my rage and hate, bursting in my throat. But still I waited. I did not want to appear until a crisis came.

Uncle Abner seemed none too pleased by the talk about money. He hurried the conversation off in another direction. "But where do you aim to go, Will?"

"West," said my father. "West, man, where old lives are forgotten and new lives are being lived. I'm going out where there's elbow room. I was never meant for this crowded country."

My heart jumped at that. A dozen times in my life I had talked with hunters from the mountains who had been west of the Mississippi, or who had heard tales from their friends about the prairies. I had in mind a vague picture of the bison of the plains and of how the Indians hunted them. To me the very word *prairie* was like a hint of heaven.

"It sounds like a good idea. Your trail would be lost there without much trouble."

"Perhaps it would, but for the West a man needs some sort of equipment . . . horses, guns, traps, and what not. A trader needs capital. That's the main reason that has brought me here."

I saw Uncle Abner's face change color. "I suppose you do," he said in a weak voice.

"Now," said Will Dorset, "I left you a thousand to put into your farm or keep for my boy, just as you pleased, and I left you another five hundred to be kept in hard cash, ready at all times in case I might ever need it. You remember you agreed to that?"

"I remember," said Abner, "I agreed under the condition the boy didn't cost more than a thousand. . . ."

"You agreed," cut in my father, "with no conditions. But now that I've come for the money, you'll tell me that you had to spend it on him?"

"A hundred dollars a year," said Uncle Abner in a fumbling voice, "isn't much to spend. . . ."

"A hundred dollars a year!" cried my father, standing up. "Why, your whole family lives on less than that, and always has, while you, like a miser, count up the pennies. You've taken that money, then?"

"Will," said my uncle, "I want to be calm and talk. . . ."

"I want money, not talk. Will you get it for me?"

"Whatever I have. . . ."

"Two hundred dollars. I'll compromise for that amount."

"Two hundred dollars! What little I have is tied up. . . ."

"By the heavens," said my father, "I don't believe it. Yonder in that old chest you used to keep spare cash, and a good deal of it."

Uncle Abner turned white. Then he raised his hand. "Listen," he said, and off through the night we could hear the baying of bloodhounds in a deep chorus. "They've put the dogs on your track, Will!"

"Damn the dogs," he said. "What I want and what I'll have is a sufficient supply of cash, and you'll give it to me. That chest. . . ."

"You're wrong, Will."

"You fool, I've seen you put money into it myself, when you thought I was sleeping on the far side of the room. I'll have a look at it now."

He started forward, and Uncle Abner, with a wild cry, snatched up a rifle. He had not time to get to the trigger. But he used it as a club. It was an old-fashioned, heavy gun, and Uncle Abner, as I've said, was a giant. But it seemed to me that my father put aside that blow as if it were delivered with a feather. He stepped in and struck with that knotted fist, and Abner slumped down against the wall.

There was a big maul nearby, used for driving posts and all manner of heavy work. It had a twenty-five pound head, but my father lifted and whirled it as though it were nothing. At the first blow the lock on the chest bulged. At the second it snapped, and the lid of the chest heaved open.

Inside there was a litter of papers and books and small boxes. Among the latter my father worked. He did not pause to unlock them. He simply crushed them in his great fingers and broke them open as I could have broken kindling wood. At last he jumped up with a shout, and there was a little time-soiled canvas bag in his hand.

"Good bye, Abner," he said. "This will do for me."

I shouted with all my might as I saw him going for the door: "Father! Oh, Father!"

But just then, as I jumped through the trap door, the wind came fresh, and the whole chorus of the big hound pack boomed and crashed around the house and drowned my voice. I saw Father tear the door open and leap out into the darkness. I tried to follow him, but a long arm reached out, a big hand caught me, and dragged me back. Uncle Abner had recovered his senses in time to make at least one arrest.

Chapter Three

YOUNG DORSET'S ESCAPE

I remember, in a wild yarn Aunt Agnes once read to me, there was an account of how a fisherman in a small boat was surprised at his lines by a white, slimy, greasy arm that writhed like a snake over the edge of his craft and fixed itself upon him by means of suckers. How he pulled against that flexible arm, and how his effort simply made the arm grip deeper, burning the flesh that it touched. How another arm came to join the first, wrapped about his body, and drew him to the gunwale over which, staring down into pale green surface water, he saw a flat, shapeless face with two huge saucer eyes. Toward that shadowy creature the arms were drawing him. He had one hand free. With it, he seized upon a wide-bladed hatchet that was near and hewed at the creature's limbs, and other arms were flung out to aid the first crippled ones.

Such a nightmare of fear came writhing up in me while I listened to that story that I had jumped to my feet and shouted: "Aunt

26

Agnes! Did the devilfish get him? Don't read any more . . . just tell me!"

It was a horror somewhat like this I felt when the great hand of Uncle Abner seized upon me and dragged me down to the floor. I writhed in his grip. I smashed at his face. It was like striking at a stone image. What was my boy's might compared to his seasoned power? He crushed me in his arms and sneered down at me.

"They'll get him. You rest easy, son. They'll get him. This time it'll be hanging, and no doubt about it. He's left dead men behind him on his trail, the fool."

I remember feeling then, in spite of my fury and my hate and the exquisite agony of my desire to get out to my fleeing father and help him against the posse, that if Uncle Abner killed a man, the outer world would never have a chance to learn of it. He would accomplish the most terrible of crimes not boldly, face to face as my poor father had done, but by stealth and from behind. No one would know. And the next Sunday he would be praying with the loudest voice in the church.

I had such a loathing for the man come upon me, I could only bow my head and submit to his grip. In the meantime the hunt reached the little house and roared past. I heard the beating of the horses' hoofs and the shouting of men, making a great undertone beneath the clamoring of the dogs. It seemed a fitting thing to me that such a man as my father, having gone on his way through the country, should drag behind him a wake of this sort, full of hatred and blind fury. I remember that I rejoiced because of the greatness of his strength — because to a boy nothing seems really worthwhile but strong hands and a stout heart.

When the leaders of the hunt had poured past, some of the tag-enders kicked open the door of the house and lunged in upon us. There must have been a score of men who swept around the shack and searched every cranny in it. Heaven alone could tell how many men had gone ahead with the main body of the hunt. Virginia has always loved the chase, whether of beast or of man. And the pursuit of my father was not that of some cowed slave, but of a whole-hearted man who could strike in his self-defense, as Will Dorset had already done and left blood behind him.

The men who rushed into the house showed me the most demoniacal faces I had ever seen. I was filled with terror. They stormed through the building. They herded my Aunt Agnes out into the one big room with the rest of us. They even tore up the flooring and went into the dark little cellar in their hunt for the lost man. They reminded me of nothing so much as of ferrets, red-eyed with the blood lust, blind to greater dangers.

I had always thought of myself as brave, even very brave. I had wondered what danger in the world could unnerve me and make me helpless, as fear made some boys when I attacked them — turning them into hulks to be pummeled or booted about at my pleasure. But I understood now what it was. I was sick at the stomach and dizzy of brain, so great was my fear. One of the biggest, a brute with an unshaven face and little pig eyes, glittering with excitement, caught me by the nape of the neck and wrenched me out upon the floor of the room.

"Here's the little Dorset, and, by the heavens, he'll grow up like the big ones! If I had my way, I'd take 'em, old and young, and stretch their necks. They'll never come to no good. Little that they'll ever do for the world."

By his looks, but more by what he had to say, I knew that this was a Connell. Another from the crowd caught at my shoulder and wrenched me around.

"Hey, you young vermin," he shouted,

"has your pa been here? D'you hear me?"

I was too sick with fear to speak. I could only stare at him. My throat was as dry as though a handful of sand had been poured down it.

The man drew back his fist and struck me in the face. "There's the Dorset blood for you," he said. "Wild horses couldn't draw out of him what he knows about his clan."

There was one place where fear was given all the credit that could have been offered to courage. They turned on Uncle Abner then, and he talked freely enough. What he said was a mere tissue of lies. Partly, I suppose, he wanted to win the favor of the crowd by showing that he was very little of a Dorset, at the best. Partly, too, he wanted to prevent the return of my father, because he feared further claims made on that stolen money which he — the hypocrite — claimed had been spent upon me. At any rate, he told them freely that my father had been there, stated that he himself, at the point of a gun, had been forced unwillingly to bring food to the fugitive, and declared that my poor father had expressed a determination to go West and there strive to find a new life.

"If he has that in his mind," said Uncle Abner, "he'll head straight up the river, I guess. If you're in doubt, you ought to go straight up the banks. That'll bring you to him if anything will."

They could not doubt his sincerity. They left almost at once with a great rush for there was a high price offered for the head of Will Dorset, and that reward, even more than the excitement of a manhunt, had brought out such a crowd on this dark night. I tried to squeeze out on the heels of the others, but Uncle Abner caught me and pulled me back. There was such a devil in his face that Aunt Agnes stammered at him and asked him, with a shaking voice, what he intended to do with me. He told her, with an oath, to get off to bed and lock her door if she wanted to keep trouble out.

She ran into her room, then, and slammed the door. I think she dreaded my uncle more than she dreaded God, and yet she was a very religious woman. But from what I have seen of the hearts of men and women, they are more governed by dread than by anything else — except hatred. Yes, I suppose that love is a stronger thing than either, now and then, but as a rule love comes in a flash and disappears again, but hate or dread can rule all of a life, as it had ruled Aunt Agnes. She married my uncle from fear of him; she had been his slave for nearly twenty years for the same reason. He gave her wages of one kind word a month, and that was all. I did not understand it then, but now that I have had time to think over it, I feel that nothing I have seen in my travels and my wild life was half so dreadful as the existence of my poor aunt.

When I was alone with Uncle Abner, he turned to me with a ghastly smile on his face. He was fairly drunk with rage and with the opportunity of spending it. He had been knocked down and abused. He had had his hoard of money broken open, and the greater part of it seized. He had been shamed and disgraced. All of these harms he was to take out on me, and I have never seen such a devilish relish for the work as was in his face. He was trembling from head to foot. His very lips were shaking, and now his tongue lolled out and went across his lips. He went to the gratification of his rage like a starved glutton, approaching a table loaded with a feast.

I knew that after he had struck me one blow he would go mad with the pleasure of it and kill me or, worse, maim me for life. He began to stroke my head, and the tips of his fingers were like iron, and there was still that loose-lipped devil's smile upon his mouth.

It may seem strange that I was not afraid of him. But that is the fact. Or perhaps there is a super fear above and beyond ordinary terror, just as there are calls and cries in the insect world, so shrill and high that they pass through the human ear and are not heard at all. I was cold with dread, but I was not trembling. I had possession of my body and my nerves. I could think swiftly and surely. There was no one to call to. I was alone with this brute, and he was so much more powerful than I, at least in this frenzy of his, that he was able to take my two wrists with one hand and keep them frozen there in helplessness.

I knew, too, that, if I showed the slightest fear of him, I should instantly feel all of his cruel strength. I had to avoid that, and I had to smile. And smile I did. You will think it strange. But I tell you on my honesty that I could have laughed aloud, if laughter would have served my purpose. But I did smile steadily into his face. And that made him hesitate. It takes a super devil to harm a thing that seems to trust it, but my uncle was a super devil, indeed. Presently I saw the black madness coming back across his face and, at the same time, there was a change in the wind that had been blowing steadily up the river. It altered now and struck straight down the valley, bearing with it a great clamoring of the hounds. I could hear the yell of Trelawney's big, spotted boar hound above the rest.

"Uncle Abner! Uncle Abner!" I cried up to that awful face of his. "They have overtaken Father. They have turned him back . . . and he's running this way again! He'll come here for shelter, and that'll bring the crowd after him. What'll we do, Uncle Abner? What'll we do?"

The last of this I let out in a wail of terror into which I put all the agony of fear that was already in me. Uncle Abner turned his back for a second to listen, while the wind carried the clamor of the dogs loudly about us. I feared that he might see, as I had seen, that it was the wind and not the approach of the dogs themselves, but his mind was too clouded by his passion to make any nice observance. He cast me away from him with a sweep of the hand that sent me crashing against the wall, and he reached for his rifle.

There was no doubt about the welcome that he intended to extend to my poor father, if he returned. At that moment, however, the wind fell away after a breath of quiet. We could hear the yelling of the dogs as far away as ever. He saw that he had been tricked, and he turned to me with a shout of fury, but I was already at the door.

"You hell brat!" screamed Uncle Abner, and lunged at me.

His great claw reached me just as I jerked the door open. The feel of his finger tips, even through my shirt, was like the feel of red hot irons grinding into my flesh, but I was already underway. If the shirt had been strong cloth — the sort of shirt I should have been wearing, if his story to my father about money spent on me had been true — he would have snatched me back. But that shirt was worn to tatters and rubbed thin with many washings. It gave like the rotten thing it was, and I, naked to the waist, leaped away into the night.

Chapter Four

ADVENTURE

He followed me for a dozen strides, but he might as well have lumbered after a whippet, for I was off in an ecstasy of speed, winging away like a driving hawk. I heard him shout and threaten to shoot. The trees were only six leaps away, and I bounded among them as the rifle crashed behind me. There was one crackle as the bullet cut through the branches before me. Then I was alone, racing for life.

I was sixteen years old, lean and hard as a hunting dog, and with the wind of a foxhound. After the first wild burst had taken me half a mile from the house, I stood leaning against a tree, taking my breath, and listening. After a time I made out the far, far cry of the hounds, still going up the river, and that was a great comfort to me. For I told myself that, if a man like my father had managed to keep his distance as long as that, they would never catch him. He would use his wits to baffle them. In the meantime the great desire in my heart was to join him, and that I could never manage to do, at present, because between us was my uncle, like an angry ghost, and beyond my uncle was the troop of men and their dogs. What was best for me was to keep straight on and put as much solid ground between me and my uncle as I could possibly manage. Now that my panting had died away, I could hear the forest whispering, and a whippoorwill was calling sadly somewhere near me, and the sharp, sweet breath of the pines was blowing about me. When I lifted up my face, I saw beyond the blackness of the trees the night blue of the sky, dotted with the gold of the stars.

I cannot find the right words to say what I felt, except that it was like taking my soul out of an old body and putting it into a new one. I suppose that most of you have heard the story of *Beauty and the Beast,* and how the Beast was transformed into a handsome prince in the end? I felt as the prince must have felt when he was restored to his true self. Freedom made that difference to me. And now, dressed up with a bright new life, all my existence with Uncle Abner was a nightmare — one forgets a nightmare under the brightness of the sun.

I started on again, running steadily down the river. There was no weariness in me;

there was no fatigue. Freedom made my toes as light as feathers. I simply swung along on wings, following the road nearest to the river for miles and miles, while the river widened, and then the salt freshness of the sea was in the air.

After a vast length of hours, when even my newly found strength was playing out, I saw a rim of gray across the horizon, and, far off in front of me, the stars seemed to be spread out on the ground, so that I knew I was near the harbor. At that, I crawled away in the brush and curled up in a sheltered spot and went to sleep. Sleep, you will say, naked to the waist, soaked with perspiration, with my back raw from the last whipping? Oh, yes, that was nothing to me. My skin was a rough leather in those days. Nothing troubled me. I expected to sleep until noon, but in a couple of hours I sat up wide awake, shuddering with the chill of the morning which had eaten its way down to my very bones. Up the road nearby I heard the cheerful clattering of a horse's hoofs. The first picture that shot across my mind was of my uncle, riding in pursuit, with his long rifle balanced across the pommel of his saddle. So I went up a tree like any squirrel and looked out. It was not Uncle Abner. I might have known that no horse he owned was capable of covering ground at such a round pace. It was a young fellow of seventeen or eighteen, riding a fine young horse that fairly danced along over the ground. But more to me than the beauty of the horse were the clothes the rider wore. He had on a thick woolen coat and mittens on his hands. He was wearing strong boots and trousers of as stout a material as the coat. At the neck I could see that his shirt was of thick flannel. And here was I, trembling in a treetop with the wind piercing my naked body.

No pirate ever felt a greater touch of joy when he saw the huge sails of some rich merchant ship, sagging down the horizon. I dropped into the lower part of the tree and ran out on a great limb that hung over the road. There I lay, stretched out flat on my belly. I kicked off my shoes, so that I could grip with toes as well as fingers. Like a mountain lion I watched him come. He was whistling. His face was red with the raw morning air. He was so full of good spirits and good food that he could not keep in his self-content. When he was just beneath, I shouted. I could not help it. It was the pure excess of savagery as I dropped, and he looked up in time to see me spread-eagled in the air with my hands stretched out at him like the talons of a bird.

That ended the fight before it even began. He was turned into a weak pulp that rolled off the horse and onto the ground as I struck him. The horse danced away, and the young chap lay with his eyes tightly closed like a child afraid to see a nightmare. He was groaning and begging me not to kill him. I was trembling too much with the cold to laugh. I simply tied his own handkerchief over his head, and there he lay like a great lump of blubber, moaning, begging, while I turned him out of his clothes. I left him naked as a newborn child, and I ran off into the forest in my new clothes.

They were warm, but after the first moment or two I did not care a great deal for my prize. They were too heavy. The boots were like steel jackets on my feet which were used to no shoes, or ragged ones. The coat was a useless weight. I tossed away the hat. I chucked the coat into a bramble bush. I kicked off shoes and socks and knifed away those good trousers at the knee. It was a shameful waste of honest materials, but I was glad to be free once more.

I went straight down to the sheds along the quays. There I sat on a pile with my bare feet hooked around it and looked out to sea. The big wind of the night before had kicked up some mighty waves, and, as far as my eye stretched off to the horizon, I saw the big, gray, white-bearded rollers, traveling. It brought my heart into my throat. If my father had been across the water, I should have spent the rest of my life at sea, I don't doubt. But he was not across the water. He was headed West and Far West. And that was my destination. I had enough of an idea of geography to know that the ocean way toward the West led to New Orleans, so I began to make inquiries. I was in luck. Before the night closed on that day, I was duly shipped on board a boat that was taking candle coal down to New Orleans. I was shipped as odd boy, to be handy generally.

It was a pleasant voyage. The captain had two jugs of whiskey, one at the wheel, and one in the cabin. He and the other three men were always mellow, and so the old boat staggered down the coast. We were as light on provisions, though, as we were heavy on liquor. Every night we dropped anchor off some little cove, and two or three went ashore to forage. After the first expedition they saw my talents and left the majority of the work to me. One man would lie back on the oars in the skiff, ready to take us fast away from shore when we came back with supplies; another hand went up with me to

41

help carry what I plundered, but the skillful tasks were all left to me.

The bidding of any older man is usually authority enough for any small boy or young fellow to do mischief. I had not a qualm of conscience. I used to slide into a chicken house and pick off the fattest birds from the roost. There is only one way to manage it. That is to snake the bird off by the neck and, with the same motion, clap him under your elbow. I learned to do it so that I could pick off a prize from a crowded line of roosters and never have the vacancy noticed. Then there were kitchens to invade. I cleaned out many a pantry on that piratical cruise down the coast, and often I secured as much as two of us could stagger under, going back to the boat. Not that it was always safe. Once the dogs took after us and followed so close that the leader came up as we took to the boat, and we had to brain the beast with an oar as it leaped after us. And once three men came after us with guns and gave us a race through the woods. However, there was only enough danger to give spice to life, and night and morning we feasted on my thefts.

With modesty put aside, I may say that I was a valued member of that crew, and all went merry as a wedding bell until we reached New Orleans, and I asked for my pay. Then the captain let out a shout and said that he would turn me over to the police for a young thief. He caught at a belaying pin as he spoke, and I had to act quickly. I dived between his knees, and, while he was flat on his back, I snatched his wallet and dived overboard. When I came up, he was pitting at my head with a rifle, but he was too poor a shot to fetch me. They tumbled into the skiff, but, before they had rowed around the stem of the ship, I was shinnying up a mossy pile and then streaking away across the docks. Some Negroes heard the captain shouting after me and offering rewards. They started after me, but they might as well have tried to tag the strong north wind. I had them gasping in half a mile, and then I dodged away to a quiet place where I could examine my prize.

By the noise that rascal of a captain had made and his effort to kill me or get his wallet back, I had naturally thought that I had a treasure. But when I opened the wallet, I found there was only nine dollars and twenty-two cents in the purse. First I wanted to go back and throw the wallet and the money in his face, but I reflected that this was more money than I had ever been able to call my own before.

So I dried myself out in the sun and then went back to the wharves. I did not meet the captain again, and two days later I managed to get a place on a passenger steamer that was bound for the mouth of the Missouri. I worked as cabin boy — that is to say, I had to do the work of a man and a boy for three weeks while the old tub of a boat butted its way up the current. But we made the big muddy wash of the Missouri at last. I was now West, but not far enough West to have found a land that would be to the taste of Will Dorset. All was too tame and too easy for him.

I had to beat about the town for a whole week before I found another steamer bound up the Missouri for Boonville, and in that boat I made the passage as a junior waiter. What with tips and wages, which were not very large, I reached Boonville with just thirty-two dollars in my pocket, and I felt myself to be a rich man. So I started out like any prosperous youngster to see the sights of the town — and in ten minutes I was seated at a poker game.

One expects, of course, to hear that I lost my money at once. I was playing with two others, both big men with wide-brimmed black hats, and long, drooping mustaches, and little bright black eyes that glittered at me and at one another. They offered me whiskey, but I could not stand the taste of this Western alcohol and filth which went by the name of whiskey, so I refused it. I remember that they praised me for having so much sense, and so the first hand was dealt. I hardly knew how to play, but I did know that four of a kind was rare good luck. So I bid high and finally won twenty dollars. Of course, that was a stacked pack the hand was dealt from, and those two rascals intended to trim me thoroughly in another ten minutes and then turn me adrift. But as I was raking in my profits, a tall, lean fellow came up to the table and stood there with his hands dropped on his hips, smiling down at the three of us.

I shall never forget what a picture he made. He had his hat in his hand, which allowed his long, sun-faded hair to tumble down about his shoulders. He had on deerskins, almost the first I had ever seen, and one of the finest suits of them that I have ever come across. The coat was very long, reaching almost to the knee, and at the shoulder, the wrist, and at the bottom, there were deep fringes cut very fine. His trousers, which fitted tight, were beaded and fringed to the heel, and he had moccasins on his feet. Around his waist there was a broad, thick belt of the finest goatskin, new and white, and in a big holster at his right hip he had a Colt revolver — a weapon I had heard about but had never seen in backward Virginia.

It was not his clothes that took my eye half so much as his brown, thin, ugly face. I could tell that this was an honest man at a glance. My two new friends seemed to be able to tell that, too, and they grew a little uncomfortable.

"Son," said this man in the deerskins, "does your pa know that you're here?"

"He doesn't," I said. "And I don't know where he is. I've come about four thousand miles, hoping to hit his trail. Maybe you could help me out."

"I'm afraid not," he said. "But I can tell you the first best step to get to him. That's to get up from this here table and get out of this dirty hole."

It seemed natural for me to obey him. I pocketed my money and stood up, but the two began to shout and swear at the stranger. He watched them for a moment, and then he said: "You sneakin' wolves . . . can't you find no man-sized meat? Have you got to eat veal? Now lemme hear no more yappin' out of you. Young man, you start for the door."

Chapter Five

HANDY WITH A COLT

I did what he ordered me to do as though he had a right to command me. When I came to the street, he backed out after me, keeping his face toward the others. Once he was beyond the door, he stopped sidewise and walked me around the corner into an alleyway.

"What's your name?" he inquired.

"My name is Lew Dorset."

"Lew Dorset, my name is Chris Hudson. Those buzzards in there was about to pick you till your bones was white and dry. If you're hunting for your father like you say you are, the nearest way is to keep outside of curs like them."

I began to see what he meant. I thanked him and promised to follow his advice. He put on his hat and brushed his hair back over his shoulders. I smiled at that, because it was like the gesture of a little girl — and yet I had seen few more manly-looking men than Chris Hudson. All this while he was looking at me with his eyes squinted a little, very much as though I were a long distance away from him. Then he asked me if I were a stranger here and without friends. I told him that I was, and a moment later I had popped out the whole story — not about Will Dorset having escaped from jail, but about how he had quarreled with my uncle and left, and how I started west after him.

Chris Hudson listened very patiently to me. When I had finished, he said: "How much of that is true, and how much a lie?"

It took me so much aback I couldn't find an easy answer. Finally I blurted out: "All that I've told you is true."

"Have you told me half the truth?" He looked at me another moment, and then he grinned. "Well," he said, "you're pretty cool. How old are you? Eighteen?"

"Sixteen."

He reached out for my hand, turned it up, and ran his thumb over the calluses.

"You'll live through it," he said.

What he meant I had no idea, then.

"What's made you think that your father will be in Boonville?" he asked me.

"He'll be farther west, I guess. He's the sort of man that will need space."

"And not too much law?" He winked at me, and I winked back.

"Not too much law," I agreed.

"Son, might he be your style of a man?"

"You could put two like me inside him. He's a *man!*"

He grinned again. Then he slapped me on the shoulder. "Would you like to go out where there's plenty of space . . . and not too much law?" he asked me. "Would you like to go out with me?"

If he had asked me if I wanted to accept a chunk of the purest gold, my answer would have been given no more quickly.

"The kind of law that goes for you," I said, "is the kind of law that goes for me."

He grew a little more serious, after that. "No, I ain't settin' up for no sort of a model that a kid might grow up by. But yonder on the prairies where the angels wear red skins and where the nighest thing to a house dog that licks your hand is a buffalo wolf that tears your throat out . . . out yonder where most folks forget all about heaven and can feel hell knocking right up ag'in' the heels of their boots . . . out yonder, old son, you got to carry your own law locked up inside of your head. And they's damned few that ain't spoiled by the chance. But, good man or bad man, nobody but a fool goes onto them prairies without a rifle and the knowledge of how to shoot straight, to say nothin' of a pistol or a brace of revolvers for the little handy inside work. Can you shoot straight, kid?"

It wasn't particularly pride that had made me learn to shoot straight. When Uncle Abner sent me out to get a mess of half a dozen squirrels, he used to give me six bullets, and no more, in an old rifle heavy enough to make my shoulder ache even now when I think about it. He didn't ask questions, because he wasn't a talkative man. But if I came back with four squirrels or even five, he reached for the hickory. After one of his hidings, I had to sit down and think — or stand up and think, because sitting wasn't particularly comfortable. You can't catch squirrels with your hands. When you're sent to shoot them, you have to shoot them. So I had to practice, and I had no bullets to practice with. What could I do? Practice without them, of course. That may sound like nonsense to men of this day, but marksmanship isn't weighed by the pound, as powder and bullets are. I've seen a great many men in these times who have burned up a thousand dollars' worth of good ammunition and who are still ten-cent marksmen — and that with rifles so light and which shoot so straight they hit the mark of their own free will, and with ammunition so clean and so cheap that every ten-year-old boy can keep his .22 rifle "in board and room."

No, the average fellow in these days says to himself with his rifle at his shoulder: "I want to hit the target." But for my part, I had to say: "I dare not miss it." I have had some compliments in my time for quick shooting and for straight shooting, but my schooling came from Virginia and Uncle Abner who taught his lessons with a hickory — not a switch, but a stick that was a handful.

I used to lie on my belly, when I was too young to hold the heavy rifle steady, and draw my bead on some small thing — the head of a nail, a bit of shining stone — anything would do. I drew my bead, until I could say: "You're dead!" I kept at it for hours — because, when I had bullets, every bullet had to mean a life. Afterward, for almost half a day at a time, as I grew bigger and stronger, I learned to snatch that big rifle to my shoulder and hold it there with hands turned into stone until the line of light on the top of the rifle barrel ran straight out into the heart of the target. Speed was necessary, too. Squirrels don't stand still, daydreaming and talking about the weather. They give you a glimpse of their head one minute and the fluff of their tail the next as they drift through the branches of a tree. I had to get hands as sensitive as the fingers of a crooked gambler and as steady as rock. And I got them. I got them by those years of steady practice with an *empty gun.* Even when times grew better with me, I don't think that I have spent a hundred rounds of ammunition in my entire life for the sake of practice.

But pistol ammunition was cheaper than rifle food, and Uncle Abner used to give me a pistol, as often as not, and send me off to bring in the family meal with that. Now, a pistol is far different from a rifle. I think that with a rifle almost anyone can be trained to become a first-rate shot through constant practice — granting a background of steady nerves. But steady nerves and practice will never make a pistol expert. Rifle shooting is a science; pistol or revolver shooting is an art. One comes from the head, and one comes from the heart. Any blockhead can learn to run a camera well enough to pass muster — if he tries to learn — but only a few can draw a picture, and one man in a century can really put paint on canvas as it should be put. I don't think it's an exaggeration to say that what the camera is to the oil painting, the rifle is to the revolver. I have seen hundreds of men so really expert with a rifle that it is not extravagant to call them "dead shots." What came in line with their sights was actually dead before they pulled a trigger. But in all my experience I have come into contact, personally, with only three true artists with the revolver, in spite of the fact that in my day I have been from cow camp to mining ground to gambling hell where every man wore at least one Colt, and where only the fools failed to practice every day if they valued their lives.

There are many reasons for this, and I think the most important reason is the six shots which lie in the Colt cylinder. Samuel Colt was a great genius, of course, but, when he gave men six chances instead of one, he divided their surety into six parts. In an oil painting every stroke ought to count. The result is that I have seen more than one barroom brawl where twenty Colts were chattering, where the mirrors and the furniture and the bar and the windows were blown to pieces — but where the total casualties were only one or two dead. People are too much abused with fiction which tells of deadly revolver play. I believe that it takes twenty revolver shots, even at close range, to accomplish what one rifle bullet brings about. On the whole, I think the old-school revolver play where the gun was fired from the shoulder and in line with the eye actually caused more execution. Afterward speed became the thing, and men shot from the elbow and then from the wrist.

But all of these schools of shooting were wrong. There is one perfect way of drawing and shooting a revolver, and that is *with the fingers only*. A mere flexion and twist of the fingers ought to snatch the revolver out of the holster and fire it. But this can only be done by men who have practiced constantly and who have, in addition, a certain genius born in their eyes and in their hands. In my entire life, as I have said, I have only known three great artists with the revolver. One was the great Andy McGruder, one was Chuck Morris, and the third was — myself!

This vanity will perhaps not be pardoned, but at least I say the words honestly. And, once again, I attribute my skill with a revolver to Uncle Abner, who made me turn bullets even from a pistol into dead squirrels or dead birds, as the case might be. I had to learn young, and childhood is the time for schooling, whether in books or in guns. I had another advantage. I learned in the hardest of all schools, with an old, badly-balanced pistol, so that, when I took the Colt from the hand of Chris Hudson, it seemed like a part of my body. I felt that I could not fail with it.

I must apologize for this long digression, but, because guns, unfortunately, were to play such a large part in my history, I thought that I would explain why it was that I had a certain skill with them. Indeed, after I went into the West, I never improved in anything except in learning to draw a revolver. I was only sixteen when I started to master that phase of the art, but even then I was almost too old. I could manage to make my draw as fast as poor old Andy McGruder, perhaps, but I never could achieve that flashing light magic with which Chuck Morris could get his weapon out of leather.

Now, after all this talk, I must come back to the point at which Chris Hudson, standing there in the street in Boonville, said to me: "Can you shoot straight?"

He might as well have asked me if I could speak English or eat food. I was not vain about my skill. It was so much a part of me and of my life that I had hardly had a chance to contrast my marksmanship with that of other people. I simply answered: "I usually hit the spot."

He gave me one of those side-ripping glances of his. Then he handed me the Colt and said: "There's a bit of a broken bottle over by the fence. Don't let that hold you back. You've got six chances in that gun."

As I have said, the balance of that Colt, conceived by an inventor who was a genius, was like a miracle to me. It was not one of those Colts everyone else has seen so often. It was not one of those double-action bits of magic that answer the finger as thought answers the eye. It was an old single-action gun, but, after all, it was a Colt, and from the first that was a wonderful gun. A glow went over me as I looked down at it. I glanced for a moment at the mechanism. I saw how the cylinder worked. I tried the weight of it in my hand. Then I tipped up the muzzle and fired.

That was a stunning blow to me. Even Uncle Abner Dorset's hickory had never inspired in me the desire to shoot straight so much as had the wish presently to impress Chris Hudson. I felt the hot blood pumping in my temples. Chris Hudson simply called out: "Look out, youngster! Don't handle that gun so careless. It's got a mighty light trigger. But dog-gone me if that wasn't a lucky accident. The bullet mighty near hit the glass."

I saw that he thought the Colt had exploded by accident, and I had to bite my lip to keep from smiling. Shooting from the hip had not yet been invented in the West.

"I won't miss this time," I said.

I called into my mind, in place of that bit of glass, the head of a squirrel darting about behind the leaves of a tree with just a glint of the sun in its bright eye. Then I tipped the muzzle of the revolver again and fired a second time. The glass crashed into nothing.

"That's a beauty, that gun," I said, as I handed the Colt back to Chris Hudson.

He brushed straight past me without any attention to the butt of the gun as I offered it. He hurried over to the post and leaned down at the base of it. He stayed there for a long moment, fumbling in the dust and staring at the hole which the bullet had clipped through the post. Then he came back to me with his hat pushed back, scratching his head.

"What's wrong?" I asked him, very much worried.

"The devil," he said, and kicked at a little stone that was in his way.

I felt that I had done something terribly wrong, and I searched my mind to find out what it might be.

"Well," he said at last, "you better come along with me."

I was sick, I was so worried by his frown. I said: "If it's the cost of that post, I'll be glad to pay for it. I've got money. I've got thirty-two . . . I mean fifty-two dollars."

I was pretty proud of having such a lot of coin, but he only turned his head a bit and glinted at me out of those long-distance eyes of his.

"Post be damned," he said. "By the way . . . you better keep that gun."

It stopped me in my stride like a blow. It was as if he had offered me a palace in fairyland. I ran after him and touched his arm.

"Look here, Mister Hudson, of course, you're joking. You don't mean that I can have this?"

"Don't I? You can, though."

"Why, it must be worth a mighty lot of money. I'd be glad to buy it. I got this fifty-two dollars for a part. . . ."

"Humph," said Chris Hudson. "I don't suppose that you ever seen a gun like that before?"

"Never. Except on the boat coming up the river."

"Maybe you hit that glass by accident, then?" he asked. He began to laugh. "Before you tell a lie like that, Lew, you want to think first. But that gun is yours. It ain't any good to me no more."

"Have I spoiled it?"

"You've spoiled it for me," he answered. "I don't know enough to handle a gun like that. I'm gonna stick to a rifle from now on, you can bet your last dollar right on that."

I went on holding that gun in both hands. It was bright, well polished, and also bright with its newness.

Chapter Six

CHUCK MORRIS

The place to which Chris Hudson led me was on the edge of Boonville. It was a great circle of huge covered wagons. There must have been twenty-five or thirty of them. All around them were horses past counting, tied to the wheels.

"Have you ever seen anything like this?" he asked.

I told him that I hadn't, and he said that it was a trappers' caravan, and they were bound due west for the prairies the very next day. While he was telling me this, we entered the circle of the wagons. All that inner circle was tossing and swaying with light and life from a big fire in the center of the enclosure. On the edges of that fire two or three men had raked out coals and were cooking. One was frying meat, and another was making coffee, for it was the dusk of the day, and they were getting ready for supper. There seemed quite a crowd of other men — at least thirty were in sight at that moment, and I felt this caravan was like a whole village ready to roll away on wheels. Except that there were no women and no children, although I did notice a number of youngsters who could not have been much older than I was.

Hudson took me up to a big wagon on the far side of the circle and called out: "Gregory!"

A big-shouldered man came, lumbering out of the wagon with a pipe in his mouth and some playing cards in his hand.

"I'll be back in a minute, boys," he was saying, as he jumped down to us.

"Gregory," said Chris Hudson, "this is Lew Dorset. He has fifty-two dollars and a new Colt. He wants to join our crowd."

"A Colt," said Gregory, "is mostly good for making trouble in camp, and fifty-two dollars ain't enough to turn around with. What can he do?"

"Ask him," said Hudson.

"Can you use a lariat?" asked Gregory.

"No," I said. I hardly knew what a lariat was.

"Can you ride a horse?"

I thought of the bony nags my uncle kept. They could hardly be called horses. "Not very well," I replied.

"Have you got a rifle?"

"No."

"Can you talk Sioux?"

61

"No," I said, never having heard that word before.

"What the devil *can* you do?" asked Gregory.

I was stumped. "I don't know. But I'm tough, and I'm willing to work."

"*Humph!* We've already got all the kids in camp we need for the odds and ends."

"Wait a minute," said Hudson, and took Gregory aside.

He began to talk quietly to him, and after a time Gregory grunted and looked back at me. I can understand now what Hudson must have been saying, but at the time it seemed very mysterious to me.

After a moment Gregory turned and walked up to me, looking me up and down. "I understand," he said, "that you're looking for your father out here." He waved his hand to the darkening western skies. "And if you come across sign of him, you're due to quit the party at any time." He grinned a little as he said this.

"I'd have to leave if I got track of him," I affirmed.

"Well, maybe you can do enough hunting for the party to be worth your keep. Do you think you can?"

"I have hunted a little," I admitted. "But it's rather hard to shoot far with a pistol."

He looked at me a minute. "Maybe we can fix you up with a rifle. As for a horse, Hudson has more than anybody else in the camp. Might be that he has one worth less than fifty dollars. I dunno."

He hurried back into the wagon without saying good bye. I asked Hudson what it meant, and he declared I was now a member of the party if I cared to join. He took me to his wagon, showed me some blankets I could use, and declared that he would sell me a horse for twenty dollars the very next morning when the caravan started. As for the rest of my money I could turn it into ammunition, or do what I pleased with it. But he advised me to get a hunting knife and a hatchet together with plenty of matches and a couple of pots for cooking.

I thanked him with all my heart. "Mister Hudson," I said, finishing up, "the Dorsets never forget good turns or bad ones."

"The devil," he said. "I've heard folks talk like that before, but words don't mean nothing . . . not out on the prairie. Now you cut loose from all this gratitude and mix around among the boys and try to pick yourself out a friend or two. Lemme tell you this . . . a friend on the prairie is worth more than his statue done in gold and set off with diamonds."

This was a manner of talk that made me very much at home. It was so much like Uncle Abner. So I went off to stir about among the other young people. I could see at a glance that they were not like the boys, black or white, that I had known in Virginia. These fellows were as brown as paint. They were all quite straight, and they seemed to be whittled down rather lean — dried out, I might better call it. They were drawn out altogether longer and finer than the people of the Eastern coast. I could see that they were tough and lasting rather than strong. When they stepped, they stepped like young horses — ready to jump out of their skins for fun or fighting at any minute. They didn't have eyes like boys I had known — that is, they didn't have a dull, tired look — but they stared around as the men did, except that they were wilder. I knew before I had seen them so much as lift a hand that they were as fast as lightning. But it seemed to me they lacked the shoulder bulk and the width of back which is only put on a youngster by hard work or a great deal of athletics. Here were boys who could ride all day on a tough mustang or run all day over the prairie, but on the whole their legs were more exercised than their arms.

Of course, there were exceptions, and it

was into the hands of the greatest of all, and one of the most remarkable men who ever carried a rifle or spurred a horse that I was to fall. I marked him the instant that I came on the outskirts of the group. He was a tall fellow with blond hair worn very long and a fine blue eye, the handsomest man I have ever seen in all my travels. He looked twenty — as a matter of fact, he was just eighteen — but he had his full height even then, which was two or three inches over six feet. He had filled out not to the great bulk that was eventually his, but to some hundred and ninety pounds of leathery muscle and iron bone. Indeed, he was fit company rather for the men than the boys, and it was only by accident that I found him among the younger crew on this occasion. He was one of those men of whom I have spoken before, who are naturally strong and who know their strength. He had a bold, high carriage of the head, the very look of a hero, a throat like a brown pillar, and a breast arched with muscle — and with pride.

I studied him with delight and terror commingled. It was a time before I paid any attention to what he was saying, for he was delivering his opinion on a subject that for years had been the most important question in the country and that was eventually to

65

bring on the saddest and the bitterest war that was ever fought. But after a moment I began to follow the thread of his talk.

"Suppose I had a black skin," he said. "Would that make me any different? I aim to say that I'd be just the same underneath. I'd need the same sort of eating and the same sort of sleeping. The same sort of things would make me happy, and the same sort of things would make me sad. But suppose you come along and you say . . . 'Look here, Chuck Morris, your dad was mine and belonged to me, and therefore I own you.' Suppose that you was to say that, how would I feel and what would I do? I'd bust loose, that's all. I tell you gentlemen, we must abolish slavery."

There was a little muttering of assent, but I began to sit up stiff and straight. I had heard of abolitionists in my life, of course, because like every boy south of the Mason-Dixon line I knew that everyone north of that line was a designing scoundrel. But for some reason I felt that in going into this far land of the West I would be where politics did not exist, and where all men were noble and free of thought. It sickened me to find myself in such a crew, and I decided on the spot that, if the others were of the same temper, I had rather die than go on with them.

The young orator was continuing. He was growing so excited that he stood up to his full height, a very splendid young god with a golden head and flashing eyes, with his big, supple body clothed in tightly-fitted deerskin all aflash with colored beads.

"It ain't a right thing, of course," he said, "but what're we gonna do about it? They got those men with the black skins, and they call them slaves. I say those black men are just as good as the white ones. I say again, slavery is wrong!"

This I could stand no longer. This was open heresy of the most damnable stamp, and I lifted my head and said: "That's not so!"

There was a dead silence. I saw Chuck Morris start and glare swiftly around the circle as though he were trying to pick out the voice that had challenged him, but, since he couldn't seem to find the man, he said: "Who said that?"

I didn't answer. I was plainly too frightened to speak, for I felt that, if I did, my head would be in the lion's mouth. He went on again, talking very slowly, his glance fixed vaguely in my direction, while he said: "Down yonder they tie a man up to a post . . . a man like you or me, except that his skin is black . . . and they whip him and his blood runs down, and I tell you folks that treat other folks like that are *worse* than devils! They're cowards, and one man that never owned slaves could lick any two that *do* own slaves."

I wanted, with all my might, to let all of these challenges slip away unnoticed. I knew that there was a great deal too much danger for me if I dared to speak out what I thought, and yet to save my soul I could not keep my rage from rushing up into words. They came tumbling out of my lips before I could check them. I found myself jumping to my feet and standing up in clear view of them all.

"That's a lie!" I shouted at him. "And an abolitionist like you isn't fit to sit with a gentleman."

Chapter Seven

A BATTLE OF FISTS

Looking back now through what I know of Chuck Morris, I can understand why the other boys in that circle were too appalled and too astonished so much as to turn their heads toward me. But most of my courage returned the moment I leaped up, and most of my old self-confidence. I had seen how big and how lion-like this fellow was, but all my life I had been fighting — fighting with my hands, and, though I had often come against youngsters almost half as big as I was, I usually found that the bigger they were, the softer they were. Indeed, with one exception, I have never seen a man over six feet in height who was really built in good proportion, well knit, well balanced. That great exception was Chuck Morris, not as he was when I first saw him, but as he afterward developed into a glorious Hercules.

At that time I had fought so many times — so many times I had beaten two and even three boys at once by the ferocity and the weight of my attack — that I looked upon the handsome blond giant as just one victim more. The bigger he was, the more satisfaction I would take in leveling him with the grass. He walked across the little circle with his hands clenched into fists, but, when he stood close and I saw how he towered a head above me, he smiled a little and stepped back.

"If you was a mite bigger and a mite older," he said, "I'd teach you how to talk to your betters. Are you a slave-keeper, maybe?"

He had spurred a willing horse with those insults. I could not speak for a moment, so great was my passion. Then I said: "Chuck Morris, lemme tell you why it's right for a Virginia gentleman to keep slaves while it isn't right for a damned Yankee. In Virginia a man with black skin knows his place when he's around a white gentleman. But when that black man goes North, he feels like bossing around the bad blood he finds there."

Chuck Morris lifted his hand, but he controlled himself, though he ground his teeth. "Boy," he said, "send your pa around to me, and I'll teach him to learn you better manners."

"Why," I said, picking my words one by one and rejoicing when I saw the sting of them madden him, "you Yankees never would have been free if it hadn't been for a general from Virginia who came up and fought your battles for you. That was General Washington. And he owned slaves, Chuck Morris."

"You lie," he said, and then, seeing that this point would not bear debating, he struck me across the mouth.

That open hand was as heavy a clenched fist wielded by any boyish arms that I had ever encountered. It gave me the first taste of what was coming, but I was not a whit dismayed. With all the skill which a thousand free fights had given me in the science of hitting, with all the power which ten years of moiling and toiling had given to my young back and shoulders, I flung my fist into his face and landed it squarely on the point of the chin where the long leverage of the jaw bone throws the shock against the base of the brain. Chuck Morris dropped upon his face.

I was astonished in spite of all my fighting. It was like felling a huge oak tree with a single blow of an axe. But my astonishment was nothing compared with the bewilderment and the rage of the other youngsters who were there. Hardly a one of them had but felt the arm of Chuck Morris in anger or in play until they had come to look upon him as an invincible hero. They shouldered past me in a wave. They picked him up. They threw water in his face. They called on him to stand up.

"You better leave him lay," I said. "Because, if he stands up, he'll get the same thing again. I tell you, no abolitionist can stand in front of a Virginia gentleman."

I blush a little as I write down these words, chiefly when I think what a real Virginia gentleman would have thought if he had heard the son of Will Dorset rank himself with them. But at that moment I felt strong enough to face Dan Donnelly himself, the big Irish blacksmith who had been a pugilist in England and who had taught me something of the art of the prize ring and filled my ears with tales of its heroes, from the matchless Jem Belcher down.

Then I heard a groan and a shout. The circle of Chuck's friends was torn apart, and Chuck Morris himself, his long golden hair floating behind his head, rushed out at me. There could not have been a better mark for me. I gave him my right again with such force that my arm turned numb to the shoulder, and a slash of crimson opened under his eye. Though that blow stopped and staggered him, the next minute he fell in on me and gripped me in his long arms. It was as though Uncle Abner had laid his giant hands on me. That bear hug crushed the wind from my body and the confidence out of my mind.

I managed to writhe loose and, bending over, as Dan Donnelly had taught me to do, I jerked both my hands upward with all my might into his body. I had used that trick twenty times before and felt each hand sink sickeningly deep into the stomach of another youngster, gasping, choking. But striking the body of Chuck Morris was like hammering at a log cushioned with wrapped sacks. The force of those punches made my wrists ache, but they did not daunt Chuck Morris. He whipped a long overhand blow into my face. I was not stunned, but the sheer weight of it smashed me to the earth. Before I could stir, he was on me.

"Fair play!" I shouted.

"I'll give you fair play," he said and sprang up again.

I rose, lurching low along the ground as Dan Donnelly had taught me to do, so that his ponderous first swing missed me, but the second, as I stood up, caught me fairly under the jaw and knocked me head over heels. That was the end of the fight. I do not mean that the battle stopped at this point, but after that stunning blow my mind was half wrapped in darkness, which lifted long enough now and again to show me my foe and let me get at him with driving fists, a darkness rent with red splashes of lightning and thunderstrokes in my brain as his heavy fists thudded home on me. I was either down on the ground and dragging myself up, or else I was leaning in against his powerful hands like one leaning into a hurricane.

Vaguely I knew that other people had come — all the men in the circle of the wagons, as well as others from the outside. My consciousness was awash with a roar of voices, like the beating of the sea against great rocks.

Friendly hands caught at me, at last. I made out the voice of Chris Hudson shouting: "He's had enough, Chuck . . . and so have you, by the looks of you."

"You lie," I managed to groan. "Lemme at him."

"All right, young tiger," said Chris. "But this goes by the ring rules from now on . . . half a minute between knockdowns . . . and the first man that fails to come to the scratch at the end of that time . . . he's beat. Gregory, you get out your watch. . . ."

His hands pushed me to my feet. I went at the shadowy form of big Chuck Morris. My brain cleared a little. I found myself standing toe to toe with Chuck, exchanging crashing blows. As my senses cleared, I was bewildered by my own skill which, out of the fighting instinct, had kept me weaving my body and head from side to side to dull the snap of his punches, while I drove my own in with more telling effect. He went back. I followed him in the midst of a sudden silence. Then he was down — lost in the blackness at my feet.

The hands of Chris Hudson caught me, and I was dragged down upon his knee. It was the last bright moment of the fight for me. Dull and distant, I saw the swarms of faces, I heard their shouts, I even heard the calling of bets as they laid wagers. Then the voice of Chris was at my ear: "You've done enough, Lew. You can stop now, before he smashes you to pieces. There's no disgrace. He's older. He weighs forty or fifty pounds more. There's not a man in the camp would stand up to him with either fists or guns."

What I answered, I do not know, but I know that the thought of surrender turned me sick and then turned me wild. Time was called. Chris Hudson pushed me to my feet, and Chuck Morris and I lurched together. I felt my hard fists literally splash twice against the running blood on his face. Then before me loomed the huge fist of Morris, striking over and down. It landed, and my knees turned to water.

Still it was not the end, though that blow is absolutely the last that I can recall of the fight. During the rest of the time I must have struggled on through perfectly instinctive motions, but my conscious brain was covered with darkness. Chris Hudson told me later how the struggle went on, with Chuck Morris literally cut to pieces, his feet braced to keep his body from falling, his eyes almost blinded, his face dripping crimson, but still hammering away at my lurching, swaying body until finally, after I had fallen upon my face for the fiftieth time at the end of the half minute, I was a mass of inert flesh in Hudson's hands.

You will say, as others have said to whom I told this story, that it was a brutal thing for those men to allow the battle to go on between two youngsters, and one so totally overmatched. But those hardy traders knew what they were about. Up to that moment both Chuck Morris and I had been ceaseless bullies. They knew about Chuck and perhaps they guessed about me, as older men usually see through boys with a glance or two. All my life I had gone about hunting for trouble. But after that fight with Morris, though I loved battle as much as ever, I had

had my lesson, and I never again hunted trouble. To my knowledge, neither did he, until the combination of events — and something, perhaps, of a predetermined fate — forced him to hunt for me, and find me, and fight with me the most dreadful battle of our lives — except the final fight that is still to come for me and that all men must eventually face.

I wakened into blackness at last. Across my face was a mass of wet cloth, and there was a pungency of some healing salve in my nostrils. I hardly could draw a breath, I was in such agony. Every inch of my body had been battered, strained, crushed. My mouth was swollen, my eyes were closed, and the pain was so dreadful that I prayed for unconsciousness again. I groaned, and Chris Hudson's voice said rather softly: "He's coming 'round. I thought he never would. I thought that we had a dead boy on our hands. Friends, we've let this go too far."

"Bah!" exclaimed Gregory. "It'll be good for both of 'em."

Chapter Eight

CHUCK FINDS A PAL

The final reason, then, that I left Boonville with that trading caravan was simply because I was unable to help myself. I could not walk; I could not stand. And so I was carted away by those abolitionists. For all of my life — let me confess it — that word has reddened my face with anger, and for a long time it would be my regret that I was unable to come out of the Far West to fight on the side of the Confederacy. I had not yet come to realize that we are a nation subject to passionate fevers, that it is in our very nature always to want to abolish *something*. After all the killing of the Civil War, the abolitionists declared to the slaves that they were free, and then proceeded to turn their backs on them. Abolition itself is the thing, and about all that ever really matters to the true abolitionist is what he wants to abolish, and damn the human consequences.

It was a whole week before I could sit on a horse, let alone walk or run. On the same day I staggered out of the wagon with a patched and purple face, I saw a huge grotesque at the same moment reel out of another wagon on the opposite side of the caravan — for they had not yet broken up their morning circle for the day's trek. I did not recognize, at first, the awful face I saw. Then I knew that it was none other than big Chuck Morris.

The men were finishing the cooking of breakfast at the central fire, and yet even breakfast stopped to watch the encounter between Chuck and myself. We went straight toward one another to the center of the circle, and there we paused and looked at one another out of our blackened eyes. I still hated him, but the change from the handsome face was so great that I could not help breaking into laughter.

"Chuck," I said, "you're a sight."

He roared with laughter at the same moment. "Lew," he said, "you little game chicken . . . you're a sight, too."

He clapped me by the shoulder. I caught him by the hand. In that instant was cemented a friendship which was to last through many years, a strange and beautiful friendship. Would to heaven that it had never been broken, Morris, and that you and I had never come to hate one another as we do now.

The men, when they saw that there was to be no more fighting, gave us a shout and a cheer and called us over to the breakfast fire. We sat down there side by side. I'll never forget how the men laughed at our smashed and purple faces. I'll never forget how the youngsters did their best to swallow their grins for fear of us. But we would not have cared if the whole world had laughed, we were each so happy to have found a friend worthy of the other. So perfect was our friendship that we even talked of the cause of the fight and of the fight itself.

"You see," I said to Chuck, "we're from different sides of the fence. You know what grows in your own back yard. I know what grows in mine. Things look different when you have only a knothole to peek through. But let that go. You can think what you want, Chuck, and I can think what I want. Leastways, there's no slaves out here to quarrel about."

He chuckled and nodded over that.

"If you'd had ten pounds' more weight, or another year of seasoning behind you, you'd have licked me, Lew," he commented so frankly I turned red at the mere thought of it. "Every time I closed with you, it was like closing with a wildcat. I had those knuckles of yours slashing me across the face. Besides, I was down and done for with the first punch . . . if the boys hadn't given me a hand."

This sort of talk made me dizzy with wonder. I had such a shame of defeat that merely to mention it made me a little sick. But he was so open and free I felt like a small-souled coward. That was a characteristic of Chuck's. He was always willing to admit when he was beaten. Yet, there is a sort of savage bulldog in me that shames me from seeing such truths. After that, we rolled our blankets down beside one another every night of the passage.

There is no voyage at sea that takes as long as the crossing of the plains did with a traders' outfit. Even with steers, in the earlier days, the outfits of the 'Forty-Niners bound for California traveled faster, because they had a definite destination, and every day they tried to put more miles behind them and press farther toward their goal. But the trader had no such goal. He was simply embarked for the prairies and for Indians in general. He never knew exactly where he could find them, and, when he found them, he never knew whether they would feel more like trading or *taking* scalps — and the whole train of goods.

That was why we traveled in such a large

band. We had, altogether, fifty-five men in that troop, and every man was familiar with the use of a rifle. Every night, or whenever the scouts brought back word of danger, the wagons were drawn into a compact circle, and the bales of forage were piled against the wagons, making a very good sort of fort. At night the horses were tethered inside, close to the wagons. If there were trouble, they were taken to the center of the corral, and their heads were pointed in, because what a horse doesn't see is not so apt to bother it. Those fifty-five rifles handled by steady fighters could turn back the rush of any wandering bands of young Indians, hunting for game and scalps and fun. If there were a gathered tribe, there was also apt to be more good sense from the old men among the Indians — wise old chaps who pointed out that wars with the white men rarely ended well, and that one massacre, no matter on how small a scale, was enough to start trouble.

For trading we had quantities of butcher knives, *et cetera,* and mostly made of cheapest steel. We had hundreds of pounds of beads, all of the biggest size and of the brightest colors. We had flashy cloths, usually cotton printed with staring dyes. We had some old rifles and pistols, usually guaranteed to explode after two or three discharges. We had a hundred kinds of foolish trinkets, to say nothing of extra flour and molasses and tea — for the Indians had the strangest love of the white man's food. But, first and last, we had firewater. Not whiskey. Make no mistake about that. The thing that ruined the Indians was not whiskey, no matter how new, how poorly made, how raw. It was alcohol — raw grain alcohol of the cheapest sort, full of impurities. It was mixed with water and with coloring matter of any kind, often sweetened a little with molasses. The effect of it was simply a terrible thing to watch. A tumbler of it could actually make a white man drunk — and I have never seen a white man who could not endure alcohol better than the poor Indians with their hair-trigger nerves and lack of centuries of drunkenness. It was a dastardly thing to trade among the Indians with such poison. But the traders who did not carry it could do no business, and money, from the beginning of time, has always weighed heavier than ethics. I did not understand, then, what the whiskey accomplished in the natures of the red men. But after I learned, I am honestly glad to say that I never used whiskey to delude any Indian — not even a Cheyenne, confound their rascally, horse-stealing hearts.

All the ways of the prairie men were made short-handed for me by Chuck Morris, and I could not have found a better teacher. He had been born to this life, and, having been in it from infancy, he knew more by instinct than most of the oldest scouts ever learned through experience. In the first place, he gave me a horse. Chris Hudson had offered to sell me one of the worst of his string. Not because he was ungenerous, but because giving things away was not in his nature. He had surrendered the Colt to me out of purest chagrin when he saw how much more master of it I was than he could ever hope to be. But Chuck Morris showed me his string. He had four horses, and all of them were fine animals. They were of fine Kentucky blood crossed with the best sort of Indian mares. The result was that they were larger than almost any Indian pony, and they had borrowed some of the toughness of their mothers. One meets hard weather on the prairies, and your real Thoroughbred is apt to be made of tender stuff. When Chuck showed me those four beauties, he pointed out a gray mare.

"You can have your choice of any of the lot," he said, "except that gray. She's my special saddle horse. And between you and me, I figgered out that she must have some of the same blood that's in White Smoke. Anyway, her mother was gray . . . almost white . . . and that mare came from the same district where White Smoke has been raising the devil the last year or two."

I asked him what White Smoke was, and he seemed a little surprised to learn I hadn't heard the name. He said that he thought nearly everyone in the world must have heard about White Smoke at one time or another. At least, everyone west of the Mississippi.

I was often surprised in this way by the talk of the prairie men. They had lived out there so long that they had forgotten the ways of the rest of the world, and they had forgotten the size of it, too. They finally came to have the viewpoint of the Indians who never could really understand that there were more white people in existence than there were Indians. It made no difference how one talked of cities and nations. I have seen a great chief wave his hand at a village of five hundred teepees and speak as though there were no greater city in existence. And so, in a way, it was with the prairie men.

Chuck explained about White Smoke in detail. He was a great white stallion with four black-stockinged legs. The horse had first appeared about three years before —

that is, it had grown up to maturity at about that time. Since then it had done all sorts of damage by running off the horses of Indians and the stock of caravans. No one could be safe unless his horses were hobbled, and that was an immense nuisance. Over a district a thousand miles wide men watched their horses every night for fear of White Smoke. For he would steal down a gully with the cunning of a wolf, leap in among the horses, and startle them away with his great clarion neigh. Once off at his heels, he knew how to lead them where they could not be easily pursued. He kept with him a band composed of a hundred or more of the finest mares that were anywhere to be found, for they were the weeded-out result of a thousand chases. They had enough food to keep away from the relayed chasing of the Indians and the whites as well. It had come to such a point that, when a man wanted a specially fine mount, he tried to get one of White Smoke's mares, and Chuck Morris told me that some men had traveled hundreds of miles trying to run down one of the stallion's band.

This mare of Chuck's, whether she was of that famous strain or not, was a pure beauty with the strength of a tiger and the eye of a lamb. When I looked at her, horseflesh for the first time entered my soul. And those who taste the lotus are no more condemned to dreams and yearning than are those who have lost their hearts to horses, waiting for the perfect horse to jog over the horizon into their lives. I knew, however, that I could not ride her. I told Chuck that I was no good in the saddle, that I didn't know a horse well enough to attempt to select one, but, if he chose to give me the gentlest animal of his quartet, I'd pay him my fifty dollars as a first installment and more money later. He wouldn't take a cent of money, though it must have been like parting from his own flesh and sinews to give up a horse to me. Every one of that quartet was worth more than two hundred dollars — in a day when a dollar meant many times over what it means in this reign of millionaires. And Chuck Morris was only eighteen. However, he did give me a horse, and it was the second best of his lot. It was a brown gelding with a white left forefoot and a big, wakeful eye. I felt that horse had brains I could trust, and I was delighted with the choice. Chuck gave me an old bridle, too, and Chris Hudson gave me a saddle that was rather in tatters. Gregory himself, who was the captain of the caravan, gave me some blankets and some good advice, every word of which I forgot.

In short, the entire caravan, young and old, treated me like a king simply because I had shown some spunk in standing up to big Chuck Morris. But after my boy's life spent like a hunted beast half the time and like a beast of burden the rest, God alone can understand what that warmth of human kindness meant to me or how my whole heart responded to it and opened up. I loved the men, and I loved the country they came from. The very word *West* has always brought joy to me from that first happy time.

In the meantime we drudged forward. No one can appreciate the incalculable slowness of a caravan. In a pinch the whole progress could have been multiplied. Most of the horses were in good condition, and most of the wagons were sound. We could have rustled away across the prairies at an excellent clip, but the leaders wished to keep a good deal of strength in reserve to be mustered in case of need. Besides, at the slightest cause of alarm or the very hint of Indians, the crawling snail drew in its horns, stopped, curled up, and prepared for an attack. Once we lay for an entire day and a half, scouting the country busily in search of Indians, and all because one boy, riding alone, thought that he had seen one creeping through the grass.

By the time we had issued from the borderland of hills and ravines and noisy little streams rushing through narrow gorges, and by the time we had left the last trees behind and were committed to the true prairie, I had had time to recover from the last of my bruises. I had learned to ride, and I had made a poor beginning in the handling of a horse-hair lariat. And, above all, I was enjoying the purest happiness, for at the suggestion of Chris Hudson I was appointed huntsman to serve with Chuck Morris.

Among the hills it was well enough to scour here and there, and a fair share of the luck fell to me — or a little more than a fair share. For, as I have said, I had learned to make bullets count, which simply means that I had learned not to miss. Chuck, genius though he was with a gun in a crisis, was always too careless. However, the game we shot we always brought in together, and neither made any claims. I never boasted, and I think that Chuck was grateful for my silence. He, as head huntsman, received the praise, and I let him take it as a very cheap way of paying off that expensive horse on which I was riding. I never could understand, however, the way in which he would accept tributes that were not his due. He was generous to a fault. Money or any other possession was nothing to him, if it would please a friend. At the same time he hated to hear others praised. That was only one of the first peculiarities I was to observe in that remarkable man. By then, however, we had embarked at last on the vast sea of the prairies.

Chapter Nine

PRAIRIE DANGERS

I realized suddenly that we were in a new world. Chuck and I had ridden foolishly far the preceding evening in pursuit of a wounded deer. We had spent half of the night in getting back to the caravan, so that, when the morning came and the caravan lurched ahead, he and I tumbled into a wagon and rode on through most of the morning. When we crawled out from under canvas at last, thoroughly slept out, I found around me a huge green ocean where all the waves were frozen in place — soft swells of ground and then irregular long stretches over which the sun rippled. Nothing lived here but the wind and the grass. And the face of every man around me was changed, just as faces change on board ship when the land drops below the horizon and the vessel is committed to the sea at last. I cannot define the change. But at first everyone was more subdued, more watchful, with a strain of anxiety beginning to tell. Perhaps it was the gradual cessation of talk that wakened both Chuck and me.

I was a bit oppressed, at first. But half an hour later Chuck and I were riding out to find fresh meat. When we had pressed on into the silence beyond the sound of the rattling caravan, it seemed to me, looking around to the great horizon, that I felt the curve of the earth's surface, pressing us up closer to the sky. The sky itself became my intimate, so that, half the time, I rode with my face up, watching the sweep of little wind-torn clouds. I looked at Chuck, smiling, and Chuck smiled back at me. We were like two children and very happy. I knew in that moment that this was the life for which I was meant, and I could see, as I stared around me, what had made Chuck Morris the man he was.

We found nothing on that day. Chuck told me, as we turned back toward the caravan that evening, that we should find hunting the prairies a very different matter from hunting through the hills, where there was life among the trees everywhere and along the streams. Coming back we crossed fully five miles over which the grass was trampled and eaten low. The ground bore myriad marks of hoofs, as though all the cattle in the world had come this way and been pooled here, milling and stamping. And we found one skeleton, of which even the bones had been torn apart.

"A buffalo herd," said Chuck.

"Good heavens!" I cried. "Are there this many buffalo in the world?"

"This is only a small herd. I've seen the prairie black with them as far as your eye could stretch. This crowd passed along here some time ago."

We reached camp and found it a gloomy place. The men were silent and all busy with the preparation of supper. When we reported that we had no game for them, they answered not a word — as though they expected no good news to come out of this land sea.

Chuck and I ate our meal hastily and then walked out to get away from that atmosphere of dread and sorrow. Before we had gone a quarter of a mile from the wagons, Chuck told me that this dismal cloud would disappear from the caravan after a day or two, and that they would all be as merry as ever. At first the prairies always made men homesick — except the few men who were born to love the prairie. He did not have to tell me that he and I were among the exceptions. He had hardly finished telling me this when he suddenly dropped flat on his face and swept me down beside him.

"Straight ahead," he whispered to me.

I looked through the grass, as he had told me to do. Up to the top of a little hummock, just before us, rode a half-naked Indian and halted there. There was a steady south wind that blew the feathers in his hair to the side. I remember wondering at his long, smooth, naked arms. He carried a rifle, and he was staring down toward the caravan. We were so close that we could see the stir of his chest as he breathed. Then he backed his horse out of sight and disappeared, and after a moment we heard a feeble drumming of hoofs.

Chuck sat up. "We'll get back to camp," he said.

"What's wrong?" I asked. "We've nothing to fear from the Indians. We've done them no harm."

"I don't like the looks of that fellow. He ought to have ridden straight into the camp and asked for something to eat and for a gift or two. That's what he would have done, probably, if he had been friendly. I don't like it at all. As for never having harmed them, that doesn't matter. The wrong that one white man does them, they lay up against all white men."

When we reached camp, he went straight to Gregory and reported what he had seen.

Gregory was playing cards and drinking a good deal more than was good for him. He looked at Chuck Morris with a flushed, reckless face and told him he was a young fool to make a ruction about one Indian.

So Chuck backed out. "The worst of it is," he said, "that we have a drunken fool at the head of this party. I don't like it. I've half a mind to break away and cut back by myself."

He talked a good deal more in this strain. That night, as we lay awake murmuring to one another after the rest were asleep, he sent my blood cold by saying: "There's no watch tonight. Have you noticed?"

Just at that moment, by an inspired accident, a long, smooth howling began far away in the night, a devilish noise that stopped my breath like a leap into icy water.

"What do you suppose it is?" I breathed.

He chuckled a little as he answered: "It's not Indians, tenderfoot. It's buffalo wolves. You saw that skeleton today? That's where they nipped off a straggler from the big herd."

I hardly more than dozed that night, expecting every moment to hear the screeching of Indians as they rushed for the attack, the beating of hoofs, and the roar of guns. But that attack did not come.

The next day Morris and I compared

notes on the ridiculous carelessness with which this caravan was heading through the prairie. But the days went by, and nothing happened. There was no sign of Indians. Ten days — and still no Indians. But there was also no fresh meat.

Gregory called us in to him and said: "Fresh meat tomorrow, boys, or the next day you can drive horses, and somebody else will take up the job."

There was no use arguing. He was half drunk, as usual, and very angry. Chuck and I knew perfectly well that we were the best hunters in the crowd, with the possible exception of Chris Hudson, and we were not sure of that. We decided that we would range farther than ever in quest of game the next day, so we were up in the cool of the dawn and started away. We ranged all morning, riding recklessly far and straight out from the caravan, but we found no sign of game. Finally we reached a low hump of ground — what passed for a real hill on the prairie — and from that vantage point we searched the horizon.

"There's not a thing," I said.

"What's yonder?" asked Chuck, stiffening his arm to point.

"The sun flashing on some rocks, I suppose."

"Antelope," said Chuck. "Damned if it ain't antelope. Now, if we have a little luck, we'll give them meat tonight."

We had luck in the very beginning, at the least, for the wind was a steady breeze, cutting straight from the antelope to us. We rode like mad straight ahead for a time. Then, in a low, shallow swale, we left the horses, which were trained to stand when the reins were thrown over their heads, like the cow ponies of the present-day ranchmen. We sneaked over the next high place, wriggling along on our stomachs and pushing the rifles ahead of us. There we saw the antelope just before us. They were not by any means in point-blank range, but we dared not risk frightening the whole herd away by climbing farther over the ridge. Even as it was we nearly lost them.

While we lay there, one of the big ones, on the farther swell of ground, suddenly tossed up his head, and his whole rump turned white with a flash like a tin pan. It was a very astonishing thing to see — as though someone had touched a match to him — except that fire would never have been so brilliant. After that, which seemed to be a signal, the heads of the others went up, and their rumps flashed white — a wave which in an instant had passed through the

97

entire herd. Then they began to run. I mean that they turned themselves into dark streaks slashed with white. I had never seen anything so lovely as those dainty-limbed creatures. When they started away, I thought, for an instant, they had taken wing.

I had occasion afterward to find out that their running is not so miraculously fast. But it is fast enough, considering that a one hundred-pound antelope can run almost as swiftly as a blooded race horse. Nothing else on the prairie can rival them — not even a jack rabbit, which is almost too fast for belief. At any rate, fast as they ran, Morris and I got in a shot apiece, and each of us dropped a buck. They were fat ones. Mine weighed one hundred pounds, by my guess. Chuck's must have been close to one hundred and twenty or one hundred and thirty. As usual, he was childishly glad because he had brought down the better game. He was singing and whistling all the time he was cleaning his kill.

We were both in such spirits, now, that we decided to tie the bodies on the horses and lead the animals for a few miles, so that we could rest them a little, rather than give them an extra burden at the very beginning of their return trip. Although we were extremely anxious to reach the caravan before night, so that they would have the meat for the evening meal, we jogged on for five or six miles in this fashion, leading the horses, then we mounted and rode. I remember asking Chuck about the flash signal of the antelope, and he pointed out to me two white disks on either side of the tail of the antelope. The hair is long on the outside of the disk — perhaps four inches. It is short in the center, and all that hair can be turned out, so that the spot is greatly increased in size, and the flat-lying white hair catches the sunlight just like a mirror does.

We were talking about that when I first saw the signal ahead of us, a white, thick column rising beyond the sun mist. I showed it to Chuck Morris, and his face turned pale in an instant.

"A prairie fire?" I asked him, because I had heard a good deal about them.

Chapter Ten

RECKONING

I stared at Chuck with a growing dread in my heart, but he did not speak. He turned and cut the antelope away from his saddle — all that precious fresh meat of which we had been so happy and so proud. I did not ask questions about that. I simply followed his example and then sent my brown after his gray. It was hard to keep pace with that flying mare. Up to that time I had thought secretly that this talk about the blood of White Smoke was a silly prejudice on the part of Chuck Morris rather than a real superiority. For it seemed to me that there was nothing the gray mare could do that my brown gelding could not manage.

I saw the difference on that wild ride across the prairie. Chuck, in spite of the greater weight which he made in the saddle, could have ridden away from me at any time, if he had chosen to do so. The gray mare was still sliding over the ground at an easy gallop when the brown gelding was utterly spent, his head bobbing, his hoofs pounding.

If I had learned to love horseflesh before this, I learned at that moment to value blood and bone and the heart that knows no weakness.

We did not speak on the whole return trip, but there was no need of talk. We thought of only one terrible possibility, and, when we reached the source of the smoke, we saw that our fears had been prophetic, indeed. There lay the caravan, a crumbled, blackened ruin. The story was told even by the smoldering remnants of the wagons. There had not been time to curl the train into a perfect circle. The danger struck too quickly after the first warning. While the rear wagons were hurrying up, and while the front wagons were slowly turning back to make the circle, the charge struck home. Through the gap the screaming riders must have poured. After that there was no chance to make an organized defense. Ten men in good positions may keep off a thousand Indians — for a time, at the least. But when it comes to scattering fight, man to man, it takes a rare good white man to beat an Indian when the latter is attacking with his first rush. At any rate, not a soul remained alive, and most of them had been burned beyond recognition. First the Indians had looted the wagons of all that was useful to them. Then they had thrown the bodies of the whites into the wagons and set them all on fire, trusting to the fire itself to wipe out the traces of their crime. But we, wandering slowly through that dreadful place, were able to identify a few of the bodies, and from every one the scalp had been ripped away. There were fifty-three dead men. Not a soul had escaped except the two of us.

I was so sick that Chuck Morris had to help me away. We climbed into the saddles, rode over the next rise, and stopped in the hollow. There I threw myself from the saddle and fell flat on my back. I stared up at the evening sky. The red of the sunset was not the only red that seemed swimming and streaming across it. Then I sat bolt erect.

"Chuck," I said, "you hear me swear that so long as I live I'll. . . ."

He clapped his hand over my mouth. "Leave the rest of that oath be," he said. "I know what you're gonna say. You'll never treat an Indian the rest of your life to nothin' but bullets. Well, don't say it, Lew. You ought to have better sense, and you'll get better sense after a while. I've known Indians all my life. They come good, and they come bad. Just the way white men do. But if they're some bad, the whiskey that they get out of the traders makes them worse. You can't give a man poison and then blame him for what he does."

"Would you let a thing like this go, Chuck?" I asked him, full of horror. "When I think of poor Chris Hudson. . . ."

"Chris was a fine fellow," said Morris. "But the average is what you got to think of. The average good that the traders have done for the Indians is to give them whiskey to turn them crazy and give them guns to do more murders with when they're crazy. Whiskey'll kill more Indians than rifles ever will, Lew, and you'll agree with me before long."

"Why?"

"When our horses are rested a mite, you and me are going to have a look at that gang and pay them back a little for the pretty piece of work that they've done."

He had such a set look about the face that I was afraid he meant what, in fact, he really *did* mean. I asked him what he intended to try.

He said: "We each have a Colt and a rifle. That gives us seven shots without reloading."

He didn't offer any more explanation, and I didn't ask for any because of pride. But I was feeling rather wobbly inside, I can tell you, when we climbed onto our horses again. It was easy to follow the trail of those Indians, of course, for they had ridden off in a solid troop.

"What mighty near kills me," said Chuck, "is the number of the Indians. Why, son, there wasn't more'n sixty or seventy of the rascals, take them altogether."

It seemed to me that was quite a number, particularly for two youngsters like ourselves to play with, but I had to follow where Chuck led me. Pure shame whipped me along. I wouldn't be first, but I wouldn't be useless.

It was dark, then twilight, then black night, with all the stars scattered over the sky. Against those stars we presently came on a scaffolding on top of which was a bundled form, and under the scaffold was a dead horse. There were other scaffolds near, built from the timber taken from the wagons, and on each scaffold was the bundled form, and beneath each frame was a dead horse.

"Five Indians," said Chuck Morris, "gone to death . . . one for every ten white men that they've murdered. Oh, this wouldn't be believed! It makes my blood boil. Ten for one."

Really, the actual murders in themselves seemed to make very little difference to Morris. It was the fact that they had not at least slaughtered twice as many Indians as the whites numbered — that was what punished him.

"But the horses?" I asked him.

"They kill a horse for each dead man. The braves have to have something to ride when they get to the happy hunting grounds, don't they?"

He said it rather testily, as though I should have guessed that oddity at a glance. Then we rode on, but I couldn't help looking back at those dead forms, turned toward the sky under which they had lived and fought and murdered.

After a time, Chuck pointed straight ahead. "There it is," he said.

"What?"

"The fire, of course."

I had no idea what he meant, but, after we had gone a little farther ahead, I made out a very faint glow beyond the next swale. Immediately after that we heard their voices.

"All drunk," said Morris. "All dead drunk. If they've taken too much of that poison that Gregory called whiskey, they'll wake up as dead as Gregory himself is."

We dismounted and ran up the swale. Underneath us was the fire, built of still more wood from the wagons that they had taken along with them and heaped higher with brush that they had cut down on the prairie. All around that fire we could see them. Most of them lay flat on the ground, the light glistening on the copper of their half-naked bodies. But a dozen or so were still staggering around the fire, falling down every step or two and then picking themselves up again to go on with the dance. I shall never forget the sound of their drunken maunderings as they tried to shout and sing their chants.

"Get down," I whispered to Chuck. "Get down . . . or they'll see you."

He said without trying to keep his voice down: "They'll never see us. The fire blinds them . . . let alone the whiskey. They'll never see us. Come on. We want to make every bullet tell."

It was plain that he intended to go through with his bloodthirsty scheme. He directed me to go to one side of the fire, and he would go to the other.

"When you begin," he said, "shoot as fast as you can . . . without missing. That'll make them think that they're surrounded by a lot of us, perhaps. Take your horse. They'll see the horse no more than they'll see you."

I never went at anything in my life that I liked so little. Not that the idea of cold-blooded slaughter troubled me any. I had seen the work of those red devils too recently. I would have been glad to blow the whole tribe into their happy hunting grounds. What I worried about was simply the safety of my own skin. Those fellows who were still trying to dance were obviously helpless. But some of the sleepers might have worn off the effects of the liquor, and they might come to their feet quite capable of fighting effectively.

However, I did as Chuck had directed me to do. I went to one side of the fire with the brown gelding and watched him go to the other. It seemed a miracle that the Indians didn't spot us. Because, even looking across the firelight, I could see Chuck, like a ghost, moving on the other side. I suppose the reason was that I was looking out from darkness to darkness, across the light, but the Indians were in the full flare of the fire, and even while I looked, taking out my revolver, one of the Indians heaped more brush on the fire and sent the flames crackling and towering into the sky.

Then Morris's gun cracked, and he who had brought the fuel leaped up into the air with a screech like a wounded cat and fell on his back in the fire, knocking up a vast cloud of sparks twice as bright as the flames themselves and showing me, I thought, the face of every prostrate Indian.

Only they weren't prostrate very long. The alcohol fumes were not able to keep them numb and stupid with that death shriek ringing in their ears. They came swaying to their feet. Out of the grass not twenty feet in front of me rose a giant I had quite overlooked.

I shot at the first human being that had ever been my target, and that man slumped to the side and lay still. He had not uttered a sound. I wish I could say that I felt a great pang of horror and remorse when I saw that Indian fall. But I didn't. Instead, there was a rush of savage delight, and I knew in a flash what the Indians themselves must have felt as they swooped in on that helpless caravan of traders. I took the ones nearest me, as they came staggering to their feet. On the far side of the fire the revolver was chattering from Morris's hand. My own work was almost as fast, and every bullet found a mark.

In the meantime the whole hornet's nest was up, screeching and waving their hands, leaping and catching up weapons, and shooting them into the air or into one another for all I knew. No, there were a good many in that lot who were not dead with drink. Half a dozen seemed to locate me at the same moment, and they lurched in my direction. I had only two shots left in the Colt, and I dropped two of that crowd and then snatched up the rifle and downed a third before the others had enough of it and broke and ran back toward the fire.

Then I swung into the saddle. Morris was already in his and was charging through the frightened herd of Indian ponies, waving his hat and shouting. They broke away before him and stormed across the prairie with Morris, whooping along in their midst. That living wall of horseflesh undoubtedly saved his life, for it was on him, for some reason, that the braves centered their fire, while they let me go galloping off with only a bullet or two singing around my head to make me ride harder.

Three miles or more away I joined Morris, who was reining the gray mare in to wait for me. I was well over my enthusiasm and covered with cold perspiration by this time, but Morris was laughing and shouting like a madman. He seemed to feel that he had performed one of the best of good deeds. I didn't pause to moralize, for I could hear those red wasps buzzing far behind us as they caught horses and rushed on in pursuit.

I have no doubt that they would have caught us in half an hour, considering the weariness of our horses, but Morris adopted a new and very brave maneuver. He turned at more than right angles to our original course, actually inclining back somewhat toward the fire, which we could still see glowing like a great, angry red eye far away. On this new course we put our tired, galloping horses. At least, I can answer for it that the gelding was so spent that every stride he took I feared might be its last. Yet the gray mare with the strain of White Smoke in it was still flaunting along with head held high. Even in my terror I could not help admiring the wonderful animal.

So we got out of the hornet's nest for the time being, though we still had not heard the last of them. At the end of an hour, when the brown no longer so much as flinched under spur, but stumbled along at a trot, head down, Morris called a halt, and we stripped the saddles from the nags and lay down to rest.

I have narrated this event with care, and, looking back over the details, one by one, I see nothing that is not the truth, as far as I can remember. The whole thing is still bright in my mind, and I can still quiver with that fear and then that savage rage which I felt as I crouched in the glimmer of that campfire and shot into the drunken crowd.

I want to be peculiarly exact, because I realize that the great fame of Chuck Morris is largely built on that slaughter of the Cheyennes. If the name of Lew Dorset is also fairly well known to some of the old-timers, I have no doubt that the same bit of slaughter is more closely connected with my name than anything else that I have ever accomplished. That story rang so loudly, for a time, that nothing else was talked about when men sat over campfires. To this day, I know that there are many honest men who lived on the prairies during the early days who contend that the whole tale is a fabrication.

To them I need only reply that old Chief Black Feather himself — and he was as honest as any horse-stealing Cheyenne who ever lived — made statements corroborating everything that I have said. Except that he always declared that, from the fact that the fire was so rapid, he was sure that more than two men were there. Also he declared that no two men would have the courage to attack a war party — even a drunken war party — from two separate sides where they would lack the support of one another. However, he also confesses that, when they struck our trail, they only found two sets of hoof prints, though he explained that away by supposing some of the party had ridden off in a different direction. Nonetheless, the truth is exactly as I have stated it. There were only two men at that fight, and no third person has ever so much as claimed a share in it.

For my part, I freely confess that I don't think the thing was so creditable as it may sound. In the first place, those Cheyennes were a pretty groggy lot with the alcohol they had in them. In the second place, the fire from the two sides undoubtedly made them feel, at first, that two large bodies of men were attacking them. In the third place, the surprise was complete. I have done other things of which I am much prouder.

Of course, the vast majority of the credit goes to Chuck Morris, because he originated the plan and led in its execution. Though when we had passed the age of foolhardy youth, neither he nor I would ever have attempted such desperate work. The Cheyennes themselves have always declared that the Great Spirit was punishing them for their sins.

Before I leave this incident, I want to call attention to the result of our attack, as we afterward learned the details from the Cheyennes themselves. We had fired fourteen shots. These killed six men outright and wounded *eleven others*. The explanation is simply that the drunken Indians, shooting off their guns at random in the first attack, sent some of their bullets into one another. I distinctly remember seeing one fellow, at whom we had not fired, leap up from the grass with a shout and fall back again, groaning.

Chapter Eleven

INTO THE RED MAN'S CAMP

I said that at the end of our day's run we lay down to rest, completely fagged. After half an hour, when I was sound asleep, I was wakened by Chuck Morris, standing up from his blanket. I saw him go to the gray mare and begin to work over her patiently, steadily. It made me wonder to see him.

"Is she sick?" I asked him.

"She's getting her rubdown," he answered. "And she's earned it."

I got up without another word and went to the brown. Not that I knew anything of the fine art of rubbing down a horse, but at least I could wipe the sweat off the poor beast. I found him, standing with his head down, trembling with the cold of the night coming on, and only making an occasional nibble at the buffalo grass. He had the look of a sick horse. He *was* sick, and another day of following that streak of gray lightning which Morris had between his legs would have killed the gelding beyond a shadow of a doubt. I worked over it until I had whipped the thickly beaded sweat out of its hair and brought a bit of a glow to the surface. I worked until it gathered itself together a bit and went ahead industriously with its feeding. Then I heard Morris's voice, speaking low. All men, except the fools, speak low on the prairie.

"A good many more would rather have walked tomorrow than worked over their nags tonight. But you and me are going to ride, Lew, and maybe we'll *have* to ride. Those red devils will be after us, I think."

"They've had enough of us," I said. "Besides, haven't you told me that they rarely stay with a trail very long?"

"That crowd is different," said Chuck. "They're all picked men."

"How could you tell that?"

"You're like others. God gave you eyes, but He didn't give you the sense to use 'em. Didn't you see that every man in that gang had a good rifle?"

"What of that?"

"I'll tell you what. The majority of the Indians have three bows to every gun, and their guns are mostly old flintlock muskets, no good at all. But these bucks had rifles . . . every one of them had a rifle. Lew, I tell you that they're the pick of the whole Cheyenne nation."

"Are they Cheyennes?" I asked.

This was too much for Chuck. He gave up on me in disgust and turned back to his blanket, though he really could not have expected me to know a Cheyenne from any other of the Indians. But he had been reading the prairie language for so many years that he could not understand those who lacked the same knowledge. I had to wait until morning to ask any more questions, and in the morning there wasn't much time for talk. I was still deeply asleep when Chuck prodded my shoulder with the toe of his boot.

"Get up," he said. "It's morning."

"You be damned! It ain't more'n midnight. Besides, I'd rather be scalped than wake up now."

I can still remember the agony of that waking. Chuck simply walked away without arguing. For the prairie kind never wasted their words; they spoke once and went about their business. It was a habit I never acquired. I always enjoyed talk, and the Indians could never grow accustomed to my garrulity. It was Chuck's silence that told me he meant business. I dragged myself into a sitting posture and saw there was only the faintest sort of a gray rim in the east. But even that had been enough for Chuck. Winter and summer, at that moment in the day he always wakened. And as soon as the sun went down he grew dull and sleepy. He seemed to need the sun, and he seemed to respond to it as flowers do.

We saddled the horses at once. The gray mare was as frisky and happy as though she had not carried a rider a mile in a fortnight. I was beginning to understand from her the value of symmetry in a horse. These hulking monsters are not necessarily the great weight carriers. There was the gray that had been flaunting along with Morris's two hundred pounds as though it was a feather. And yet she was really a small horse. I don't think that she stood more than fifteen hands and one or two inches. But she was made with a wonderful neatness and aptness that gave her strength where she needed strength. I looked at her with wonder and with delight this morning. For that matter, the brown had come through the struggle astonishingly well. But there was simply no comparison between the two.

Five minutes later, as the dawn brightened and spilled from the horizon across the faintly rolling waves of the prairie, we were riding for our lives again. I saw nothing. My eyes were still filmed with sleep, and I was sick for the want of it when Morris brought me to my senses with a cruel jerk.

"Cheyennes!" he said.

I sat my saddle, while Morris was already scudding away. I thought for a chilly instant that he intended to ride right away from me, he was so seriously bent on jockeying the gray along. Then I saw the Cheyennes. There were nine of them in sight, four whooping in on the right and five on the left, beating and kicking their nags along. They could do nothing with Morris, of course, and even my brown was too much for them. Indeed, the astonishing thing about Indian horsemanship was always the great average speed of a large body. One hundred Indians would travel twice as fast as one hundred ordinary mounted white men. But, individual against individual, I don't think that they either rode as well or raced as well as a white man.

At a certain point in the chasing they were apt to smell blood and stop thinking. And thinking's what one should be doing all the time, whether it's whittling a piece of wood or reading a book or shooting a gun. One should be thinking hard of what one is doing. Perhaps that sounds like Mother Goose wisdom, but too many men in these days are giving one half of themselves to their work, and with the other half of their brain they are wondering how the accounts of their greatness will appear in the newspapers. While I was riding to put myself out of reach of those nine Cheyennes, I was not thinking of what would happen if they caught me, or how a scalping knife would feel against my skull as I lay half dead on the ground. I was thinking of only one thing, and that was how to put the brown through the gap in time.

Chuck Morris now looked back and brought the gray beside me. It was a very fine thing. He could have shot the mare through to an easy escape, but he preferred taking that terrible chance at my side.

"God bless you, Chuck!" I shouted at him, with tears stinging my eyes.

He did not even hear me, he was so busy watching the Indians, and now his hand began to fumble eagerly at his rifle. It was a beautiful thing to see him. To keep the mare at the brown's speed required no effort from him. He simply dropped the reins and rode her with his heels and his knees, leaving both his hands free. He sat very erect, with the wind whistling under his hat and combing his yellow hair out behind his head. He was smiling, too, in a sort of devilish, happy way that said as plain as day that he loved the danger more than he loved his life.

We flew past them. Then they straightened out behind us until they came to the next little hummock of ground. There they halted, dropped on their bellies on the ground, and began to take pot shots at us. However, I almost fear bows and arrows more than I fear an Indian's gun. They simply are not natural marksmen, and the exceptions are mighty few and far between. There seems to be a desire in them to close the eyes as they pull the trigger.

We slipped out from the danger zone in ten seconds, and not a bullet came closer than humming distance. I felt that this was the last of the Cheyennes, but a moment later I saw that Chuck Morris was a little excited and a little angered — I could not say that there was any fear in such a man.

"They're still after us," he said, "and that means that we may have a month of hell dodging in front of us, Lew. If they turn into bloodhounds, they'll stay with the scent a long, long time. Probably we killed a chief or a chief's son."

That, of course, was exactly what had happened. Morris's very first bullet of all had killed the only son of Chief Black Feather, and that chief himself was among the nine who gave us that early morning rush.

I did not see exactly what we had to fear when we could ride away from the fastest horses in that party. Morris merely shrugged his shoulders. "You wait," he said.

About mid-morning he called my attention to two columns of smoke rising close, side by side in the rear. An hour later he showed me two more smoke columns straight before us, for the air was clear with no wind, and those streams of smoke seemed to go like shadow hands into the heart of heaven.

"Now watch these prairies grow Cheyennes thicker'n grass!" said Chuck Morris.

He was right. In the mid-afternoon we came on a party of a dozen braves, headed out of the north, whereas we had been running up from the south. They did not have to be told that we were their quarry. They merely made for us with a yell, and the only reason that we escaped was, again, owing to the superior foot of our nags.

"They can never catch us!" I shouted, as they dropped away on the rolling green sea of the prairie.

"Why, you fool," said Morris as calmly as you can imagine, "your horse will not be able to raise a gallop tomorrow. There's no real heart in that mongrel dog."

There was no doubt that the brown lacked strength of spirit. It was failing fast when, later, we saw tiny forms bobbing against the southern horizon. Our original friends were catching up with us. When I tried to raise a gallop from the gelding, the spur made it groan, but it only broke into a faltering trot.

"Go on and save yourself!" I cried to Morris.

His silence made me fear that he would take me at my word. Then I saw him, sitting perfectly still, and staring straight ahead of him.

"Don't talk like a fool," said Morris.

He began to push the gray mare straight ahead toward something he made out, though I could not. What an eye he had, like an eagle's, always marking down prey. We had gone on for some time when, at last, I saw what he had seen long before — the crisp little outline of an Indian village against the sky. There were scores and scores of teepees.

"Chuck," I called to him, "are those friendly Indians?"

"I don't know," he said.

"You don't *know*. Then we may be running bang into the fire. They may be more Cheyennes."

"They may."

The very name turned me sick. He answered my thought: "It's either that or else those fellows behind. They'll have you in a few minutes at this rate."

He pointed to the streaking figures coming out of the south, far away.

"They may get me," I said, speaking with lips that were stiffer than actual cold ever made them, "but they can never catch the gray mare."

At that he turned on me with a frown, and Morris's frown, even when he was a boy, was something to remember.

"Look here, Dorset," he said to me, "as long as I'm your friend, your luck is my luck. The minute I'm your enemy, I'll tell you about it, and then heaven help one of us. Now don't let me hear any more nonsense. Whatever comes to you today, comes to me."

It seemed to me then, and it seems to me now, that was the finest speech I ever heard a man make. Afterward I was to learn what the second promise meant.

I got the brown into a gallop after that, and we rolled straight on toward those teepees that meant either heaven or a very real hell to us. When we were a furlong from the tents, a swarm of young bucks came shooting out toward us, all armed to the teeth, but chiefly with bows and arrows. When they saw that there were only two of us, and that we were apparently running away from the horsemen to the rear, they opened up and let us go through to the teepees.

As we galloped on, Morris turned his head to me and said: "Sioux!"

My heart jumped into my throat with joy. "What'll we do in the village?" I called to Morris.

"Keep your mouth shut and do what I do," he said.

Chapter Twelve

IN THE CAMP OF THE SIOUX

The whole village was astir as we rode in. The women and the children were raising a tremendous ruction, and the men were leaping onto the backs of their horses and whirling away to meet whatever danger might be coming on. Morris made for the biggest teepee in the lot. When he came to it, he jumped down from the gray and walked up to a tall Indian who was standing in front of the tent. He was very big for an Indian — within an inch of Morris's own great height and very well made. He was partially gathered in a robe, but the folds of it had slipped from his right shoulder and exposed a huge arm that glistened and bulged with strength. He had the most savage and impassive face I have ever seen, even among his own kind. Behind him stood a squaw with his rifle ready. On the other side was a young girl, holding his horse by the reins. I dismounted as Morris had done and waited.

Chuck went straight to the big chief and waved to his gray mare. He said something in a harsh guttural, and it was not hard for me to tell that he was offering the chief the mare as a present. It was as if he had offered part of his own flesh and blood. The big fellow gave the mare one glance, then he turned to my brown gelding and walked around it, searching it from head to foot. I could see what was going on inside his brain. That gelding was a beauty, as I have said before, and built for both strength and speed, yet it had been run to a rag, and here was the mare, carrying forty pounds more and comparatively as fresh as a daisy. When he had satisfied himself that the brown was a real horse, he gave one more glance at the mare, and then he turned to meet the Cheyennes.

There were a dozen of them who had been brought into the village by a sizable escort of the Sioux. There were perhaps fifty more gathering beyond the outskirts of the little town, waiting to learn what luck their spokesmen would have. The oldest of the twelve walked in advance of the others. He was a wicked-looking old rascal, and, as he came closer, he gave me a glance that was a foretaste of fire and other torments that would be mine if he got me into his hands. From that instant I never left my revolver out of my grip. If they tried to take me, I was determined to die fighting and keep a last bullet for myself.

Black Feather — for it was he — went to the Sioux chief and began to talk with a good deal of excitement. Now and again he turned to give a point to his remarks by waving at us, and every time he turned there was a red glint from his eyes and a white flash of his teeth. I've never seen anything so wolfish. Sometimes, as he talked, great shudders ran through his body, he was so eager to get at us.

The Sioux let him talk himself out without saying a word. As Black Feather ended, he laid a perfectly good rifle and a quantity of beads at the feet of the big chief. Then the rest of the twelve came up and each had his say, most of them using fewer words than Black Feather, but every whit as much emotion. Each, as he finished, put down something in front of the big fellow. It was as plain as plain could be that they were offering a price for the pair of us. And in terms of Indian wealth, what a price they were offering in rifles, powder and lead, and beads and knives and little trinkets. When the last of the twelve had spoken, Black Feather stepped up for a final shot. He pointed to the heap of plunder at the feet of our host. Then he waved to the sky and struck his breast. He was declaring, I suppose, that, if the ugly giant would take the bribe, he would also receive the eternal friendship of the Cheyennes, both past and present.

The manner of the Sioux, in the meantime, was thoroughly Roman and perfectly delightful. Not a muscle in his face stirred. He looked each man in the face, in turn. When Black Feather had ended his second jargon, the Cheyenne horse thief turned on me, because I was nearest, and reached out a hand toward me. I was ready to sink a bullet in his brain when I heard a deepvoiced monosyllable from the Sioux. I did not need a translator to tell me that the word was "No!" Oh, sweetest of all music and most beautiful of all words.

There stood the Sioux, pointing down to the heap of loot and shaking his head. The price was not high enough. There began a hurried roar of voices, each of the twelve registering his protest, but the Sioux stopped it with a single wave of his hand. After that, all talk ended. Each of the twelve emissaries in silence picked up his rejected gift, and they trooped out. Each, as he went, gave me a side glance that cut like a whip.

Black Feather, the rearmost of the procession, turned suddenly around and delivered himself of half a minute of concentrated hate and defiance. I knew that he was telling the Sioux that another day was coming when the memory of what was happening now would be poison. Our host said nothing in reply. Not until the Cheyennes were well out of the village — not until on their return a wild yell of disappointment and rage had gone up from their fellow wolves — did the big man speak, and then it was only a guttural murmur. It brought another squaw straightway from the tent. She went to the gray mare, stripped off saddle and bridle, and led the gentle beauty away by the mane, until they disappeared behind the tent. Oh, wise chief. He had been able to read horseflesh value with a very sure eye. Now that the mare was his, he turned on his heel, lifted the flap of the teepee, and disappeared inside. The two other squaws went off. Morris and I were left alone, except for a few gaping, naked children.

"I'm sorry about the mare," I told him.

He gave me a frowning glance that said it would be best to avoid that tender topic. Then he said: "I don't know whether we're lucky or unlucky. This fellow who has turned the Cheyennes about their business is Standing Bear himself."

"I never heard of him," I said.

"You've never heard of a great deal that

you ought to know," said Morris tersely. "Anyway, he is a great man in his nation. No one agrees about him. Everyone admits that he's a bang-up warrior . . . a real fighter fit for any company. But some say he's a cunning devil. Others swear that he's a fine fellow. The first guess looks nearest the truth to me."

"A great deal," I agreed. "He's taken one of our horses, and now he as much as says . . . go about your business. He's saved us from the Cheyennes for a moment, but what will happen when we try to leave this village?"

Morris nodded. He dropped his head for a moment in thought, then he nodded to me, as much as to say: "I have it." Then he stepped forward, lifted the flap of the teepee, and entered. I was at his heels. Inside we found the three squaws I had noticed already, together with a fourth one. By that I knew that whatever he might be in war, Standing Bear was certainly a great man in time of peace. There was much more comfort in this teepee than I had expected to find in an Indian's habitation. The tent itself was stretched around very long, strong poles, and it was made of buffalo skins sewed firmly together with rawhide. These skins were painted on the inside with flaring pictures of hunting scenes. As studies of anatomy the figures were not masterpieces, of course, but they always seemed wonderfully bright and cheerful to me. There were four small basket beds, filled with buffalo robes, and one big one. In a corner were packages of dried meat. There were clumsily made racks, here and there. Some of them were filled with bows and arrows. And there were three excellent rifles of the latest make. I could not help wondering if the chief had secured them by honest purchase. There were other things in the tent. For instance, there were heaps of buffalo robes for everyone to sit on. The other details I can't remember. At least, these were the main articles of every Indian household.

It was an ideal scene of domestic thrift, in a way. Standing Bear was looking over the mechanism of a rifle, taking it carefully apart and knotting his brows over it. I knew by that he was an exceptional Indian, for as a rule they are willing to take a rifle for granted. They class all machinery with the mysteries of life. The four squaws were beading moccasins. Every hand in the group was busy. Their tongues were not a whit less active. Only Standing Bear went on with his work without giving us a glance, but the women poured out a tide of talk that never ended. All the time they were prying at us with their eyes, making new discoveries, and then talking over their opinions with one another in the most naïve manner. I was frightfully embarrassed, both because of their chatter, and because I felt that we were forcibly intruding ourselves on the chief's household. However, Morris was magnificent. He took a pipe out of his pocket and lighted it. He went on smoking as though this were the most ordinary scene in his life, and he gave them back look for look. Those big, clear blue eyes of his were always a heavy weight for even a white man to bear, and I have never seen an Indian, man or woman, whose glance did not flick downward after fronting Morris for a moment.

After a time he finished his pipe, knocked the ashes out, and made a motion with his hand to his lips. The youngest squaw got up at once and brought us some dried buffalo meat. It was tough chewing, but I was famished and thought I had never tasted anything so good. After that, they brought us water. And there we sat. What would be the end of the play I could not imagine.

Presently Standing Bear got up, threw open the flap of the teepee, and, looking at us, he pointed outdoors. He could not have said more plainly: "You have rested enough.

Now kindly take yourselves off." I got ready to stand up until I saw that Morris had no intention of stirring. He was smoking again, and he continued to puff in a dreamy, contented way, looking at big Standing Bear as though the chief were no more than another painting on the side of the tent.

I would not have been surprised if the Indian had snatched out his knife and come for us, but after a frowning moment he went out. Then the squaws tried their hands at us. Gestures, fluent Indian prattle, were nothing to Morris. He kept a face as composed as granite. The youngest sat down beside him, began to smile and nod, and then rose, still talking, and went toward the entrance, looking back at him. Even this was not enough. Morris looked at her with a bland lack of understanding.

Night dropped over the village. The fire in the center of the teepee threw a wild, red light on the faces of the Indians and over the long golden hair of Morris. Then Standing Bear returned. He gave us a dark look, then muttered a word to the squaws, and they brought us two buffalo robes apiece. Morris had won again.

Chapter Thirteen

A LAST STAND

There we spent the night. At first I thought that I should never close my eyes in so strange a place. For, if I did, might I not be wakened by the point of a knife? Might not my last glimpse of life be the thousandth part of a second during which the blade slid into my heart? My own scalp would not be very highly prized, of course, but the long blond tresses of Chuck Morris would be an immense addition to the trophies of even so great a chief as Standing Bear. Just as this thought came to me, I heard the deep, regular breathing of Morris, and an instant later I was buried under a towering wave of sleep.

In the morning we were up at daybreak, as the whole camp began to stir. Standing Bear's squaws gave us breakfast, and then we ventured out of the teepee. The first thing we saw, on a hillock outside of the village, was a Cheyenne, sitting on his horse like a copper statue, waiting. Waiting for us, of course. The moment we left the Sioux, the wolves would be after us. Morris and I stared at that rascal and then at one another. We did not need to speak, but we decided silently at that moment that nothing but sheer physical force should drive us out of the village.

We received a good deal of attention and quite a bit of admiration. Afterward we understood why. The Cheyennes, in telling their reasons for wanting us, had described the night attack on them, and that description put us down as great warriors in spite of our youth. We were allowed to go where we pleased, and we put ourselves out to be agreeable, smiling and nodding whenever anyone looked at us. I asked Morris if we were safe now, and he said that he did not know. One could never tell what would come into the heads of Indians, whether they were Sioux or others. What most impressed me was the immense cheerfulness in that little town. There was a continual babble of voices, and there was a great air of industry. That was given by the women, of course. Your real Sioux warrior knows that work is beneath him. He supplies the food and does the fighting. As for the disagreeable duties that must be performed about the teepee every day, he does not even notice them.

When the mid-morning sun grew hot, almost the entire lot of young braves and boys went down to the river that flowed near the village. We dived in with the rest, where the current flowed wide through a little lake. The water was warm and clear; the bottom was sprinkled with shining pebbles and great golden drifts of sand. It was very pleasant to drift down the stream, then turn and fight one's way up again. I soon saw that I was the worst swimmer in the lot. Morris was magnificent in the water, as he was on the land. His long, powerful strokes carried him along with the foam bubbling around his big shoulders. But for actual speed Morris could not compare with even the worst of the Indians. Boys and men, they glided along like watersnakes. They seemed almost as fast under the surface as on top, and they were repeatedly going down for pebbles and coming up laughing with a prize, only to throw it away again when, out of the water, it appeared as merely a dull rock.

In the midst of the fun, a gleaming, copper shadow slid along under me. I was caught suddenly by the neck, and down I went. I struck out with my fists, but the water dulled the force of my blows. I had only a confused impression of a bronze-skinned monster, dragging me down. When I was almost choked, he released me, and I came gasping and spitting to the surface with the laughter and the mockery sounding far and faint through the roaring in my ears.

Just as my head began to clear, the attacker shot through the water again and dumped me under the surface once more. I was furious because he was making a fool of me. This time, when I came up to the surface, I had sense enough to head in for the shore. By the time I had reached the shallows, the big fellow was after me once more, but now I could turn on him with a firm footing to hold me up. That made a different story of it at once.

I grappled him, and, although he was a full-grown warrior, he was nothing in my hands. My grip was twice his. In addition, he knew little of wrestling, because the Indians show little science in that art. So, after a brief flurry, I had him lying on his face in the water, struggling and kicking in vain. Not until he began to grow weak did I let him out. Then he was so far gone that I had to drag him ashore. He lay for a time on his back, gasping and coughing. Then he got up and went slowly back into the village. I looked about, expecting a little applause, but everyone was very sober. Morris came up to me at once.

"Go ashore," he said as he came by. "You've made a fool of yourself, and maybe you've put us both in danger again."

"What have I done?" I asked. "Was I to get myself half drowned without hitting back?"

"Play is play among the Sioux, and nobody ever dreams of making a fight out of a game."

I could see that he was rather disgusted with me. But I saw nothing wrong in what I had done until Standing Bear himself came over the horizon and made for me, riding Morris's beautiful gray mare. He pulled up in front of us, but he addressed Morris, not me. He spoke to us in very good English, the rascal, though I had not dreamed that he understood a word of the language.

"A wise chief," he said, "keeps his young men in order. Spotted Buck" — that was the name of the young brave who had had the tussle with me — "is very sad and is stringing his bow. The Cheyennes have gone. The trails from this city are easy to follow, friend."

Morris nodded, then he answered: "This young man," he said, pointing to me, "is very simple. He knows how to fight, but not how to play. He is not a beaver at home in the water. He is a badger. He is very sorry about Spotted Buck and wishes to smoke a pipe with him. Besides, he says that Standing

Bear is his father, and he wishes to give his father a knife which cuts leather as the sun cuts through ice. It has an edge that never turns."

With that, he reached out and took my hunting knife out of its sheath and gave the handle into the palm of Standing Bear. The chief weighed it for a moment with a blank face. Then he flipped back his hand and shot the knife down. It was buried to the hilt in the hard ground and remained there, humming. Then Standing Bear turned his back on us and rode away.

"You see?" Morris said. "You've managed to get us thrown out of the camp by your infernal fighting. Great heavens, Lew, were your hands given to you for nothing but tussling?"

I was sorry we were in such a scrape, but I was glad to have that knife back, and I reached for it.

Morris caught me by the shoulder and jerked me upright. "You idiot," he said. "After giving a thing away, do you think you can take it back again? Standing Bear will probably send a squaw after that knife pretty soon, and, if he finds that it is gone, he'll probably turn us out of the village at once."

"He has as good as done that already," I suggested.

"Not at all. He rode away without ordering us off, because he was in doubt."

"What will happen now? Some other buck will happen along and pick up that knife."

"Certainly not. You see no one in sight, but you can be sure that at least a dozen people have seen that knife. It will stay there, fixed in the dirt, unless Standing Bear decides to send for it. Now come along with me."

He led me back to Standing Bear's teepee, but, when we went to enter, a big brave was standing there with a bow and some arrows ready. He did not speak to us, and we did not speak to him, but we simply drifted away. Words were quite unnecessary.

"And now?" I said.

"Do your own guessing," said Morris. "I'm not a mind reader. They may be waiting until night to throw us out of the camp and then send a scalping party on our trail, or they may be waiting for Spotted Buck to take his chance at you. In that case, heaven help Spotted Buck . . . and us after you've sent a bullet through his poor, misguided head. Of course, he has to try to kill you if he can. Otherwise, he has lost his honor."

That was the beginning of a wretched day. We went back to the river's edge and remained there under a willow until late in the afternoon. Then we came back into the village, but no one saw us. We stopped in front of a teepee where two squaws were cooking and made signs that we were hungry, but they paid not the slightest attention to us.

"I understand now," said Morris. "Standing Bear took my horse, and, therefore, he can't very well have our throats cut and our scalps taken at his front door. First, he'll starve us out. When we've left the village, he'll let the young braves do what they want with us. Well, it will be a sorry day for these Sioux when they corner the pair of us."

"I've brought you into trouble again," I told him sadly.

"Bah," said Morris. "No man can live forever."

In the meantime the twilight came, and then a great moon stood up on the eastern skyline and turned the prairies to white silver. Morris and I sat down back to back, because there was no telling when Spotted Buck would come snaking along toward us with his gun or his bow and arrows. I was beginning to get cold and stiff, and the barrel of my rifle was freezing my hand, when a commotion started on the farther side of the village.

In ten seconds every soul in the place was screeching a word that sent shudders through me.

"What's wrong?" I asked Morris.

"Pawnees," he explained.

"What are they?"

"They're enemies of the Sioux. Fighting devils, too. If there were as many Pawnees as there are Sioux in the world, I suppose they'd wipe our friends out."

"I hope they do," I said gloomily, "if they'll wipe out the Cheyennes at the same time."

The village had really gone mad, it seemed to me. The boys darted out and rushed in the horses. The bucks went whooping out to make a battle line. We were left alone in a trice with the women, the youngsters, and the old men, together with two or three of the young warriors who were sick.

The fighting had started. The Sioux and the Pawnees were screeching out on the prairie, hidden from our eyes. By the sound of the guns and the diminished noise of yelling, we guessed that the fight was gradually rolling farther and farther away from us. The squaws, the children, and the old men seemed to think the same thing. They had been half frightened to death a moment before. Now they began to yell again in a new key, get out knives, and do scalp dances that turned one's blood cold. They used us for their little game. They would come prancing straight up to us, making the most hideous faces and screaming at the top of their lungs, wave the knives in the air, and then do a foolish, hopping dance around us.

I asked Morris if we were in any danger, and he said we were, because the women, when they got excited, were ten times as frightful in action as the men. The really expert torturing was always done by them.

It was a fit ending for the sort of a day we had been passing. I was beginning to think that one of those knives would slice across my throat when there was a new babble breaking out, and this time it came from *our* side of the town. I could not imagine what it was all about, but Morris figured it out quickly enough.

"There's a Napoleon among those Pawnees," he said. "They've engaged the braves with part of their band, and the other part is going to eat up the village and get away with the horses."

There was no doubt about that. The Pawnees came shrieking into the teepee town, letting off their guns and shooting their arrows at everything in sight. Like deer and vermin scared out of a forest by a fire, the old men, women, and children began to scoot away from the danger line. But there was one young buck, really too sick to stand, who refused to run. He stuck a couple of broken feathers in his scalp lock and grabbed up a bow with a quiver full of arrows. Then he stood out in plain sight and began to warm himself up for his work by doing a war dance — but his knees were so weak that he could only shuffle his feet along the ground. Only his lungs were in good working order, and the whoops he let out are still ringing in my ears. Morris knew enough Sioux to give me a free translation.

"He says that he's Gray Buffalo, and that he has never turned his head from a Pawnee and never intends to. This is where he figures on dying. Lew, we'd better range up beside the poor cripple."

We had to make our last stand somewhere, and, even if Gray Buffalo were small comfort, he was better than nothing. We ran out beside him. When he saw us drop on our knees and get our rifles ready, he turned stark, staring mad, and began to scream at the others. He had an effect on them, too. Some of the boys and the old men got up their nerve when they saw this example and came running to join our lost cause.

Chapter Fourteen

SITTING WOLF

We had a little army around us in an instant. And what an army. We had little boys of ten years with their amateur bows that shot arrows just strongly enough to stick the heads into the hide of the village cows. We had women swinging clubs. We had men too weak to bend the big war bows. We had sick young braves like that real hero, Gray Buffalo, who had organized the defense.

We were no longer outcasts. I may tell you that, in the few seconds remaining before the Pawnees broke in on us, we were given a rare welcome, because anyone could see with half an eye that Morris and I, with our rifles and revolvers, were the real strength of the defense. We were patted on the back and stroked and made much of — and then a drove of frightened horses came crashing straight toward us. The Pawnees had sent them ahead as a screen to shelter their main attack on the village, and they nearly ground to bits our staggering line of last defense. But just as they were about to sweep over us, the horses broke to either side and sloped past us, giving us an open view of the Pawnees, raging in the rear.

Have you ever seen an Indian charge by moonlight? Those who have will understand why I don't try to describe it. There was not enough dust raised to obscure that sight. And we had a free glimpse into hell with half a hundred devils, raging through the mist. They were shooting as they came. An arrow clipped Gray Buffalo in the throat, and he went down on his face, scratching at the dirt with both hands for a second, until he died. A poor little child of ten or eleven stood up beside me and sent an arrow from his play bow. The next instant he had a shaft through his leg and went down — went down without a murmur.

By that time I had forgotten to be afraid. I was too hot for that. I barely heard Morris call: "Now, Lew!"

Then we let them have it. They were coming in a flying wedge, and our two shots chipped off the two riders who were the point of the wedge. Our little army of cripples raised an immense din when they saw the leaders of the Pawnees drop, and they turned loose a wild volley of arrows, bullets, sticks, and stones. I could see the Pawnees swaying back on their horses, tugging at the reins. An Indian likes to see the other fellow running before he charges home. While they were swaying — the front men checking their horses and kicking up clouds of dust, and the rear trying to press through and get at our scalps — Chuck and I opened up with our revolvers.

When a man has shot squirrels out of trees, he doesn't miss a grown man at point-blank range even when only the moon is out. We took our time. There was no hurry. The Pawnees began to drop fast enough to take the heart out of them. Besides, the moment they halted, half a hundred of the Sioux women and old men and cripples rushed them. I saw a big squaw swing a club I could hardly have managed myself and knock down a rider at one clip.

It was over in ten seconds. The Pawnees lost heart in the first five and began to struggle to get back in the next five counts. Then they bolted off into the moon mist just as a troop of our own Sioux, returning from the main battle to the rescue, came thundering through the town. They went after those Pawnees like timber wolves after coyotes. Another instant and the trouble was over. There was nothing but victory. I didn't mind the racket that the squaws and the children put up. I felt like doing a little yelling myself.

Then I remembered the youngster who had gone down with the arrow through his leg. He had pulled himself a little to one side and had braced his back against a teepee. There he had shot one arrow after another at the Pawnees while the battle lasted. After that, he put down his bow, folded his arms, and waited for help to come — if help was coming. None of the Sioux paid the slightest attention to that little hero. They were too busy celebrating. I went over to him. He gave me a smile I shall never forget and waved me off as though he were saying: "Go join the fun. I'm quite all right."

I took him to a quieter nook between two tents. The arrow had gone clean through his thigh. I cut off the head. Then I pulled out the shaft. The youngster didn't make a sound, but the agony wilted him. He fainted dead away, and I was glad of it. While he was senseless, I washed that wound clean, more thoroughly than I would have had the heart to do if his eyes had been open. Then I cut up my shirt and began to bandage his leg in tiptop fashion. Before the bandaging was finished, the boy woke up with a groan. The instant he realized that he had made a sound of complaint, he clapped his hand over his mouth and stared at me as though he expected a beating. I brought him plenty of cold water next, and he drank like one with a fever. As a matter of fact, he had lost a good deal of blood, for it was a nasty wound. Then I picked him up in my arms and carried him off to find his parents, if I could.

I had hardly come out into the crowd before I saw that the two battles were not only over, but that the Sioux had gained a whacking big victory. The braves were coming in singly and in groups, telling what they had done and showing the scalps they had taken. From what I learned afterward, it seems that the Pawnees ventured to stand their ground a bit too long, and, although they intended to act merely as a mask for the really vital attack on the village, they allowed themselves to get entangled in the sweep of the Sioux charge. The result was a pretty severe butchery before the Pawnees disentangled themselves again and scooted across the prairie, but even in the hunt many were cut down, because their horses were not comparable in freshness with those of the villagers. Nearly half of the braves of the village, it seemed to me, had at least one scalp. Those who had more were sure to be centers of interest, but no one was more densely surrounded than a tall young man with golden hair that flowed down over his shoulders. It was Morris, of course. They were making an immense fuss over him, but, when he saw me, he broke through the circle and came wading through the Indians.

"Half the party is taking the praise, Lew," he said, laughing at me. "Step in for your share."

"You talk like a fool," I told him. "I have a poor boy here more than half dead. I want to find his mother. Will you ask these chattering blockheads to find the right teepee for me?"

He asked the question and got his reply quickly enough.

"Standing Bear has a brother, Three Buck Elk, almost as important a chief as the Bear himself. This youngster is Sitting Wolf, the only son in either family. You've done yourself a good turn in taking care of that youngster, Lew."

He had barely gotten this out when a squaw came twisting through the crowd and snatched at little Sitting Wolf. I only had one arm free, and I didn't feel like wasting politeness. I put my palm in her face and pushed her away. But right behind her came an Indian every whit as tall as Standing Bear, except that he was not nearly so ponderous of shoulder. He was dabbled with blood from neck to waist, and he had four scalps at his belt. I knew by that as well as by his dignity that he was quite a man in his nation. In another moment I knew that he must be Three Buck Elk and the boy's father. I could tell by the way he stood over the youngster and looked down to him, and by the way Sitting Wolf smiled back in his face. He laid a hand on my shoulder, this blood-stained brave, and the word that he spoke came up from his heart. Whatever the word was, the sound of it is the same in all languages spoken by men. It was: "My brother."

He took Sitting Wolf in his arms tenderly. The squaw trotted along at his side, wringing her hands. I brought up the rear, because I wanted to see that the youngster was well taken care of. They waded through the wrangling crowd to one of the biggest teepees — the same one that had refused us food that afternoon. There they put Sitting Wolf on a buffalo robe, and presently they brought in a cross-eyed old woman who began to mumble over the youngster and knead his wound right through the bandage. The pain of it must have been frightful, and Sitting Wolf's face shone with perspiration. I couldn't stand that, so I took the old hag by the shoulder and sent her right about. Then I sat down by the boy. The leg was swelling and feverish. I cut the bandage away and washed the wound again with warm water. The relief was so immense that Sitting Wolf actually moaned. Then I dressed the leg again. I smoothed out the buffalo robe on which he was lying and put a pad under his hip and his knee, so that the weight of the leg would not lie on the wound. Then I made Three Buck Elk's squaw stew up some meat and gave the broth to the boy. A little while later Sitting Wolf fell asleep.

All this time the chief and his squaw had been fiddling around. She was tremendously worried because the old witch had been sent away. Besides, she wanted to take a hand with her son herself. Three Buck Elk took her by the shoulder and sat her down with a thump, for he seemed to guess that the white man's magic of common sense was a great deal better than any folderol made up of words and foolishness. When the boy finally went to sleep, the chief pointed to him and then to me, and the squaw came up and peered at her child.

He made a wonderful picture as he lay there on his back with the firelight flickering and leaping over his smooth young body. The mother went over him from head to foot with a touch as light as a feather. Then she covered him carefully and tucked him in. When she finished, she sat down by his head, and, looking up at me, she said something with a voice as soft as cooing doves.

Of all the pictures with which my mind is crowded and in which Sitting Wolf plays a leading part, this picture is the most lasting one. I can still see his head turn into his mother's arm with a smile. As for Three Buck Elk, he was in an agony because he could not tell me what he felt toward me. He took up a fine new rifle and pressed it into my hands. He dragged together a heap of buffalo robes and made signs that they were mine. Finally he signified everything in the teepee was mine, if I would take it, and, pointing to a picture of a horse painted on the side of the tent, he held up his fingers many times to indicate that I should have ten — twenty horses.

I shook my head. It is amazing how much a person can say without words. I was able to tell Three Buck Elk and his squaw, by signs, how Sitting Wolf had come into the fighting line with his toy bow, how he had been wounded, how he had dragged himself to the side, and continued his fight after he was struck down. The face of the chief, while I talked, was that of one who is drinking the most delicious wine. His lips moved, translating my gestures into his own language, and the big muscles of his arms worked as he labored at the war bow in imitation of his boy in the combat. When I ended, Three Buck Elk was too moved to speak or move. He stood there with his head down, and his blood-stained chest heaving.

I knew that he was afraid lest I should see the tears of pride and of sorrow and of utter happiness in his eyes, and so I sneaked out of the teepee as quietly and as quickly as I could. Outside, a couple of young bucks spied me. They took hold of me and swept me along with or without my will to a place in the center of the village where a big fire was shaking its head high above the tops of the tallest trees. There was the whole band except the wounded and their families. Their howling brought echoes from the coyotes and the buffalo wolves out on the prairie. They were dancing and prancing around the flames, generally making themselves happy and foolish.

I found Chuck Morris drawn back into the shadow, looking on. I went to him as soon as possible.

"We're made men among the Sioux," he said. "The main thing is not the fighting we did, it seems. Standing Bear has just left me. He has been telling me that the sun would never have risen in his life again, if Sitting Wolf had died of bleeding, as he would have done if it hadn't been for you. Those were his words, or something like those words, except that he was a lot more grand. He put in that Spotted Buck is both a young man and a young fool, and that it is best to forget him. He, Standing Bear, is my father, it seems, and Three Buck Elk is yours. I am to have the gray mare back, if I'll take her. Anything else we want is ours. If we want to touch a match to the whole village, we're free and welcome to it. Now, old son, the thing for us to do is to speak soft and walk small, because they may change their minds about us."

Chapter Fifteen

STANDING BEAR HEAPS HONORS

I want to say why the Sioux made such a fuss over us. In the first place, those who have never been on the prairies in the old days must understand that the Indian is the most generous person in the world. He is a white man turned inside out. The white man is aiming to collect more and more all the time; the Indian wants to give away. It's more honorable for an Indian to give away a thousand dollars than it is for a white man to make a million. And that is not an exaggeration. If you give an Indian one horse, he immediately wants to give you two, and yet horses mean more to Indians than anything in the world, except their children.

Now the great point was that Standing Bear was already a little ashamed, as well as I can understand it, because, after taking our best horse, he had contemplated turning us out on the prairie for the benefit of the Cheyennes. Just when his remorse was beginning to work on him, the Pawnees jumped the town, and Chuck and I saved the horses and the women and children from a massacre, whereas the logical thing was for us to join the Pawnees and help them gut the town. In addition, Sitting Wolf had been saved from bleeding to death, and the total result was such a number of benefactions heaped upon that tribe by the pair of us that Standing Bear was in an agony of humiliation. He wanted to give us all his earthly possessions, and, in conclusion, he offered to adopt us into the tribe.

"Of course, you'll join," said Chuck in the most matter-of-fact way, "and I think I'll join, too."

I was astonished and also a little irritated, because I felt that Chuck was talking down to me.

"Why should I join?" I asked him.

"Well, you want to find your father, don't you? That's your whole reason for coming out here on the prairies, isn't it?"

I admitted that it was.

"What better chance could you have than with these Sioux? If your father is the sort of man you tell me he is, he's probably out here, trading or trapping, or some such thing. He's in the out-of-the-way corners where the law doesn't bother a man too much and where questions aren't asked. That's just where the Sioux will take you, or, if you want to cut away from them, you're free to do that whenever you please and make a search by yourself."

"But why should *you* join?" I asked him.

"Because I like the life," he said frankly. "I'm not quite nineteen. It doesn't much matter what I do with the next few years. They're pretty sure to be wasted. If I go back among our own people, I'll still be treated like a boy for three or four years. Out here among the Sioux I'll be treated like a man, and a chief at that."

The first naming of the idea had shocked me, I admit. After I had listened to Chuck's reasons, it seemed rather a natural thing to do. *I* liked the life, too, as well as any white man who was ever born. The prairies were made for just such men as I, and the unchecked freedom was the purest heaven to me after a life with Uncle Abner and Uncle Abner's whip.

We told Standing Bear the next day that we had made up our minds to become Sioux, and he seemed to be delighted. He let the news go around the village, and we had to hold a reception that lasted all this day and the next. Everyone down to the children came to us and gave us some sort of present, saying the name of each article over and over until it was fixed in our minds.

That was the way we began to learn the Sioux language. We were given a teepee, and it was completely fitted up with the best that the tribe could offer. Everything from dried meat to buffalo robes of the finest quality were in it, and we were told to select what horses we wanted from the herds of Standing Bear and Three Buck Elk. It was quite a temptation, but we limited ourselves to three horses apiece. Morris always advised moderation.

After this, there had to be a ceremony. The mere saying of a word could not make us members of the tribe. First, they sent away for several famous chiefs of the Sioux nations. I think that there were five, altogether, who responded. They came, bringing some of their principal braves, and, when they had all arrived, there was a great feast of roasted venison — and dogs. It was a real celebration. Some of the chiefs had been trading with whites lately, and they carted in a supply of firewater. Five Indians were dead and a number of others wounded before that firewater had been used up. For five days the racket continued, and, when it ended, the visiting chiefs came to me, and each made a little speech, welcoming me into the tribe and telling me that his teepee was my teepee and his horses were mine, and *vice versa*. Standing Bear and Three Buck Elk did the same thing, and so the ceremony ended. We were Sioux Indians.

It was very odd, and not at all unpleasant. I looked on the whole thing as a mere experiment and felt that in a year or two I would turn my back on them and never see any more of my red brothers. But two whole years passed like a drawn breath. That is to say, I was nearly seventeen when we joined the Sioux, and I was nineteen before the next great event happened in my life.

I say that the two years passed like a drawn breath, and I mean just that. There was never a simpler nor, in a way, a more beautiful life than that of those prairie Indians. The summer was a long frolic. The fall was the season of laying in heavy buffalo robes and trapping beaver — also watching those wise little animals, for if they stored a great deal of food against the cold season, we knew that the snow would be deep and the winds outrageous. And the beavers never fail as weather prophets.

Those winters were sometimes a bit monotonous, but there was usually something to amuse us in the village, and all winter long there was always buffalo hunting to keep us active. What a waste of valuable food were those buffalo hunts. I have seen fifteen hundred animals cut off from the outer edge of one of the vast black herds and then shot down to the last bull in the lot. Of the whole carcass nothing would be taken except the tongue and that tenderloin on the inside over the kidney. Even this we considered too much trouble to carve out half the time, and only the tongues were taken. If the skins were prime, they were ripped away. The rest of the animal remained for the buzzards and the eagles.

I suppose that in those two years I should have been forming my mind with hard work. But I have always looked back to that period as the golden season of my life. All the bitterness of my boyhood was melting out of my soul. Also I was busy on the trail of my father. Whenever I heard of a solitary trapper, I made a point of looking him up, although he never turned out to be the man. For some reason I was sure that my father would live alone like an outcast buffalo bull. Whenever we met traders, I described Will Dorset and asked if they had heard of such a man, but I never received a satisfactory answer.

Those were prosperous days for Standing Bear and his tribe. Chuck and I were a great windfall for him. He already had the backing of his brother, who was talented enough to have led a tribe on his own account. Now, in addition, he had two white Indians who were famous enough to have drawn a select band of warriors to follow them. This does not have a modest sound, but it is very true. As a rule, one important action is enough to make the fame of an Indian. The Cheyenne, Black Feather, was always celebrated because in his youth he had killed two Pawnees in one battle. If other braves were inclined to forget a warrior's achievements, he freshened their minds by whooping it up on his own account at a feast. Such tales were not considered boasting but were necessary statements of fact, proving that a warrior had self-respect and reflecting credit on the whole tribe, and these narratives were supposed to fill the brains of the young braves with a noble emulation.

All of which has a certain degree of truth in it. If Chuck and I never had the art of chanting about ourselves, the others filled in the gaps. We had two exploits to our credit. One was the harrying of Black Feather and his crew; the other was the turning of that Pawnee charge. Chuck was much more famous than I was, partly because he deserved to be, partly because he was a picture that filled the eye of every Indian, and partly because he was by nature dignified and reserved. However, we were both constant attractions, and our tribe never visited another section of the Sioux nations without detaching a few of the most select young braves to follow our standard.

As for my education, I had learned to ride and to swim, though I am afraid that I was never as expert at either art as nine-tenths of the Indian youths. They were inclined to smile at me on most occasions, except when I had a gun in my hand or when I doubled my fist. But in order to be respected by Indians, one needs to excel in only one thing. As I have said, I was never a genius on horseback or in the water. I was never more than an A-B-C scholar when it came to reading sign on the prairies. And, though big Chuck Morris learned to handle a bow and arrow as well as the best of the braves, I could not manage those tough war bows at all. I had no natural talent for the thing. Indeed, except what I learned in the hard school of Abner Dorset, nothing was ever thoroughly mastered by me.

Since I had only the ability to fight, I recognized that fact and clung to it. I studied wrestling and boxing and mixed in with the traders to practice my craft whenever I could. I had filled out to my full bulk, which was never more than one hundred and sixty-five pounds. But every one of those pounds was composed of the most necessary sort of muscle and bone. I looked like a mere morsel beside Chuck Morris, but I could lift pound for pound with him, and the Indians knew it. As for Chuck, he was a dreadful fighter as well as a wise man much prized in their councils, whereas I never opened my mouth in their debates. They had only one thing to say about me, and therefore they gave me a more concentrated celebrity. It was a belief among the Sioux that I *could* not miss a target. This belief, acting naturally on my pride, made me as anxious with my guns as when Uncle Abner had threatened a hiding to me every time I failed to convert a bullet into dead meat.

Since those two years did little for me except to bring me to maturity, I am going to give a picture of myself at the age of nineteen. I was five feet and ten inches high. I weighed exactly one hundred and sixty-five pounds — which was a weight I kept for thirty years. I was rather light in the legs and gaunt bellied, but thick and heavy around the shoulders. I had very long arms, and my hands were actually larger than those of big Chuck Morris. I was never very particular in my dress. In fact, I was rather an eyesore to my tribe. My deerskins were usually out at the elbow. My moccasins were crude and unbeaded, and my hair was chopped off close to my head. I had a big, blunt jaw, a hooked nose, or at least a very high-arched one, and those bright black eyes which are born in every Dorset I have ever seen. I was not an imposing figure, and not at all close to the romantic hero type. I blush a little even now when I recall the name the Indians gave me — that is to say, my enemies, the Pawnees. The Sioux called me Black Bear, but the name by which I was known among the Pawnees and all the other Indians, together with the trappers and traders, was Stink Bear. Please let me add that there was no olfactory evidence against me. But my ragged, rough appearance was like that of the wolverine, and Stink Bear is the Indian name for that strange animal.

Perhaps one will wonder what name they gave to Chuck Morris, yet you could almost guess it before I say what they selected. They could not have chosen better. When I think of him as he was in those days, with his glorious presence, his beautiful face forever smiling, his bright blue eyes, and the sweeping mass of his hair of purest gold, his Indian name rushes back upon me, and I call him, naturally, Rising Sun. I have said that nothing happened to me during those two years, and I have said the truth, but something did happen to Rising Sun. It was a great deal more important than either he or I, young fools that we were, thought at the time.

I must begin at the beginning in due order and tell the whole thing out, from the moment when Standing Bear walked into my teepee and ordered me to send for Rising Sun. It seemed an immense joke to me, then — it seemed a joke to Chuck, also. The tragedy began later on.

Chapter Sixteen

RISING SUN, A SQUAW MAN

It began, as I said, in my teepee which was kept in order. My cooking was done by the squaws of Three Buck Elk, partly because Three Buck was fond of me, partly, because by taking care of me they were also taking care of young Sitting Wolf, and because he was always with me, refused to eat except at my side, and refused to sleep except in my teepee. I had taken the education of the young rascal in hand, and a woeful time I had of it. It was like trying to teach a young eagle to read and write the English language. He wanted to be riding or swimming or hunting — I made him sit quietly. His grave face would never betray a sign of impatience, but sometimes every muscle in his wild body would be twitching. I was reading to him out of ROBINSON CRUSOE and, at the end of every few pages, I used to put down the book — I had traded a fine beaver skin for it the winter before — and would ask him what I had read. I had to make sure that he had heard me.

"What is the name of the man who Crusoe saved?" I asked him.

"Friday," he responded.

"Who did he save him from?"

He answered in guttural, rattling Sioux: "Men who ate the flesh of other men. Foh."

"When you are with me," I said, "talk English."

"If I do, the father of Sitting Wolf will think that he has a white heart under a red skin."

We had had that argument over and over again, and I was angry because I had to drudge through it once more. I said: "Boy, we'll not argue about this any more. You are to speak English to me, because it is better than Sioux."

He shook his head.

"What is there in Sioux that cannot be said more quickly in English?"

He did not hesitate an instant, but brought out in his native tongue, as quick as a flash: "Stink Bear." Then he leaped for the open flap of the teepee. I was squatting on crossed legs at the moment, and I nearly missed him which would have meant that he would have got clean away. But I managed to lay my grip on his ankle, by lunging along the floor the length of my body. That sudden check threw him on his face, but he writhed about again like a snake and whirled on me with his knife already in his hand. With the edge of my palm I chopped him on the wrist, and the knife dropped from his numbed fingers.

He was paralyzed not so much by my blow as by the fact that he had drawn a knife on me, though that was as instinctive an act with him as the baring of teeth is with a wolf. He would never have struck me with the weapon, and I knew it. However, the face of Sitting Wolf was gray. He did not alter a muscle, and he stared at me with his unwinking eyes. I wanted to laugh, but I knew that I must make this a lesson for him, so I stood up and pointed.

"Go," I said in his own language. "The teepee of the Stink Bear is too small for the son of a great chief like Three Buck Elk."

He shuddered under every word as though it had been the stroke of a blacksnake and, for a soul like Sitting Wolf's, that speech of mine was worse than any beating. But he turned on his heel and walked out of the tent with the dignity of a grown Indian brave.

I had hardly time to fling ROBINSON CRUSOE the width of the tent and damn all books and what they did to men, when Three Buck Elk's youngest squaw came running to me. She caught me by the arm and pulled me after her.

"What have you done to Sitting Wolf?" she asked. "He is dying."

I hurried after her full of horror until she had brought me behind the teepee, and there she showed me Sitting Wolf, lying on his face, hidden in some shrubs. Not a sound came from him, but he twisted his whole body as if in agony. His face was buried in his arms; his fingers were clutched in his hair. That was his remorse, his shame because he had insulted me. It cut me to the heart. Yet, I have heard fools say that Indians have no emotion. However, I dared not interfere. I couldn't do it without losing my dignity and showing the tears in my eyes, and then even Sitting Wolf himself would have despised me a little as long as he lived. So I said to the girl: "Keep your eyes off him. Sitting Wolf is a little sick now. I shall make him well before the next sunrise."

Then I went back to my teepee with a very dark heart. I had hardly gone inside when Standing Bear came to the entrance, wrapped in his robe, with a splendid set of feathers in his hair — true eagle quills, stained blue and crimson and yellow. His eyes fell on the spot where the book lay, and by that single glance I knew that he had been nearby and had heard the entire scene between me and the boy. I expected that he would deliver a lecture to me on the subject. He was greatly worried, and so was Three Buck Elk, I knew, because of those English lessons. But he said: "I have not seen Rising Sun."

"Have you looked for him in his teepee?"

"I have looked there. So I come to his brother."

"He is probably gadding about with some of the young braves, practicing with his bow and arrows," I suggested.

"The bow has a small voice," he said, "but it has many tongues." This was his way of saying that the rifle has a single shot, and that a bow in a strong hand can turn loose a steady stream of arrows. He went on: "I have found a thought in my heart that I will give to Rising Sun."

I went out and whistled through my fingers — you can make a shriek like a siren in that way, if you know how. Almost at once Chuck came in view, racing his pony toward me. He leaped off while the little brute was still in full gallop.

"What's up?" he asked, for that whistle was our signal to call one another for important matters.

"Old Standing Bear has something on his mind," I told him. "He looks more like a storm than ever. I think he wants to send us out on a war party."

"I hope so," said Chuck. "This time I'm going after scalps."

He strode into the teepee. I went to the entrance, and Standing Bear waved me in.

"What a man thinks, his brother must think also," explained Standing Bear.

He said not another word, but remained gravely seated on a buffalo robe. I saw what he wanted and so took out and loaded a pipe, which I lighted and puffed, then passed to Chuck, who took a whiff and handed it to Standing Bear. The old fellow kept it, nodding his satisfaction.

"Rising Sun," he said at last, "how many horses have you?"

"Five," said Chuck.

"They are all chosen horses," said Standing Bear. "You have a teepee also."

"Yes."

"It is filled with robes, with food, with guns, with arrows and bows, with moccasins."

"Yes."

"And yet," said Standing Bear, "your teepee is empty."

"I am contented," Chuck replied.

"If the sun sets, when will the sun rise again?"

Chuck looked at me. I had seen the drift of Standing Bear at once.

"If you die, Chuck," I translated, "there will be no sun left . . . not even a moon. You have no children."

"The devil," said Chuck and then grinned in the foolish way that most men do when a certain subject is mentioned.

"If an unlucky bullet or an arrow found the heart of Rising Sun," said the chief, between his puffs, "my tribe would be left in darkness."

Chuck shook his head.

"It is good that a man have a squaw," said Standing Bear. "You are now one of my nation. You must have children. Their hands will be strong for you when your hands are weak, friend." He stretched out his own huge paws. "I, Standing Bear," he continued, "have empty hands. I have many horses and many squaws, and my teepee is filled, and still it is empty, and the heart of Standing Bear is empty also. I have no children."

He dropped his head for a moment. For the first time in my life I pitied that fellow.

"There was only my brother's son," went on the chief, "but what we thought was a hawk now wears the feathers of an eagle and begins to fly with his kind."

Here he looked at me — a left-handed

compliment, along with a black look that gave me a chill.

"He has left the nest of his father," said Standing Bear. "He strikes with Black Bear's claws" — here he touched my rifle — "and he speaks with Black Bear's tongue. But that is good. An eagle is greater than a hawk."

Another compliment, but it did not mask the soreness of his heart.

"But you, friend," said Standing Bear to Chuck, "have taken no hawk from our tribe and made it your own. It is good that you should have a squaw."

Chuck Morris stared at me, and I stared back at him. Then he shrugged his shoulders. "Well, Standing Bear," he said, "if you really wish it, I suppose. . . ."

I broke in: "We must talk this over, Morris."

Chuck scowled at me, as a man scowls when he hears the voice of his own conscience. "I suppose that I must," he calmly stated.

"It is good," said Standing Bear, favoring me with another black look. "I shall wait in my teepee to learn what Black Bear has said to Rising Sun."

He got up and walked out with that measured stride that belongs to nothing on earth but an Indian chief. The moment he was out of hearing, I said to Morris: "Good heavens, Chuck, you don't mean that you'll make yourself a squaw man?"

It was the most brutal way of putting it, and I had chosen that way on purpose.

"We've been here a couple of years," said Chuck uneasily. "We may be here a couple of years more."

"But at the end of that time, or some time, you'll go back to your own kind. Then what will you do with your wife?"

"Squaw," said Chuck sharply. "Not wife . . . squaw."

"It's the same thing."

"Not at all. There'll be no marriage ceremony."

"Not our kind of ceremony, but what serves just as well for these people."

"There's a difference. You know as well as I do that they shuffle their wives about pretty freely. A man can divorce his wife at any sun feast, and she can do the same by him with a stroke on the drum. Is that a real marriage . . . when it can be broken up at any time either the man or the squaw feels like breaking it up?"

I was afraid to argue with him, because argument merely fixes a man's mind on what he has already decided. I said: "There's another angle. What about the children?"

Chuck flinched again. "They'd be happy with the tribe," he said.

"Maybe they would, but would you be happy without them? They'd be a part of you. They'd belong to you. Confound it, Chuck, half of their blood would be white."

"You take it too seriously," said Chuck. "Besides, I'm lonely as the devil in my teepee. You have Sitting Wolf to amuse you. And his mother and stepmothers are glad enough to do your cooking and take care of your teepee. But Standing Bear's squaws are mighty tired of working for me as well as the chief. I really need a servant, Lew. I really do. Besides, some of these Indian girls are pretty."

"You mustn't do it," I said, getting a little hot.

He looked very gravely at me. Then he dropped his hand on my shoulder. "Why, Lew, if you really don't approve, of course I'll let the thing drop right here."

I knew he meant it. He would have chopped off a leg to please me in those days, and how many times since I have wished to heaven that I had forbade the whole thing on the spot. But I thought, as I looked up at him, that I was a fool to try to control the ways of such a man as Chuck Morris. He was twice as wise as I — older, more experienced. Besides, I hated to buy him off through his affection for me. It rarely pays to bribe a person through affection. It costs you part of their love. They may give up what they want in order to take your advice, but they never forget. All of this came storming through my brain.

At last I said: "I don't know enough to lay down the law to you, Chuck. If you marry an Indian girl . . . call it something else if you don't want to call it marriage . . . it will be a horrible thing in the end."

"Tut," said Chuck. "These matings have happened before, and the Indian girl always gets tired of her white man and runs off with one of her own kind."

I smiled at the idea of one of the girls running away from Chuck Morris. "Think it over, backward and forward and, when you come to a conclusion, go tell Standing Bear what you've decided. I haven't a right to persuade you."

He let out a big breath of relief. I could see how much he had been dreading my ban on this affair.

"As far as that goes," he said, "I've already pretty well decided what I want to do. I can talk to Standing Bear now."

I went with him, pretty sick at heart. We found the old warrior in his teepee with a couple of his squaws whom he sent away on the run with a single grunt. One glance at Rising Sun set a glitter of triumph in his eyes, and he smiled at me a little, as much as to say that he had discovered I was not so strong with my friend as he had thought.

"Very well," said Chuck, "I've thought it over and talked it over with my wise friend, Black Bear, and I've decided that you're right. A squaw would be good for me. But what squaw should I take?"

Standing Bear said: "There is no girl in the tribe too beautiful or too proud to be the squaw of Rising Sun. You must let your eye and your heart choose for you. Standing Bear will not speak."

"How am I to go about this thing? Do I simply begin to pay court to some girl?"

"In the evening and in the morning," said the chief, "the girls go down to the stream for water, and the young braves wait for them on the bank. When they see the girl they love coming, they throw a blanket around her, because it is not good that other eyes should see the face of the woman who listens to the man. If she does not wish to hear him, she will send him away at once. If she cares to listen, she will hear him on ten evenings, and on the tenth she will make him an answer. When you hear that answer, come back to me, Rising Sun, and tell me what you have heard. Then I will give you counsel."

That was all. I could tell by Chuck's light step as he went out of the tent that he was very happy and very excited about the whole affair. I did not need to ask him what girl he had in mind. There was only one of whom he could think for an instant, and that was Zintcallasappa, The Blackbird. She was by no means the pure Sioux strain. Her mother had been the daughter of a trapper who had gone back to her kind, and the white blood was visible at a glance in the girl. She had black hair and eyes, to be sure, but no Indian ever had eyes so big and so tender, or hair so soft and thick, or such a mouth. And her smile was the smile of a white woman. It had always startled me when I saw it, and it really made my heart jump a little.

I simply said: "It's The Blackbird?"

He shrugged his shoulders. He was too keen for the business to give me an answer in words.

Chapter Seventeen

BLACKBIRD GIVES HER ANSWER

I was sitting in my teepee that evening — as gloomy as any man in the world — and waiting for news, when a shadow fell across the entrance. I saw Sitting Wolf standing there with an unstrung bow in his hand. I jumped up at once and went to him.

He made his voice big and strong so that no womanish tremor might come into it. "The white men," he said, "beat their dogs when they snarl and snap. Sitting Wolf has been a snapping dog. He has brought a whip to Black Bear."

He offered me the bow, and I took it. There were half a dozen passing, and they paused to look on. An Indian who offers himself for punishment is a strange sight, and an Indian, no matter how young, who is willing to endure a public shame is simply a miracle. Yet, Sitting Wolf folded his arms across his breast and waited. That was a tough piece of wood, that bow, but there was such a burst of emotion in me that I snapped the bow in two in my hands and threw the pieces away.

"A white man," I said, "never strikes his brother. It is near the time for the evening meal, Sitting Wolf. Sit here with me."

We sat down side by side, until he saw where the book lay, crumpled in a corner. He jumped up, ran to it, sat down by the firelight, and tried to read, smoothing the wrinkled pages tenderly. I think that, take them all in all, there were never other Indians like the Sioux, and there was never a Sioux like Sitting Wolf.

Before dark Chuck Morris came in, and I saw what had happened in his face. I sent Sitting Wolf out, and he broke into his story at once.

"Do you know how old she is?" he asked.

"Seventeen."

"You know a good deal about her, then?"

"Yes."

"You rascal, Lew, have you had an eye on her, too?"

Now that he had committed himself, I thought, there was no use in holding him back. I merely said: "She's beautiful, Chuck."

"You've never seen her. You've never seen her," he repeated. "Well, she's seventeen, and I suppose that it's been a year since any young brave popped a blanket over her head and asked her to be his squaw."

I could understand that. "She's sent them all about their business," I said. "They are tired of feeling the sting of her tongue. She told Spotted Buck, I believe, that he ought to become a man before he wanted to have a squaw."

Morris smiled. "I waited by the bank," he explained. "This springtime has the blood of the braves up. There were a round dozen of them, waiting for the girls . . . five or six at a time huddled under blankets, muttering. Finally The Blackbird came. What can I call her besides that stupid name . . . Zintcallas-appa? It takes an hour to get it off the tongue. When I saw her coming, I began to feel a bit uneasy. I wanted to put the thing off until tomorrow. Confound it, I remembered that I had never spoken half a dozen words to her since I came into the tribe. There's always something about her that discourages familiarity. Those young fellows, who would give their eyeteeth for her, don't know what to do when she looks at them with frost in her eye. And I felt just that way."

He fell to dreaming, with a strange little smile about the corners of his lips.

I urged him on: "What happened, Chuck?" Because I knew that he *had* spoken to her.

"Oh," said Chuck, "when she came nearer and saw me, she stopped a little, and I thought that her head went up just a trifle. And she went on past me, hurrying a little with her eyes fixed straight before her. But I knew that she was seeing me, and I thought there was a bit more color in her face . . . in a word, I did exactly what the chief suggested. I went up to her with half my blanket trailing over my arm. I didn't throw it over her head. I simply took her inside it."

He paused again. I was immensely excited. I said: "Get it over with, Chuck, will you?"

"Oh, well, there's no one like her!"

"She said she was willing to marry you, I suppose?"

He corrected me like a shot. "She said nothing . . . and I said nothing about marriage. I simply told her how pretty she is, and how devilishly restless it made me to see her . . . and such stuff, you know. I forget all of it." He made one of his irritating pauses again.

"Well?" I shouted at him.

"Did you ever see a prairie fire start, Lew?"

"What the devil has a prairie fire got to do with her?" I thundered.

He leaned back against a lodgepole and began to smoke his pipe, lifting his head to watch every rising puff, as though he saw a face in it. "Did you ever watch May come rippling over the prairie?"

"Damn May," I said. "I'm waiting to hear something about Zintcallasappa."

"Did you ever watch a still lake blossom when sunset came along, Lew?"

I could stand it no longer. "You're talking like a jackass, Chuck. I don't want to hear any more of your maunderings."

He waved his hand, still with the same wonderful smile and the same far-looking eyes. "She was like that," he said. "She seemed a little frightened, just at first. Then she put up her face and looked me over as though I were a new book." Morris sighed and shook his head, as though he regretted that some of the picture was already fading in his memory. "She said, 'Do you wish to take me to your teepee?'

" 'I do,' I said. 'But will you come, Zintcallasappa?'

" 'I cannot speak until the tenth day,' she said.

" 'But what shall I guess?' I asked. 'I shall lose my mind waiting ten whole days and wondering. Let me guess only one little thing . . . that you do not hate me.'

"Ah, Lew, I would give ten years of my life to see her always as she was just then

184

when she smiled at me. She went on down the riverbank, still smiling back to me, not caring a damn how many of the young bucks saw her. After that . . . well, I came staggering home here with my head full of fire."

That was the story of how Chuck Morris won The Blackbird, put down in his exact words, because I have them all in my mind, exactly as they were when he spoke them. But it was not over a minute before the end of the ten days — not a minute. Most Indian girls would not have given him so much as a glance, no matter how they loved him. But though The Blackbird had let him know instantly that she loved him, she would not give her promise. And when he saw her for the tenth time on the bank of the river, she simply said: "I shall go to your teepee, if you have the consent of my father."

Her father was Lame Beaver and a notorious lover of firewater, but he was a good-natured brave and had enough courage to fight one hundred men at once. We both went to Standing Bear and told him the good news.

He said: "I knew that Zintcallasappa was not a fool. Now take two or three of your best horses and tie them at the lodge of Lame Beaver. If they are taken into his herd, then his daughter will be brought to you . . . she is yours and has been bought. If the horses are returned to you, Lame Beaver is not satisfied. You must take him more horses. If he sends those back . . . up to nine or ten horses . . . then you know that he does not wish to give you his daughter."

"What can be done then?" asked Morris with anxiety.

"Nothing," said the chief.

"I'd find something to do, though," said Morris, and he doubled his big fist.

"There is no need to worry," said Standing Bear. "Lame Beaver is not drinking firewater. He will do as a man of good sense should do."

We picked out four horses from among Morris's five. I gave him two of my own four, and then he went to the lodge of Lame Beaver and tied the gift at the entrance. Half an hour later they were in Lame Beaver's herd! Of course, the entire village knew about it instantly. They made a procession past Morris's lodge all that evening, grinning at him, giving him little presents, and wishing him well. Morris himself was in second heaven.

Finally I said to him: "Chuck, why not marry her? You certainly will never care more for anyone else."

He snapped his hand at the sky. "No man could ever care for any woman as much as I care for her. But where is there a minister to marry us?"

"We'll be at a settlement or near one by the fall."

"By the fall? By the end of ten years, you might as well say. I may be dead and bleaching on top of a rack of poles by that time. Lew, are you made of steel and ice? I'm only a man, and I love The Blackbird. What a delicate and lovely thing she is."

Every minute there was a weight on my heart. I half trusted in what he said. He swore that as soon as they came near whites, he'd marry her in the white man's way. But I had a doubt. No one could be sure what Chuck Morris would be thinking when he had turned around the corner of tomorrow.

All of Zintcallasappa's family came around the next morning and brought The Blackbird herself in their van, while they followed, carrying all sorts of presents for the new family that was starting up. I watched her go in at the entrance and stand there, looking up to golden-haired Morris without a smile, but with a sort of worship. Then she passed on into the shadow of his teepee. That was the clue, after all, to the whole affair, I think, now that I have the long road

187

of the years to look down. She not only loved Morris, but she worshipped him as a sort of god, as though he were in fact the rising sun.

Chapter Eighteen

BALD EAGLE

I have talked as though all were peace and quiet during this time. As a matter of fact, it was about a month before the day when Chuck Morris took The Blackbird for his squaw that the shadow of Bald Eagle fell across the Sioux. You must understand that there was never any real peace between the Pawnees and the Sioux. Those horse-stealing Pawnees were never so badly beaten that for the sake of a fine young stallion they wouldn't risk another war. But, as a rule, they were routed. They simply hadn't the numbers to combat us. Sometimes they beat a war party of the Dakotas. Sometimes they stepped down and blotted out a village. But in the end they always had the worst of it, so far as I know. The Pawnees were a strong people and hard fighters. But there were three hundred thousand Sioux — as the United States government itself was to learn one day. If the Pawnees grew too daring, the Sioux banded together and sent out a great wave of warriors that washed the Pawnees dizzily west and north and left great villages a drift of white ashes, a few small heaps of black cinders.

Now a new chief appeared among them and began to strike right and left. First he appeared when a tribe of the Sioux called the Brulês were towing their household stuffs across a narrow river. That was done by putting a lot of lodgepoles together to make a raft. Then the poles were lashed together, the belongings were heaped on the raft, and thirty or forty braves jumped in and harnessed themselves to the raft to pull it across. That was the way it was always done.

Chuck and I rigged up a pair of light sculls and used to jog across the rivers in no time, but, even in Standing Bear's own tribe, the old ways were considered the best ways. Standing Bear finally took to the oars himself, but Three Buck Elk never would have anything to do with such dangerously advanced doings. It was while the Brulês were making one of these passages over water that a little war party of Pawnees made their appearance. They had no horses with them. They had crawled miles perhaps, through the long prairie grass of the early summer, and now they popped out on the edge of the river. There were nearly one hundred bucks in the water. The braves on shore were butchered straightaway, though even they outnumbered the Pawnees — an Indian taken by surprise is no good for fighting. After the ones on dry land were finished, the rest was perfectly simple. Those Pawnees started picking off the swimmers, and they dropped every one of them. Not a soul among the braves escaped.

The rest of the Sioux were not slaughtered, however, and that was one of the odd things about the affair. As a rule, the whole lot would have been blotted out, but the chief in command of the Pawnees simply gathered in the women and the children and carted them away as prisoners. The moment I heard of this little exploit, I guessed that a new hero had appeared in Indian warfare, though, of course, I never dreamed that he would come to such fame as he afterwards did. The chief was Bald Eagle, and before long his name was enough to send a chill through every Dakota in the land. The Brulês, when they heard that part of their tribe had been blotted out, gathered a big war party and went whooping it up across the prairie.

Ten days later they overtook the Pawnees, who were traveling slowly because they had so many prisoners. When the Brulês showed up from the east, the Pawnees wanted to murder all their prisoners, even the babies, so that their hands would be free for the fun that was coming — especially since the Sioux outnumbered them almost three to one. But Bald Eagle swore that he would throttle with his own hands the first man who touched a captive. Then he made his preparations for the fight.

The Sioux scouts reported the enemy getting in line of battle on the far side of a low hill. So the Brulês got together and started a charge. An Indian charge has no order to it and only one idea — that is for each man to get at the enemy first. They whirled across the top of the hill and went crash into a solid wall of fire. Old Bald Eagle had used the few minutes left to him to make his men form in a line and scoop out a shallow ditch. The captives were forced to fall to help in the work. In a minute or two they had sunk themselves into a neat little trench. Then they lay on their bellies in the cool of the sod and blew that Sioux charge into atoms. As I've said before, Indians are not very accurate, but Bald Eagle had brought up the average in his tribe amazingly. At any rate, they rolled about two score and ten Brulê braves in the grass on the strength of that first charge.

The Sioux went scattering and staggering

back to the far side of the hill to gather their forces and think over what should be done next with this difficult Pawnee lot. While they were sitting and thinking, they heard a brief rumble of hoofs, and the whole Pawnee lot, with big Bald Eagle in front, came swarming over the hilltop and dropped right in among them like a bomb. That Pawnee chief had decided to follow up the first repulse, and he had clapped his men on horseback instantly. But the charge had other queer features.

Usually an Indian uses his lungs as his chief weapon, shooting bullets and arrows more or less at random, and hoping to frighten the other fellow into bolting for the rear. But Bald Eagle had taught his fellows new tactics. They came over the top of that hill in a solid mass, without uttering a single cry. They had neither guns nor bows; but each man had a broad-bladed hatchet in his hand. They went into the Brulês in a deadly silence and made the sun dance on their working hatchets. In about thirty seconds the Sioux had enough of it. They decided that the devil had taken possession of those unlucky Pawnees. Each Brulê turned and combed away for the farthest horizon. Altogether, it was a catastrophe. But still that was not all.

Whereas the ordinary Indian makes one raid and then goes home with all of his plunder to have a dance and a big smoke and talk about what he has done, Bald Eagle followed up every success like a regular Napoleon. He left his party of captives under a small guard, working their way steadily along toward the heart of the Pawnee nation. He himself kept right on with his warriors after their charge. They rode for three days, straight east and south until they came to the main village of the Brulês. I should say that there were not more than one hundred and fifty men with Bald Eagle. And there were five hundred Brulê warriors, at the very least, in that village. However, they had not the slightest suspicion that anything was wrong. They supposed their youngest and best braves were away *chasing* this Bald Eagle.

The first thing Bald Eagle did was to bunch his horses together. Whereas most Indians like to fight from horseback — because, if they miss, they have faster legs to run away on — Bald Eagle had an odd habit of getting his braves on foot. A man on foot shoots ten times straighter than a man on horseback and fights ten times harder — simply because he *can't* run away. Then, without waiting for the darkness to come, he marched down on that village in two lines, seventy-five men in a line. The Brulês came foaming out like so many hornets. Bald Eagle blew the foam off the cup with a volley from his first line. Then as the Brulês staggered, riding around in circles, the first line lay down on their bellies, and the second line sent a smashing volley home.

That was quite enough. The Sioux went reeling back into the village, and the Pawnees went after them, not in a rush, but marching slowly. When the Sioux turned and charged, there was always that implacable line to receive them and two volleys in deliberate succession. They filled that village with blood and gore. They scattered the Brulê warriors to the four winds, and they marched off with five thousand head of horses, loaded down with all the belongings of the teepees. Included in their plunder was the whole bulk of the women and the children.

Here were three blows delivered in swift succession, each harder than the last, each more unexpected, each more decisive. The Sioux had not received such a check in the memory of man. Bald Eagle became the hero of the Pawnee tribe. As for the Brulês, they were too badly hurt to do anything for the moment. The rest of the Sioux made a great noise about wiping the Pawnees off the face of the earth, but nothing was done. As a matter of fact, they were all a little bit frightened, as the Allies in Europe must have been frightened when they heard of the thin-faced young general who had stolen through the Alps, won Montenotte, and slid suddenly into the heart of Italy. Here were brains; here was real generalship. No wonder the Sioux rubbed their chins and became thoughtful.

Morris made up his mind on the spot. "No Indian that ever lived could have done it," he declared. "It may be a half-breed . . . more likely it's a white man turned Indian . . . because there are white man's brains in that work. See how he worked like a good fighter. When he hit a really hard blow, he followed it up at once. Look at his new tactics, too. He turned cavalry into infantry at the right time, and then turned the infantry back into cavalry again. Think of that hatchet charge. Confound me, I'm glad that I didn't have to stand up against it."

I agreed with him, except that it seemed odd that any white man should ever be accepted among them as a chief. However, there was no more of Bald Eagle for the time being. Bald Eagle and the rest of the Pawnees were having new trouble to the west of their lands, and we got only scattered reports now and then of the havoc that the new war chief of the Pawnees was making. These were very prosperous times with Standing Bear and his tribe. We passed that winter and came into the next spring, and then a real war party was made up to punish the Pawnees. It was not large. But it was choice. I was away at the time, or I should have ridden with them, and Rising Sun was too happy in his teepee with his squaw to pay any attention to a little thing like a war. Zintcallasappa turned out a true home-maker, poor girl, and, since Morris was now "rich," they had everything that an Indian could dream of to make them happy, from pounds and pounds of beads to a whole herd of horses.

I was away because I had heard of a big white trapper, a sour-faced hermit of a fel-low, and decided that it might be my father. I had made a two-hundred-mile trip until I found him. It was a false clue again, and I went back to the village only in time to hear about the calamity.

I found that the whole village was in mourning, and the teepee of Three Buck Elk was under a deep cloud. This was what had happened. A war party of about three hun-dred and fifty braves had been picked up here and there under the leadership of Little Buffalo, a Brulê chief, and had ridden off to find the Pawnees. After they were gone, taking some of Standing Bear's men along with them, Sitting Wolf sneaked away and joined them two days out. He was only a shade over fourteen at the time, but he was tall and strong, and he not only had a rifle, but he knew how to use it better than anyone in the tribe except Morris and myself. I had seen to his teaching. He was accepted into the war party as a token of good luck, and they rambled on until they reached a Pawnee town, just a small place. It was big enough, however, to make a satisfactory massacre. They drenched that place in blood, without taking a single captive. Young and old were put to the knife, and they started back with a harvest of scalps when they stumbled across Bald Eagle. He had swooped at them out of a clear sky — like his namesake. He beat them in a fair fight and then rounded them up on top of a hill. There he sat down and waited for thirst to beat them. They had no water, though there was a stream in full sight. They went through the agony for a day, then they began to make rushes for water, and every rush cluttered the hillside with dead bodies until all were gone except Sitting Wolf and one other brave. They both were then captured, being too weak to help themselves. The brave was sent back to tell the story of what the Pawnees had done to his people. Sitting Wolf was taken prisoner by Bald Eagle's party.

The brave who lived to tell the story to the tribe was the one who told it to me. I went mad for a time. I caught him by the throat and nearly throttled him. Then I went raging into Three Buck Elk's teepee, where the chief sat with his head in his hands.

"Is the father of Sitting Wolf a dog?" I yelled at him. "Does he sit and whine while his son is carried away to be tortured by Pawnee devils?"

Then I rushed out and mounted my best horse. I remember that Zintcallasappa ran to me while I was saddling. My fingers were fumbling with the straps, and I was half blind, for every moment I was seeing Sitting Wolf lashed to a tree while cruel fiends stood around him, thrusting burning splinters into his flesh. She took hold of my hands.

"Oh, my brother, Black Bear," she said, "they will not harm Sitting Wolf. He is only a boy, and Bald Eagle does not strike children. But, if you leave me, there will be sadness in my teepee."

I was so much surprised that I forgot my own sorrow for a moment. I asked her what she meant, and she said in that simple way of hers that was always so touching: "Half the heart of Rising Sun is still with his own people. A little is with me . . . and the rest is with you, my brother. If you leave us, I cannot keep him."

"I shall come again," I told her.

She shook her head. "You are going to do some terrible and great thing," she said. "When a white man turns pale, it is because he is very frightened or very angry. And you are never afraid, Black Bear. If you go, you will not help Sitting Wolf, but it will make my teepee empty, my brother."

I took her under the chin and tipped up her face. "Look at me. Now tell me the truth with one tongue. Does Rising Sun seem unhappy?"

Those dark, soft eyes of hers were swimming with tears. "I cannot tell," she said, "but I am always afraid . . . I am always afraid."

Her trouble seemed such a tiny thing compared with mine at that moment I smiled at her and patted her cheek. "You are only a child, Zintcallasappa," I said, and then I was in the saddle and away. What a fool — and what a young fool — I was, and how deep and clear she had looked into her future.

Chapter Nineteen

IN THE CAMP OF THE PAWNEES

After I had started on the way, I wished that I had taken Chuck Morris along with me. But, when I thought of Zintcallasappa, I knew that I had no right to take him into such danger as that toward which I was now going. I had two horses with me, riding one and leading the other, and each day I changed horses. In this way I made excellent time, but, even with that change of mounts, my eagerness was such that I wore both horses to rags before I got to the enemy's land. I myself had only the vaguest idea where that boundary might be, but one afternoon I was told by a bullet that whistled past my ear.

I used one of the oldest ruses in the world, which Standing Bear himself had taught me and which he said had given him four scalps — the old rascal. The instant I heard the sing of that bullet — and before even the report of the gun, like a great handclap, came to me — I tumbled off my horse and lay like one dead, except that for a dead man

I had my rifle astonishingly handy. Another bullet cut the grass at my head. Then I saw the scoundrel coming toward me, and I knew at once that he was a Pawnee hunter. He came at the full speed of his horse, leaning forward, with his rifle slung once more. When that second bullet didn't make me stir, he was confident that his first shot had gone through my head. Now he was bent on the scalp. I waited until he was thirty yards away. Then I rolled onto my knee and tucked the butt of my rifle into the hollow of my shoulder. He made a futile grab at his own gun, then he seemed to realize all at once that it was too late. He threw out his hands with a howl of despair and brought his horse to a stop almost on top of me.

I said: "Brother, you shoot well, but your rifle is not good. It carries to the left."

He grunted and then folded his arms. I could not make this fellow out. He had the look and the manner of a real warrior. He sat on his horse and looked down at me with a perfect calm. The manner of a man surrounded by the most hopeless odds.

"The Great Spirit," he said, "has charmed the rifle of Black Bear so that he cannot help but kill. But you shall not wear the scalp of Two Feather long. Bald Eagle shall stoop and strike you down."

I was twenty years old, and at that age flattery has a sharp tooth. I was tickled to the core to find that I was so well known to these fellows. So much nonsense had gone abroad about my marksmanship that, I suppose, Two Feather decided it was useless to try to fight once I had the drop on him. I grounded my rifle but kept my hand near the butt of my revolver. He saw the position of that hand and attempted nothing.

"Friend," I said, "I have done you no harm. Why do you wish to kill me?"

"The scalp of Black Bear would make the hearts of the Pawnees glad, and even Bald Eagle would smile."

"Could you know me at that distance?" I asked him.

"The eye of Two Feather is not the eye of an old woman."

Another thought came to me. "What scalps," I asked, "dry in your lodge?"

Even in the face of an enemy he could not help boasting.

"Three scalps of the Dakotas hang in the teepee of Two Feather, so that his sons may see them and their hearts grow as strong as the heart of Two Feather."

I began to gather that this fellow was a man of some mark among his people. He was an ugly villain. A knife scar crossed his face and gave one eye a continual squint and an odd, knowing look. I could believe that he had taken two scalps, or even twenty, for that matter.

"How far is it," I said, "to your people?"

Not a muscle of his face stirred. Plainly he did not intend to betray his tribe, and a little warmth of admiration came over me. Here was a man, whether his skin were red or white.

"You have among your people," I said, "a great chief and a wise man, Bald Eagle."

"Yes, his wisdom is as wide as the sky."

"And he has in his teepee a prisoner taken from the Sioux?"

A savage satisfaction gleamed in his eye again. "The brother of Black Bear is with him," he admitted.

"Can you take me to the lodge of Bald Eagle?"

He stared at me a moment, as though I had asked him if he could take me to the gates of death.

"You shall ride freely with me," I assured him, "and you shall not die. There are no scalps at the belt of Black Bear, and no scalps dry in his lodge. He cannot stop to take the trophies. He touches his rifle, and the prairies are covered with the dead of the Pawnees."

I blush a little as I write this down, but, after all, that was exactly what I said, and a man had to blow his horn a little among the Indians or he would be put down as a person of little note. Two Feather swallowed this brag without winking an eye.

I went on: "Two Feather shall not die. He shall have the promise of Black Bear, whose word is never broken, that, if he leads Black Bear safely to the lodge of Bald Eagle, all will be well, and we shall part like brothers."

There was a sudden softening of those hard features as hope came tardily back to him. But, instead of answering, he turned his back on me and trotted his horse slowly across the prairie — slowly, with just one quiver of the naked muscles between his shoulders, as if just there he expected the bullet to plow its way to his heart. However, I jogged my horse after him. In this way we kept on for a long time, until the sun slipped under the edge of the prairie. A moment later, before the darkness dropped around us, still in the bright afterglow, we came in view of a village. Two Feather halted and pointed before him.

"It is Bald Eagle," he said.

I assure you that brought my heart up into my mouth. Here, there, and yonder, were three men on horseback, keeping guard.

Certainly Bald Eagle, like a good captain, took no chances of being surprised. His sentinels were always on watch.

"Ride by my side," I said, "into the city and to the entrance of his teepee."

He gave me one look, again as though he wondered why a young man chose to throw away his life. Then he went on, and I trotted my horse beside him. We reached a sentinel.

"Black Bear and Two Feather," said the Pawnee, "come to the teepee of Bald Eagle."

It brought a shout of wonder from the young brave. He rode up close and stared at me as though he were seeing the devil in person, then he shot down into the village. After that, we rode through a jumbled mass of people. The braves stalked out, wrapped in their blankets, to watch me pass. The women and the children kept up a rattle of comment as I went through their ranks. We came in front of a sort of double teepee, taller and twice as broad as any I had ever seen before. Two young braves stood before the entrance. Two Feather spoke to them softly and rapidly. Presently one of them disappeared into the teepee and came out again after a moment, leading with him an old, bent Indian with the ugliest face that ever saw the sun.

"Bald Eagle," he said, "rests after much

thinking and sends Dark Water to speak with Black Bear."

"Dark Water," I said, "Black Bear is not a child. Neither is he a woman. He is not answered by two men, but by one. Go back to Bald Eagle and tell him."

The old chief shook his head.

"Black Bear," he said, "is a great warrior. He has filled the teepees of the Pawnees with tears and with weeping. He has covered the ground with our dead. The Great Spirit has given to him a charmed rifle that cannot miss. But Bald Eagle never speaks twice. The Great Spirit is in him, also. I dare not go back to him, warrior. But I am his other tongue. Speak to me and I shall listen."

He was a smooth old demon, there was no denying that. He spoke like a reverend councilor, and to hear a tribute like this from such a chief made very easy listening. I began to feel that I was quite a person, after all. I was beginning to grow uneasy, too. The various notes of muttered wonder and admiration at the effrontery with which I had dared to ride in among them were beginning to include new sounds. Relatives of warriors who had fallen in the charge on Standing Bear's village were joining the crowd, and one old woman was crying out repeatedly that only my scalp, hanging in her lodge, could comfort her heart for the loss of her dead son.

I saw that it would not do to stand too much on my dignity. I said: "Dark Water, pleasant words fall from the lips of old men like rain from the black clouds. Hear me, then, and carry my message to Bald Eagle. I, Black Bear, have taken in battle a great warrior of the Pawnees, Two Feather. His heart was strong, but the claws of Black Bear were lightning in his eyes. He was blinded and could not see. But his scalp is not at my belt. He has ridden back to the teepee which he left today. Let him stay there. Let his sons be glad and let his squaws make offering at the next feast of the sun. All this is well. Therefore, give me the young boy, Sitting Wolf, to take back to my people, the Sioux, that there may be peace between the Dakotas and the Pawnees, for friendship is better than war."

Dark Water turned into the tent. I heard the stir of his voice. I heard the rumbling of a deep bass, making answer. That was Bald Eagle, I had no doubt, and even the distant sound of his voice filled me with dread and a certain cold uneasiness at the pit of the stomach such as I had not felt since I left the shack of Uncle Abner Dorset. Then Dark Water came again.

He said: "Bald Eagle has spoken to his heart, and his heart says that Two Feather is a brave man and a great warrior . . . he is the arrow on the bow string, the knife ready to strike. But Sitting Wolf is the son of a chief and the nephew of a great chief. While he is in the teepee of Bald Eagle, Standing Bear will not come nor will his people come. Their knives and their arrows will be blunt against the Pawnees."

It was a tremendous blow to me, but, at the same time, I could not help admiring the craft of Bald Eagle. I was also more suspicious than ever that he was white, for his diplomacy did not have the ring of the true Indian way about it.

"A life has been offered for a life," I said. "If there is still a difference, the horses of the Sioux are many and fleet as the wind, and they have guns that shoot straight and beaded moccasins and buffalo robes by the thousand. They will give what the great Bald Eagle asks for the sake of Sitting Wolf, who is only a boy."

Dark Water shook his head.

"Bald Eagle has spoken," he said.

I saw that there was nothing to be gained, and my heart ached for the poor youngster imprisoned among these devils. So I said: "Let me see Sitting Wolf. Let me know that he is among you. Or else I may return to Standing Bear and tell him that his nephew is dead. Then he will come with his warriors. Black Bear shall ride with him with a rifle that cannot help but kill, and Rising Sun shall ride with him and blind the eyes of the Pawnees. Many men shall die."

There was a murmur through the crowd. Dark Water turned into the teepee and was gone for some time while the young men jostled around me, staring and whispering to one another. Then the old chief came out again. "It is well," he said. "Let my brother, Black Bear, follow."

I dismounted and went through the crowd at the heels of Dark Water until we came to the next teepee where, at a word from him, two braves who stood guard stepped aside for us to enter.

I found myself in a small teepee in the center of which a few embers glowed, and at one side, sitting on a buffalo robe, was Sitting Wolf, with his hands tied behind his back. He drew himself up when he saw us enter, and, the moment his eyes found my face, he uttered a cry of joy and leaped to his feet.

Chapter Twenty

A RIFLE TEST

The others left us, though presently, by the stir of feet around the teepee, I knew that new guards had been posted there. In the meantime questions ran like water out of Sitting Wolf's lips. I answered them all. When he finally asked me what strange power had brought me safely through the lines of the Pawnees and into their village, I told him the story. He listened to it, smiling and nodding.

"I have done nothing," he said, "to be worth the love of such a brother, but, before I die, I shall find a way."

I asked him about Bald Eagle and the fight. He told me practically what I had already heard, but with a good many more details. The war party with which Bald Eagle had overtaken them, it seemed, was nearly a hundred men fewer than the Sioux, but all the Pawnees were armed with excellent rifles, and they shot amazingly straight. The fight had not lasted five minutes before the Sioux broke and were herded back to the hill where they entrenched themselves to make a last stand. It had been a wretched slaughter from the first.

"How do they come to shoot so straight?" I asked.

"They practice with the guns all day. I hear the noises," he said. "And Bald Eagle teaches them to fight on foot, so that their guns shoot straighter."

I asked him, then, if Bald Eagle were not a white man. He said that he did not know. The skin of the great chief was red, but that it might have been dyed. He himself had had the same thought. At least he was sure that Bald Eagle was not a Pawnee, because he spoke the language haltingly. When he asked the tribesmen, however, they maintained a resolute silence about their war leader. In person he said that Bald Eagle was a huge man with a great, savage face — *two men in one,* was the way Sitting Wolf put it. I remembered the volume of that rolling bass voice and believed it. He told me, too, that Bald Eagle never mixed with the tribe ordinarily, but sent out Dark Water with his commands. Only when a war party was ready, he put himself at their head. The Pawnees swore that he remained by himself so much because the Great Spirit was constantly in communion with him.

It was Bald Eagle who had saved him when a knife was at his throat. And he said that the great chief was said never to slaughter the young if he could avoid it. So we chatted on until the night came. Food was brought to us. Still we talked until very late, and the evening noises in the Indian village grew less. Then I decided to depart. I told Sitting Wolf that I should never rest until I had captured men of such importance among the Pawnees that Bald Eagle would be glad to trade me Sitting Wolf in exchange. The youngster gave me a dozen messages for his family, then I turned to the entrance of the teepee and walked out — to find two guns leveled at my breast.

Such treachery amazed me. And yet, after all, I was a prize not to be passed over lightly. When I demanded what it meant, the young braves grinned mockingly at me, and I went back into the teepee to think the thing over. Sitting Wolf was in an agony of sorrow because this had come on me for his sake. He wanted me to cut his bonds, then he would arm himself with my knife, and we both could rush out at them and try to cut our way through the camp. It was very brave, but very foolish, talk, and it did not tempt me for a moment. A man like Bald Eagle would never close his hand upon a nettle that he could not hold. So I told the boy the only thing to do was to wait for the morning and see what would happen. I told him I had not the slightest doubt as to my safety. Such a chief as Bald Eagle would not allow me to be murdered after I had come to him of my own free will, bringing in safely one of his best warriors.

That served to convince Sitting Wolf. After he had gone to sleep that night, I sat there awake, chewing the stem of my pipe and wondering what deviltry lay before me. Finally I dozed off, and in the morning I found old Dark Water standing in the entrance to the teepee, looking down at me as blandly as you please.

I merely said: "I have had a Pawnee sleep, friend, but it is not as good as a Pawnee scalp."

He nodded as though he understood my feelings exactly and even sympathized with them.

"Bald Eagle is very sad," said the scoundrel. "He wishes to send Black Bear safely home to his people, but the Pawnees are angry. They say that many warriors of their blood have died with the bullets of Black Bear in their hearts. Therefore, they will not let him go before a great price has been paid."

Sitting Wolf growled deep in his throat. I swallowed my emotions. There is no use quarreling with a man who has a knife at your breast. I said quietly: "Very well . . . what is the price to be?"

Dark Water heaved a sigh. I suppose he had been prepared to listen to a torrent of abuse.

"You are to take your rifle and come with me."

I wondered what my rifle could have to do with my price, unless the idiots really thought it was charmed. I was taken along with a party of twenty or thirty warriors who acted as a bodyguard. Practically the entire tribe accompanied us at a distance, most of the men with arms. I could see the cause of the fighting successes of Bald Eagle at a glance. More than discipline and good, daring generalship, these fellows had secured excellent rifles, and, what was more, I could see that they were kept in good condition. The Pawnees had been taught to handle their guns as though they were sacred things. Altogether, they made a striking appearance, and I decided on the spot that I never wanted to meet these Pawnees on terms of equal numbers, not with the Sioux or any other Indians at my back. The more I saw of the work of Bald Eagle, the more I wanted to see the old villain face to face.

We had gone into the prairie near the village, and there I found, tethered to pegs in the ground, three skinny old horses, down-headed, ragged of mane and tail, their backbones and their ribs thrusting out through the skin, but still clinging to life by a miracle. Dark Water pointed them out to me and told me in a few words why I had been brought there. It was known that if a bullet grazed the neck of a horse close to the ears, just nicking the spinal cord, the animal could be stunned. I had heard of that method being used to catch wild horses. But I had also heard that for every one that was stunned, a hundred more were killed out-right, and several hundred more were missed altogether. Dark Water finished this part of his little speech and then went on to another part that was still more interesting to me.

"The Pawnees sigh," he said, "when they think of Black Bear leaving them in safety and going back to the Dakotas to bring them on our trail. They say that Black Bear has done enough for one life, and that it is time for him to rest." It was a diplomatic way for the ruffians to hint that they thought of sending a bullet through my head. The chief went on: "Bald Eagle has a great need of a man who can do what men talk of but never perform . . . throw a horse senseless on the prairie but not take his life with the touch of a bullet. If Black Bear could do this thing, Bald Eagle would find a use for him and afterward set him free."

Nothing could have been plainer. Some wild horse had caught the eye of the chief. He had tried to catch the horse in vain. Now he wanted to use the last desperate expedient that would either catch or kill it. It sounded very much more like an Indian's desire than a white man's. I changed my mind about Bald Eagle for the hundredth time.

"Bald Eagle," I said, "wishes to have stronger wings. Dark Water, if I should be able to get them for him, will he set free both Sitting Wolf *and* me?"

Dark Water favored me with a strange smile. "The old men say that no man shall ever sit on the back of the horse Bald Eagle has seen. But if you, Black Bear, should catch him, Bald Eagle will set you and Sitting Wolf free. And here," he concluded, "are three horses."

He waved toward them and stepped back. The other warriors drew away from me, and I saw that I was expected to try my hand on these wretched nags. I lay down on my side, found a comfortable elbow rest, and tucked the butt of the rifle into the hollow of my shoulder. Then I drew my bead on the nearest horse. I aimed high up on the back of the neck. A long aim is a useless thing — after an instant of holding on a target, even the strongest hand begins to waver. The moment I had my goal in the sight, I fired, and the horse dropped. A dozen warriors rushed out to the spot and lifted its head. It dropped back with an audible, loose thump. They felt its heart — then they stood up and waved their hands. I had failed, for the horse was dead.

There was a rapid chattering of surprise. Those rascals really expected me to do magic with that rifle. I went out and looked at the bullet mark. I had simply snapped the spinal cord — that was all there was to it — and the brute was dead. I returned to my place and tried again, and again the horse dropped. Once more they surrounded the fallen body. They felt the heart, then they began to shout all at once, and I knew that this time the trick had been turned. Yes, a moment later the old horse got staggering to his feet and went about at the length of his tether, shaking his head. I tried the third brute. I felt a certain surety, now, in my work. Again I nipped the neck of the horse, and once more it fell stunned, not dead.

They brought me back in triumph to the

village. Dark Water, in much excitement, hurried into the teepee of Bald Eagle and returned, after a time, to tell me that a hunting party would start at once and take me with them. In the meantime Bald Eagle asked to see my rifle. I sent it in to him, and Dark Water returned in a short time, bringing back my own weapon and a brand new rifle, as tight as a drum, a good pound lighter than my old gun, and in every way better. I tried it only once and knew that it was meant for me. It was not only lighter, but it had more power also. I took it with thanks and then sent for Two Feather.

"My friend," I said, "the Great Spirit has breathed upon my rifle. Take it with my good wishes. Bald Eagle has given me one of his talons in its place."

Two Feather took my rifle in both hands and was like a happy boy. From that moment I knew that I could count on at least one real friend among the Pawnees. Meanwhile a dozen braves, including Two Feather himself, had gathered. They were the cream of the tribe. Each had three horses, and those horses were the best the Pawnees could find. Then Dark Water made us a farewell speech. He told us that we were about to start on a long trail, and that before the end of it we might find whether the great horse for which

Bald Eagle had yearned was a horse, indeed, or a form of the Great Spirit. "But," he said finally, "if the bullet stuns him not but strikes him dead, and if you come not back with White Smoke, never come again in the sight of Bald Eagle, for your faces will be hateful to him."

Chapter Twenty-One

WHITE SMOKE

I should have guessed from the very beginning that the goal of the quest was White Smoke — that strange horse haunted the minds of the Indians like a fairy tale, just as it haunted the white traders and trappers. The very thought of leveling at that matchless stallion a rifle bullet that might drop it dead made my heart jump. However, I would be shooting for the sake of Sitting Wolf as well as my own.

We traveled steadily westward. I was kept under a constant watch every moment. I was never allowed to carry a weapon, but each day I was allowed to take my rifle — under the eye of the entire detachment — and practice with it as much as I pleased. I kept my hand in a good hour every day. I no longer tried to center things. It was always the outer and upper edge that I made my target — a mere nip off the edge of a rock or the top of a trunk. A slight graze of the bullet was what I always tried for. Invariably my horse was tethered to the saddle of someone among the Indians, which was only to be expected. They handled me as if I were a fire that might go out, and like a fire that might burn them to a crisp.

We marched for ten days. A dozen times we crossed the old trails of herds of wild horses, and on each occasion one of the band took a coil of rope and went over the tracks. Wherever it was found that a horse had galloped, they measured the tracks. And finally I learned why. No two horses take the same span in striding, and a horse at full speed never varies the length of his reach. It is as certain a method as fingerprinting.

I think it was the ninth or the tenth day when one of the younger braves, searching fresh-made tracks, discovered what he wanted. He let out a yell like a war cry. The whole lot of them swarmed around the spot and saw that the rope exactly fitted the stretch between hoofmarks. Then we held a consultation. That is to say, they consulted and I listened, for I would never have dared to lift my voice among such expert trackers. Finally they adopted a scheme that I should never have dreamed of. The wind was blowing steadily from the north, and we cut to the south in a shallow detour, riding hard for the rest of that day and continuing, once more, with the dawn. About midday we came to a pass through some high hills — for we had been striking steadily toward the Rockies and out of the prairies. Two of the men took fresh horses and headed north and south across the pass, while the rest of us hid the horses among a grove of poplars and then went back to lie in wait in a thicket. The Indian maneuver had been made in the simple hope that White Smoke was leading his band toward this cleft, and that we might have headed him.

In a quarter of an hour the two scouts swept back to assure us that there were no tracks in sight. So we waited, broiling in the heat that seeped through the scant and speckled shade under the brush. We waited until the deadening heat of the mid-afternoon had scalded us and diminished. We waited until the golden time of the late day arrived, and it was at this moment that Two Feather, who had eyes like a hawk, as I could bear testimony from our first encounter, suddenly whispered and pointed. We hardly dared lift our heads, but presently we made out a thin cloud of dust, rolling in from the east, growing thicker and larger, until at last it took shape as a mist, sweeping above the gleaming backs of horses.

I felt faint with excitement. They dipped out of sight in a hollow. Then they swept over a knoll just beneath us, and there I had my first view of White Smoke. He was running well in front of the rest, and how he ran! I have seen Thoroughbreds of the finest, but I have never seen an animal that moved so grandly. The desert blood of Arabia was in him; he was a throwback to some of those fine stallions the Spaniards had brought over at the time of the Mexican conquest. It needed no horse lover or expert to tell his points. He filled the eye. He fitted neatly into that place in the brain which holds the picture of a perfect horse.

I write the word soberly, judiciously — perfect! There is no other word for him. Behind him came half a hundred chosen mares and their foals. There was not an animal in the lot unworthy to seat a duke. There could not be, for a horse capable of following White Smoke in his arrowy flights across country had to have limbs of steel and a heart of brass. Yes, they were fifty queens of their kind — take them one by one, and it would have been hard to pick flaws in them. And yet, when the king was with them, they were not visible. He was gloriously alone. The wind was rippling in his mane and his arched tail. He carried his head high, with his ears ever pricked alertly. He lived like a tiger, ever on the watch.

I looked aside, dizzy and amazed, and I saw the Indians around me, quaking like sick children, their mouths gaping, their eyes burning with a fever like the fever of thirst. Straight down the pass he galloped, flicking the earth with winged feet, and yet for all his lightness he was big. I could understand how a large man like Bald Eagle might pine for such a charger, for I put him down as sixteen hands at least. As a matter of fact, he proved to be even taller than that. Then he reached the tracks of one of our scouts and stopped the rest of the band. The wind whipped the dust cloud away from them. Like fifty statues they stood, except for the life in their manes and in their eyes. And in White Smoke one could see the fear, hate, suspicion working.

I tucked the butt of my rifle into the hollow of my shoulder and prayed. Prayed a wordless, formless prayer that God would give this eagle of the earth into my hands. I drew down on him carefully. I took the edge of the neck just above the top arch of his crest. Then I fired.

He was off like thought. The mares burst into full speed behind him, but they seemed to be laboring with all their might and standing still — so tremendously fast did he leave them behind. Never was such running. Never since the world began such running as White Smoke, hurling himself through the air to reach freedom. I had missed.

The Indians looked at one another as though that were almost as great a miracle as the beauty of White Smoke. Then Two Feather breathed: "The old men have spoken the truth. This is no horse, but a thing dear to the Great Spirit."

How shall I say what I felt? Like one who stands in the harbor and sees the ship go out to sea and vanish with all the human lives that are dear to him on board. So I felt as I watched White Smoke flash across the horizon. From that instant I knew that I could never be truly happy until I sat on his back. I jumped up and screamed at the Pawnees: "Follow! Follow! Every second is floating him away from us!"

They merely looked at one another and smiled until Two Feather, who was more or less in command, said: "Let us follow, then. He must learn."

We flew to our horses and galloped like mad. Twice we changed mounts and still raced on until the dusk, but we reached not even the sight of their dust. Then I understood what Two Feather had meant. Truly I had learned what White Smoke was. As well try to follow the flash of lightning as to follow that great stallion and his mares with anything that moved on feet.

But we were not done. The fever had us. We became twelve silent men, filled with a single thought of which we never spoke. No one dreamed of giving up the hunt. For a fortnight we trailed the herd, looping back and forth among the hills, the trail growing always fainter and fainter. Then we lost it.

A month later we picked up the sign once more as we cut for it in huge circles — this time it led us far, far out onto the prairie. It circled back toward the mountains, but not before we had been scarred by the first danger of the hunt, for a flying war party of Cheyennes chased us and emptied three of our saddles before we drew clear of them.

We regained the mountains with the cold of the winter drawing near us. The first cold brought with it a fever that carried away two more of our men. Seven remained beside Black Bear. Of the three dozen horses with which we had started, a scant score were left, but these were the hardened best of the lot, inured to speed and bitter work. It was mid-December before we found the next sign of White Smoke, and on a white morning I had my second glimpse of him — but he was far, far away from rifle range, a glistening crystal form, standing on the shoulder of a mountain with a cluster of down-headed mares behind him. Then he disappeared once more, and the faint clarion note of his challenge floated dimly back to us.

The mares, at least, had been worn down one by one by the tenacity of the pursuit. Hardly a dozen remained to him, and time and again we passed the outworn creatures, beautiful even in their starved exhaustion, each of them worth fifty common nags, each of them an Indian's fortune. We passed them by like dirt. Who cares for a common jewel when he has before his eyes a diamond that fills the whole hand with electric fires?

So, through the winter, we dragged a blind and wretched existence among the mountains. Now lone hunters gave us word of the great horse. He traveled by himself. His herd was gone. He was thinner. A vague hope of wearing him down made our hearts leap. But never once during that lone, bleak season, while we starved and groaned in our miseries, did we lay eyes on him again. We had lost one man in a fall on an iced trail. We were seven when the spring brought us back among the hills and once again on the hot trail of the stallion. Then Two Feather said: "We can never follow him . . . our horses are too weak. But by the gate through which he went out, he may return, and he may return with mares behind him."

We took him at his word. After all, though we were keener than ever for the trail, we were worn to shadows. So we rested by the side of that pass and hunted through the hills behind us, while the horses grew fatter and began to lift their heads. We waited for weeks. But what are weeks to those who have labored on the actual trail for months? And each day, like men on a ship eager for sight of land, we kept our look-out posted on the ridge of a hill, scanning the lower hills and the prairies beyond in the hope of seeing the flash of a bright form. When the hail came, it was like a voice in a dream.

"White Smoke!"

We were already in our covert. We only needed to lie quietly, all saving myself, for I was desperately massaging the numbness of the morning chill out of the fingers of my right hand which must grasp the stock and manage the trigger. This time I meant to capture or kill. I had shot a fraction of an inch too high before. Now I meant to cut deep, deep — and God preserve his life, for I should not miss.

The Indians were like trembling children, eager to help, not knowing how. They smoothed the place for me. They parted the brush before me. Then they retreated, and I felt six pairs of eyes burning steadily at me.

Chapter Twenty-Two

THE MIGHTY STALLION FALLS

I have heard men — and wise ones, too — affirm with much certainty that the Indian never lived who really loved his horse. There is no doubt that usually they do not love them enough to fondle them and give them careful handling. But if to love a thing is to prize it highly, then I say that no miser ever loved gold as a Plains Indian loved a fast horse. And with excellent reason. In those prairie lands one's life often depended on nothing but the speed of the four strong legs beneath. The difference between a good horse and a great one was the difference between life and death. It meant, too, that the proud owner could range at will, like an eagle through the air, striking where he pleased, and then defying pursuit. Still, their love was something more than this even. Six prayers went soundlessly up to the Great Spirit as I leveled my rifle at the stallion.

And here he was, all in a trice. Even after the first view of him, I had wondered how it was that he could have kept away from us during those many months of hard search. Now I could understand. He blew up out of the prairie like a storm cloud over the sea, and all as effortless as the very wind. So he galloped into our sight with a band of some twenty-five mares behind him. In the rush from the inhabited lands, from the pursuit of the Indians or the white traders he had robbed, the weaker spirits were already weeded out, and these twenty-five were as beautiful and as chosen as the hardy band that we had first seen at his flying heels.

I caught him in my sights instantly and held my bead on him with a steady hand as he poured along over the ground. I repeat solemnly, with all the gravity of a very old man with little of the long trail left before him, that never did the world behold another such horse. They tell me of their modern flyers, and their miles in a minute and thirty-five seconds. But I tell them that they never saw White Smoke, sliding across the hills or turning himself into a white streak, lost on the horizon.

The wind, what there was of it, had been wavering and faltering all the day. Now, it seemed to me, it had died away utterly, but just as White Smoke came into the hollow mouth of the pass, he stopped with such a sudden violence that his mane fluffed forward over his head and his tail went high. He stopped not like the giant that he was, but like a small dog playing tag, or like a cat ready to spring one way or another.

He was too far away, much too far away. God knows I never should have risked it. For such nice work as mine I should have had him at the most point-blank range. I had no such luck. Worst of all, I had to take him at a slant — not at dead right angles. However, I could not risk letting him go by. There were the many months of that bitter trail behind me. In the instant of his pause, before he could whirl away, I steadied my rifle and fired.

I saw him fall, and I saw no more. I lay on my own face in the grass like a dead man. Indeed, I could barely see — my head was swimming as the Indians beside me caught up their lariats and raced for him. I dared not think; I dared not breathe. I only lay there, saying to myself over and over again: *He is dead! He is dead!* And then a blinding light struck a glory across my mind. It was the exultant shout of the Indians. I caught up my own rope and staggered out toward the place, shouting, laughing, reeling like a drunkard — drunk with the purest joy.

I came in time to see a white giant bound up from the ground — no, there was not a chance for him. Four lariats were already around his feet. He strove to whirl and struggle toward the flying cloud of mares, but he floundered and went down at once, again. I stood by. I was not needed in the brutal struggle that followed. He was sleek as a white seal as he lay there writhing, twisting, snorting, with hatred and terror in his eyes and with a crimson streak across the top of his neck. At least he was netted in a mesh of ropes so that struggle was useless.

The battle was over. The victory was ours. They began a wild celebration, those stoic Pawnees. While their yells were echoing over the hollow pass, I sat down at the sweating head of the stallion. From the Indians he had had the first taste of man's might, man's weapons of torment. But I, who had been the thunderbolt that struck him down unseen, was the first man to lay a hand of kindness on him, and out of my throat he heard the first gentle human speech. What did it mean to him? Well, my sincere conviction is that all the dumb beasts, high and low, feel a magic in the voice of man. They may tremble in terror at it; they may strike because they are afraid; but behind the fear there is a foundation of love also. At least, it seemed to me that some of the wildness left the eyes of White Smoke in the few minutes during which I sat at his head.

For the first two weeks we did nothing but work him slowly along on hobbles — hobbles against which he fought until his legs were cut and bleeding. Sometimes we did not make more than three or four miles, for I insisted that we should not force the horse too far or too fast. He must have plenty of time to rest and to feed. At every halt I was beside him. On the fifth day, for the first time, I sat on his back. He did not attempt to pitch. He merely crouched like an immense panther beneath me, trembling. Then, when he saw that I did not do him any peculiar harm, he stood up and hobbled on once more, but with his ears flattened to his neck and his eyes rolled back with twin devils in them.

After that I spent each day's march on his back. First with a saddle cinched on, and then with a bridle with which I began gradually to control him. All that time I performed every act of service for him. I brought him to water. I unhoused his head that he might drink. I groomed him twice a day until, as my hand with the wisp of dried grass went down his neck, he lifted his ears a little at each stroke, half automatically, I suppose, at first. But it was pleasant to him.

I have no doubt that during those first

days he was constantly, constantly biding his time. Two Feather took me aside to remonstrate.

"Friend," he said, "the squaws of the Pawnees would be glad if Black Bear went to the happy hunting grounds. But the Pawnee men, brother, would not see so great a warrior killed by a horse. He is a tiger."

We had been journeying on for a full three weeks or more by this time, and the struggle to win White Smoke had gained me such small returns that I was beginning to despair. Out of an impulse of a foolish moment I said: "Two Feather, you are wise in the ways of horses, but not of White Smoke. I could go this moment and stand at his head."

The gambler's glint shone in his eyes. Next to the old rifle that I had given him, his greatest treasure was the brown horse he was riding at that moment. He leaped to the ground and gestured at it.

"This horse is yours, my brother," he said, "if you stand at the head of White Smoke."

The other Indians had marked that conversation, and by this I knew I should have to go on with the experiment no matter how I disliked it. There they stood, waiting and watching, keeping their faces calm, but unable to control the savage gleam of their eyes and the faint quiver of their nostrils.

I dismounted and went in front of White Smoke. I took a quiet and a careful view of him. He was not then what he had been before or what he was afterward to become; the weight of captivity had bowed him a little, but still he was glorious as he must have been from birth. He looked at me, I thought, as a caged tiger eyes an enemy. I stretched out my hand, palm up. If there is any gesture which both beasts and men understand, it is this. I began to speak gently, softly. And I walked straight up to him. He flinched from me a little in horror at first. Then his ears flicked back, and his head went out as a snake's goes in striking. My right forearm beneath the elbow was caught in his mouth. Would he wrench me under his hoofs and stamp me to death? Would he close those jaws and crush the bones of the arm? Or would he simply strip all the flesh away?

While I stood there for a second with the arm imprisoned, by the tremor that passed through his head, I knew that all of these impulses were rushing through his savage brain. The Indians made not a move to succor me. Rather than destroy the stallion, they would have seen him tear a dozen men limb from limb. For what were a few lives to the followers of Bald Eagle who crushed humans like ants with the treading of his feet?

But the teeth did not close, except hard enough to paralyze the hand and wrist of that arm for a week. They loosed me, and White Smoke threw up his head and looked at me out of mischievous, coltish eyes. I let my injured arm hang in agony at my side. I went straight in and laid my left hand upon his neck, while a little murmur came from the Indians. White Smoke submitted to my caress — yes, and pricked his ears at it.

I have never had an extraordinary power over animals as some men have. Dogs bark at me as readily as at any man, and more than one Indian pony has tried to dash my brains out with his heels. Perhaps I may be allowed to think that between White Smoke and me there was a special affinity. Or perhaps it was something less mysterious, for mine was the first kind touch he had ever felt, the first kind voice. The turn of a hair would have changed the thing. He might have torn me to pieces, but he let his mind waver, and after that he was mine!

It was a simple thing. Every animal trainer has a dozen tales to overmatch it, but to the Indians there was something miraculous in the scene. They looked upon me with a greater awe from that moment. Moreover, I went straight on in the conquest of White

Smoke. He never felt spur or whip. With a gentle hand and a gentle voice I worked over him for the simple reason that I felt the enormous danger of his superior might. By sheer strength I could not subdue him, and by sheer cunning I knew not how to work. It was all done by patience, by scores of hours of closest companionship, as we worked our way over the prairie.

But this, at least, was the end. When we came in view of the teepees of Bald Eagle's camp, my six companions accorded me the place of honor, and I rode into the village at their head, without a controlling rope on the neck or the legs of the stallion, with only saddle and bridle to manage him. More than this, I let the reins hang loose on his neck, and by the pressure of my knees and the voice alone I worked him through the press of horses and men and women and children that had poured out around us.

I have said that the ownership of my first Colt was one of the great days of my life, but it was nothing compared with this second great day. And there was still a third mighty moment to come.

Chapter Twenty-Three

THE TEEPEE OF THE RISING SUN

When I dismounted, it was among the crowds in front of Bald Eagle's tent. My companions stood near me. What lean and hungry-looking wolves we were from that year of arduous trailing, but that price and all our time, our suffering, seemed nothing for the reward. We stared at White Smoke with eyes newly appreciative, because we saw him with the wonder and the joy of that whole tribe of Pawnees. They were like men among whom a gift had dropped from heaven, visibly, through the clouds. They pointed out his features one by one: the satin black stockings that clad him almost to the knee, the hoofs like polished ebony, the thin silver of mane and tail, and perhaps most of all his coat. It was not white. Only at a distance did it seem so. Close at hand one noted a dark patterning like the faded spots of a panther worked thickly over the surface. But he shone in the sun like burnished metal — pure, flaming silver at a little distance.

But even for this Bald Eagle did not come

forth from his teepee. I was bitterly disappointed. I had been looking forward to the time when I should see the face and features of the famous chief and hear, perhaps, some word of praise from him. Yet there was not a hint of him. Only old Dark Water stepped out and hobbled away with a dozen braves, leading the stallion on ropes. They had not gone ten paces before White Smoke broke from them and came rushing back to me. I spoke to him, and he followed me like a house dog, while, with a swelling heart, I led him through the press and saw him tethered. There I left him and went back to the tent that was appointed for me.

There, Sitting Wolf came in to see me, but not with a boyish rush and a shout, as I had expected. I had left him a boy. I came back to find him a man. He was only fifteen, but a year among an alien nation had done a great deal for him. He was tall, still slender, but with a promise of bigness. He had a grave and quiet face, more finely featured than any Indian I ever saw with the exception of Zintcallasappa, and she had a strain of white blood, while Sitting Wolf was purest Dakota. Only when he spoke of White Smoke did he become a child again. He had seen the stallion, but he had not been able to come to me through the crowd. He wished to know if it was true that, by magic, I had trained the horse so that he would answer my hand, my voice, and come rushing at my whistle? I told him that it was no magic, simply kindness and patience, but he shook his head. He was irresistibly determined, always, to make me out a superman.

I asked him how he had been treated, and he told me that Bald Eagle had allowed him perfect freedom after I left, telling him simply that, if he ran home to the Sioux, I, Black Bear, should lose my life with torments, whether or not I came back with White Smoke. Once again I felt surety that the mysterious chief was a white man. What Indian would have trusted so much to the loyalty of a boy — even such a boy as the son of Three Buck Elk?

He told me, too, the history of the Pawnee-Dakota war since myself and the twelve had disappeared into the west. In the year the Sioux had organized a great expedition that amounted almost to the dimensions of an army. According to Sitting Wolf, they were as many as a great herd of buffalo, darkening the plains. But no Indians have ever looked at facts without a magnifying glass. They detest scrupulous truth, not like liars but like children. This horde brushed the outlying divisions of the Pawnees before them until Bald Eagle threw himself into their path. He had not numbers, no matter how well trained, to meet the shock of such a swarm. But on the edge of a river, so that he might be sure of water, he entrenched himself, throwing up big mounds — twice as high as a teepee, according to Sitting Wolf. He stored that rude fort with heaps of dried meat and with corn. He brought in scores of loads of ammunition. Then he waited for the Sioux.

When they came, they tried to swallow the little fort in one charge. He blew the van of their charge to bits and drove them back. For a whole month they remained before the fort, but it was a miserable month for the Sioux. Their provisions ran out almost at once, and they found no buffalo herds near to supply them with meat. Every night or two Bald Eagle rushed out from the fort and struck them with the sledgehammer-stroke tactics against which barbarians have never known how to stand. They lost men by hundreds and hundreds while the Pawnees were scarcely touched. Finally the Sioux broke up the siege and began a retreat.

Bald Eagle was not content with this mere repulse. He mounted his men on fat, strong horses, preserved all this time in the center of the camp, and with these he hung on the rear of the Sioux. Twice or thrice they turned back. He evaded their starved ponies easily and returned. Every man who fell behind on the march was swallowed by Bald Eagle. And they straggled by hundreds. It was a cowed and desperate army that finally reached the proper domains of the Dakotas and thence dispersed to their homes. The fame of Bald Eagle was greater than ever. He was both chief and enchanter in the eyes of the Pawnees and of their enemies.

Sitting Wolf had hardly concluded when Dark Water came to us and showed us two fine horses, saddled, bridled, with bags of provisions tied on. They were for us, and we were free. Bald Eagle was keeping his promise.

Who has said the Indian does not love horses? Sitting Wolf turned to me and said very gravely: "Do you ride with me, brother, or will you stay here with White Smoke?"

I did not make an answer until we had ridden clear of the outskirts of the village. Then I said, as I drew my rein: "They have tethered White Smoke with only one rope. I myself saw to that. Perhaps he will prefer us to the Pawnees."

There were half a dozen Pawnee scoundrels on the edge of the horizon at that moment, but I put two fingers against my lips and raised a whistle like the scream of hawk that swings to earth through half a mile of rushing wind. White Smoke would hear, and he would either come or break his neck, of that I had no doubt. I knew at once what had happened. There was a dull roar of shouting from the town, then a silver streak flashed toward us through the sunset light with mounted men rushing behind him. Oh, how he came to me, like a creature of the air, scorning the ground he touched with his bright hoofs. I did not wait to change saddles. I stripped the bridle from my horse, tossed its rope to Sitting Wolf, and was instantly on the back of the stallion. By the time I was sitting there, the Pawnee hoofbeats were loud behind me as they came screeching like demons, and Sitting Wolf streaked far away.

My danger ended there. In half a minute I had put those Pawnee scoundrels hopelessly behind me, and Sitting Wolf was drawing back at every stride. I had never loosed White Smoke before. I felt as though I were clinging to the back of a great arrow launched from the bow of a giant, save that the flight of this shaft that bore me never slackened, never failed. The wind of that gallop cut my face and seared my eyes. I found myself yelling like an Indian — and half with fear that White Smoke was beyond my control. But, when Sitting Wolf was just before me again, a single word brought him down to the pace of the other horses. Those horses were gallant runners. The pride of Bald Eagle would not have allowed him to mount us on any but the best for our return from his people. Now Sitting Wolf was jockeying the uttermost speed from them, but White Smoke floated effortlessly over the ground as he ran at their side. Never, never, was such a horse before or since.

I was as safe as though I rode a thunderbolt. Sitting Wolf was another matter, but the second horse attended to that. For three miles he whipped the mount he bestrode until it staggered — and still some half dozen in the van of the Pawnees gained on us. Then we halted our horses. I jerked my rifle to my shoulder and dropped the leader of the Pawnees into eternity, the others scattering to the side, yelling. By that time Sitting Wolf was on the back of the led horse and off to a fresh start. The danger ended. The Pawnees had given the best that was in their horses, and now they dropped gradually to the rear, until at last we rode into the darkness of the eastern horizon alone, untroubled by any fear.

There followed one of the merriest fortnights of my life as Sitting Wolf and I roamed over the prairies, hunting for a sign of the Dakotas. He was keen as starvation to find his people once more, but also he was reveling in his freedom and, like myself, in the magic beauty of the white stallion. We found a trail and a broken arrow of a make that assured us we were after a band of Sioux. Sitting Wolf even declared that he recognized the handicraft of one of the old arrow makers of his uncle's band. Three days later he proved that he was right, for we came into the village of Standing Bear himself. That chief was away hunting buffalo. We went straight to the teepee of Three Buck Elk with the entire camp laughing and shouting for joy around us. It was as though I had come back to my own people. The young children held up their hands to me joyously. The young braves waved and shouted. The women were screaming like so many hawks. But, of course, if they cheered me, they went mad over the return of Sitting Wolf. He had been given up for dead long, long ago, just as I had been given up. Now they were looking on two ghosts, one of whom came back from the dead on the horse that the Great Spirit Himself might have been proud to ride.

There was a cleavage through the mass of

people before us. Through this opened lane the mother of Sitting Wolf came running, and in an instant he was off his horse and in her arms. Three Buck Elk left his son, who was the hope of the tribe, to the arms of his mother. He himself looked on with shining eyes. Joyous laughter kept swelling in his throat. He choked it back and subdued it to a groan.

"Brother, brother," he said to me, "the Great Spirit has sent you back to us as a sign that our troubles are ended. Three Buck Elk has become an old man, ready to die. The sun had no warmth for his cold blood. Now he is young again."

The braves were beginning to cluster around me and my horse. It was growing embarrassing. I said: "I do not see my brother, Rising Sun. Just where is his teepee?"

There was a little pause at this. Then Three Buck Elk said in a marked voice: "His teepee is yonder."

I found it at once by the yellow disk that was painted near its top. When I raised the flap and entered, I found Zintcallasappa sitting on a robe with a nursing infant at her breast — a child whose hair was a tender fluff of gold. She was as lovely as ever, but how changed. When she raised her great dark eyes to me, full of fear of a dying hope, I knew without a word from her all that had happened. Chuck Morris had left her and gone back to his kind.

Chapter Twenty-Four

AT THE FORT

I was too choked with pity and with a sort of horror to speak. But The Blackbird? She simply rolled the infant in a blanket and then made herself come to me with a smile and welcomed me with both hands. Then, because White Smoke had put his head through the entrance flap, sniffing and snorting because he wanted to come to me but feared the fire, she went up to him with a handful of corn. I have seen one other woman, as lovely, as gentle of voice and eye, but even she could never come near his head. To my bewilderment, he submitted quietly to her touch and began to nibble the corn from her palm. So, stroking his neck, she turned back to me, smiling still.

"I knew that you would come safely home," said Zintcallasappa. "And I have heard them shouting. You brought Sitting Wolf also. Ah, what happiness there is in the teepee of Three Buck Elk . . . for him who has returned."

There was the slightest tremor in her

voice, as she ended, and a shade across her eyes through which I could look into her soul and see, for an instant, the deep agony of her grief. But then, in another moment, she was smiling again.

Afterward, I got the story from Three Buck Elk — a story brutally simple. Morris had simply gone in to a new frontier trading post and fort, and, while he was there, he had seen a white girl. He had not come back. He had sent back a rich present of horses, loaded with a thousand trinkets, together with a message that he was not worthy of her, that she was free, and that she should find happiness with one of her own kind.

I had no doubt that it was a gentle message, for I knew Morris. But when I listened to Three Buck Elk, the first foreshadowing of anger and sadness came over my heart. All the happiness of that return was wiped out of my soul. I cannot tell you what a bitter loneliness came to me at the same time. What a pull there is of like to like — of dog to dog, of hawk to hawk, of white man to his kin. But Zintcallasappa was neither white nor red. She lived on a sad borderland with her heart turned from her people.

I could not endure remaining near her, inactive in her cause. I could not even wait for the great feast that on the next day was to celebrate our return from the land of the dead. In the morning I saddled White Smoke, and I said a brief farewell to Three Buck Elk. I shall never forget how the great chief looked silently at me before he said: "You leave us, my son?"

"I shall come again," I said, "and bring Rising Sun with me."

He merely said: "When the bear sees his brother trapped, he should run from the place before he himself is caught."

I hardly appreciated that. My mind was full of only one thing, and that was how I should bring Morris back to his duty. For it seemed to my blind self then that, when I put the picture of the poor girl and his child before him, he could not help but come with me.

For an ordinary horse, traveling fast, the journey to the fort on the river from the place where I started was a full fifteen-day march. But on the tenth morning I rode into the fort. The fort itself was simply a big, low structure of wood, faced with heaps of dirt and a palisade around it. The town was a scattering street that half surrounded the fortress. It was composed chiefly of canvas and of little wretched shacks. No one would invest in permanent structures when they could not tell at what moment an Indian raid might sweep everything flat as the palm of the hand. In the streets of the village I saw such a population as one might have expected in that country — Indians, half-breeds, trappers who were more wild than the Indians themselves, hunters, scouts in deerskins, and now and then the shrewd face of a trader, full of anxiety, full of schemes. I looked not half as wild as most of the people I passed. What drew their eyes to me, of course, was White Smoke. He would have made a congress of wise elders leap to their feet and gape as he came in from his ten-day whirl across the prairie as fresh as a lark.

Their voices I paid not the slightest attention to. How long it had been since I had seen any white face other than Morris's I could hardly guess, but this return to my kind meant nothing to me. I was too full of the sorrows of Zintcallasappa, who waited yonder in the huge bosom of the prairie, hoping, praying, begging the Great Spirit or the white man's God to put wisdom and eloquence in the words I spoke to Morris. Their voices did not really touch my ears, until I heard the golden voice of a girl cry out: "Look, Dad, look! Oh, what a king of horses!"

I turned like a horse that starts under a spur, and, riding up the street beside her big-shouldered father, I had my first sight of Mary Kearney. To me, fresh from the Dakotas, she looked very like an Indian girl at first, what with her dark olive skin and her glossy black hair. Yet, even before she came near enough for me to see that her eyes were blue, I could have had no doubt of her race. For she rode with an easy, graceful carelessness, and she had a way as bold as a man's, except that it was all a woman's — and more than all this, there was something of mind that spoke in her face.

I knew in a trice everything about her, except her name. I knew that she was brave, that she was gay, that she was full of wit and laughter, and that at heart she was as honest as she was gentle. I knew more than this — that here was the girl who had swept Chuck Morris out of his old life and into a new one. There could not be two like her — not at a small trading post or even in a great city — no more than two horses like White Smoke have ever trod the earth.

They pressed straight up to me, she still full of excitement, chattering to her father while he smiled and nodded. With every step of their horses her beauty grew out on me as though I were watching the unfolding of a great rose from bud to fall flower in a single moment.

Her father said, as he came closer and reined his horse: "My man, I wish to buy that horse for my daughter. What is your price? My name," he added, "is John Kearney."

To the end he had always a lofty manner and a proud habit of speech. But to me, accustomed to Three Buck Elk and Standing Bear and other chiefs with their natural dignity, the pride of white men, even the greatest of them, has always seemed an affectation. I prefer a downright, plain, frank man who doesn't wear his name as if it were a title.

"My name," I said, "is Lewis Dorset."

Before I could go any further he broke in: "Dorset? Dorset? My dear boy, are you one of the Rhode Island Dorsets? I heard that young Harry Dorset came west. . . ."

I said: "I am not a Rhode Island Dorset, Mister Kearney. I come from Virginia."

I saw the nose of the girl go up in the air a bit, and I said to myself: *Young filly, for all your pride, perhaps I could teach you your paces.* The face of Kearney had turned cold at once as he went on: "Very well, Dorset. Now, the price of your horse. I'm in a trifling hurry and cannot wait."

"This horse," I said, "no woman can ride."

There was a faint exclamation of injured pride from the girl. "Give me time, Dad," she hastened to assure him, "and I'll ride anything that calls itself a horse. You know that I can."

"Certainly. Certainly," said Kearney, and he brushed my objection into the thinnest air. He continued: "Now, Dorset, let me have your price, if you please. I suppose it will be high enough. But I am not here to strike a bargain. I must have that horse."

"Very well," I said, "then we have to find a basis for working out the price. What would you say the lives of six men are worth?"

He stared at me for a moment, and then he said with a bit of acid in his voice: "You come from a slave state, Dorset. I abhor slavery. Therefore, I presume you can answer that question better than I?"

There was a flare of red across my eyes. He was only about forty-five, fit as a fiddle, not a whit too old for a fight. I wanted to smash him to bits. But the very sense of my greater strength held me back, as such a sense will hold any man of decency.

"I am speaking of free men," I said.

"The price of freedom," said Kearney with

a ring in his voice, "is ten hundredweight of diamonds."

He had been in politics, and he couldn't help turning out these stump-speech phrases every now and then. No more than he could help running his eyes over the little crowd that had gathered around us, harvesting the murmur of their applause and smiling as they nodded.

"Well, pay down sixty hundredweight of diamonds, and you get my horse, but not before."

It was his turn to grow hot then. He glared at me and surveyed my rough deerskins. I have said before that I never was famous even among the Indians for a good appearance. I wore now the same ragged suit that had been on me when I finished the hunt for White Smoke. It was a mass of tatters, held together with rough patching.

"I am not a professional jester," said Kearney stiffly. "Now, Dorset, I shall pay real money. That is a fine animal. I'll give you four hundred dollars."

He reached for his purse. It was as big as a provision bag, and it clinked with the gold in it. It was too good an opening for me to miss. I hit back as straight as I could.

"If your own horse was gold, and the saddle on its back was gold, and the man in the saddle was gold, you could not trade yourself and your horse for White Smoke."

I had not meant to bring out that famous name — it simply slipped out of my lips naturally, and I could have cursed, afterward, because I knew that if men wanted to buy that horse before, they would want to murder me for the stallion now. At least that name did one good thing — it covered up the insulting manner of my remark to Kearney and brought a gasp from him and from the crowd while Mary was simply turned speechless. Kearney jerked back his horse to get a better view of the big animal.

"Great heavens, man," he said, "is that the horse of the fable? Is that White Smoke?"

"It is."

Here a big voice from a big man sounded. "That's a lie and a loud lie! I've hunted White Smoke for a month and seen him a dozen times. Why, this here hoss ain't white at all . . . he's gray."

What kept me from putting a bullet through his head I have never understood. My good angel must have laid a hand on my arm. I merely turned on him while he was still blustering.

"Among the people where I have been living," I said, "the rule is to kill a fool while he's still talking. But white men give fools a second chance and a warning. I give you that warning and that second chance now. But if I put eyes on you again, I'll skin you alive, you sneaking coyote. Get out of my sight!"

The greatest miracle was that there was not a killing on the spot. The fellow hesitated half an instant, but then he saw certain death in my eyes, and he turned and waded through the crowd.

I was in the true killing humor now, and, from the way men shrank from me, they must have seen the humor in my face. I looked around at them and said: "As for you, Kearney, and any of the rest of you abolitionists, all I want from you is news of where I can find Chuck Morris."

I heard an oath from Kearney and saw him move a hand to his gun, as I watched him from the corner of my eye. I was not too far gone with madness. I only intended to put a bullet through his shoulder. But Mary caught his hand. "Dad, Dad," she gasped out. "Are you thinking of fighting with a common ruffian?"

"Oh Lord," groaned Kearney, "to put up with such a speech from even such a man."

He let his daughter take him through the crowd. And that was my introduction to Mary Kearney.

Chapter Twenty-Five

LEW PLEADS FOR THE INDIAN GIRL

I suppose that a dozen hands were working at a dozen gunbutts during that moment. I might have killed one or two, but the third or the fourth would surely have nailed me when someone sang out: "Here's Chuck Morris himself! Maybe he has first call on this man."

At that I saw Chuck moving down the street, and at the same instant he saw me. He threw up both hands with a shout like the roar of a buffalo bull, and then he came for me. He was at me before I could get out of the saddle, and he lifted me down as though I were a child. What a giant's power was in those hands of his. There he held me in one great bear arm and brandished the other in the air.

"Lew! Lew!" he cried. "Have you come back from the dead, boy? Have you come back from the dead?"

"Back from the Pawnees," I said, "which to some is the same thing."

"And here . . . dear Lord, it's White Smoke."

That name from Morris settled any doubts about the identity of the stallion that might have been in the minds of the crowd. And, seeing Morris greet me like more than a brother, most of the sting of my last speech was rubbed out of their minds. They stood about with good-natured grins, watching Morris lead me up the street, stopping every now and then to wring my hand, or I to wring his, laughing, shouting, and — on my part at least — weeping like a child. He got me into his own cabin at last.

"The Pawnee villains told the truth, then," he said. "I caught one of the red demons, and he swore that Bald Eagle had sent you hunting White Smoke as a ransom for yourself and Sitting Wolf. I thought that was another way of saying that he had sent you to heaven. I strangled the poor dog. But you're here, Lew . . . you're here past my hopes. Ah, man, when I thought you were gone, it wrung my heart. I hated every redskin. I hated the damned prairies. They were haunted for me. I couldn't stand it . . . and so I came in here."

So I, after all, was the first cause of the tragedy. If it had not been that loneliness for me had driven him away from the tribe, he would have stayed with Zintcallasappa until she and their child held him with a greater strength than steel. But my loss was the knife that cut the bond, just as she, poor, wise girl, had prophesied. Hearing him say it sent something like ice to my heart. I was dumb. I could only stare miserably at him. Then most of the brightness left his face.

He muttered: "You saw Zintcallasappa, of course?"

"The boy has your hair, Chuck," I said, fumbling for the surest means of wounding him and finding it well enough. "Yellow hair like yours, Chuck. When I saw it, the firelight was shining through it and turning it into gold."

He blanched as the words struck him. But I was brutal for the sake of Zintcallasappa. I thought I might as well let him know that I knew everything.

I said: "I've seen the other woman, too."

At this, he put up his great hand, and it was trembling. "Don't, Lew. Not any more for a minute."

He got up and went to the door where he stood a moment, and the noise of his breathing filled the room. Then he turned about and came slowly back to me.

I looked about the room. There was such a strain in the shack that I couldn't go on tormenting him for a time — and this in the first moments of our meeting. It was a big place, heaped in every corner to the very ceiling with all manner of stuffs from flour to beads.

"Who owns all this?" I asked him.

He nodded at it vaguely. "I do."

"Why, Chuck, have you gone into partnership with some rich man?"

"It's all mine," he answered, as though it were so much dirt. "I'm doing a new kind of trading."

"What's that?"

"Most of these fellows are risking their necks, trading straight with the Indians. That takes oceans of time. Of course, they make huge profits, but every third time they get wiped out by accidents or Indians. Well, they need partners, too, to share the danger and the profits with them, but I had a new idea. I cleaned up five thousand in less than a week when I first came to the fort. It's a lucky place . . . a lucky place for me, Lew."

How his face lighted as he said it and gave me a glimpse again of Rising Sun.

"I chartered an old river steamer for that . . . too crazy to run, people said, but I got an old Scotchman who can make a steam engine talk Sioux, if he wants to. He took it down the river and mortgaged the ship together with the rest of my cash. He sank it all in the sort of goods I'd named to him, and he brought it back to the highest point on the Missouri that his old tub would take it. Then I pulled it up here on canal boats . . . horses on the banks, you see? Well, I turned five thousand into fifteen thousand on the first trip, simply by selling the cargo directly to the traders. I'm a wholesaler, you might say. I went right back at the job myself. We patched up the ship, shot her down to New Orleans, and brought her back again with my entire capital turned into flour, rifles, beads, and. . . ."

He paused quickly and glanced askance at me.

"Firewater?" I asked him.

He knew my opinion about that traffic, and he said: "Well, that's what they want. If they didn't get it from me, they'd get it from someone else. Why not from me? I really don't like the business any more than you do."

I looked down at the floor. I was afraid to face him.

"I finished that second trip with close to forty-five thousand dollars. Another man up here caught my idea and offered me a ridiculously high price for my charter on the steamer. Well, he offered more than the old tub was worth. I took my Scotchman, dropped down to New Orleans, and bought another ship outright, twice as big and twice as fast as the one I had chartered. I poured the rest of my money and all I could raise with a mortgage into a cargo that jammed her to the gunwales, as my Scotchman says."

He lowered his voice a little and looked at me with shining eyes.

"Lew, I cleared a hundred thousand dollars on that voyage! I cleared a hundred thousand, and besides that I have the new steamer. I mean she's new in this trade. This stuff in the house is all that is left of the cargo, and I could sell it all today . . . but I'm waiting for a little rise in prices. In a word, Lew, I'm a rich man." He brought it out with a ring. "A rich man in eight months of work, Lew."

It was like a miracle. I found myself changing my mind about him again. I had always been changing my mind about him, off and on. My last estimate of him had been as a careless lounger who would smile his way through life in easy fashion and do no good for himself or anyone else except to spread a sort of festival spirit around him. Yet, I found it as easy to understand why he had been able to take these huge business ventures and succeed in them. The mere thought of investing one's total profits after each trip in a crazy old river boat that was overdue in Davy Jones's locker made my blood run cold, but, whereas I was the poorest gambler in the world, Morris was one of the best. In eight months he had piled up a huge fortune. In these days of billions one may think a hundred thousand is a very small sum, but, before the war, a hundred thousand was a tidy fortune. Besides, it was only the beginning for Morris. Already he seemed to be drawing away from me. He was becoming a figure, I felt, of national importance. I digested all of this news in a moment of quiet.

"You are going to be a rich man, Chuck," I said. "I thank God for it. Because you're the sort of a fellow who will use money in the right way. No poor devil will ever be broken-hearted by your business ways. But what became of the man who bought the charter from you?"

"Of him? The ship sank on the way down . . . rammed a submerged wreck of a scow, I think. The poor devil who had invested in it blew his brains out . . . after he'd swum ashore. A fool, you see, with no nerve at all. Should have been in a foundling's asylum. I gave his wife and his youngster money enough to take them home."

Once more I had to look down to the floor. Yet, I could not accuse Morris of sharp practice. It was simply business, I suppose. The next moment his heart was running over again.

"And now, boy," he said to me, "you're coming in with me, and we're going to be partners. I have it worked out. The whole scheme jumped out of my brain alive and running the minute I saw you. I'm going to New Orleans to handle that end. I have some ideas about shipping in stuff cheap, directly from England and France and Boston. I can cut our costs in two, now that I'm able to handle things on a larger scale. I'll work down there. You'll handle this end of it. I've only had one outlet, and that's here. I want others. I need others. I have growing pains with this business, old man. I want twenty forts and posts to be fed directly from me at a rate that will break the hearts of the little fellows that cart their stuff three thousand miles overland and *have* to ask ridiculous prices. Waterway transportation . . . nothing but waterway transportation is my motto. It beats dry land ten ways. I have a scheme for getting a couple of big depots up these little side rivers to the forts. Very well . . . this will be the firing line, and on it I need a fighter. I need you, Lew! You know Indians better than anyone in the world. It was always play with me, but some of their stuff got into your blood. You *are* an Indian, you tiger, you. Very well, you know what the red devils want better than they do. I . . . I . . . why, I'd almost cut out the firewater trade, if you'd come in with me, Lew."

He was striding about the room as he said this, and I watched his magnificent enthusiasm in a sort of dream. Finally he stopped and frowned at me.

"Well?" he snapped out. "Well?"

"What?" I asked him blankly.

"Damnation, man. I'm asking you if you want to be a partner in a hundred-and-fifty-thousand-dollar business. Isn't that enough to keep you awake?"

I roused myself at that. "You're too generous," I told him, "but I have something to work at for a while. There's something else on my mind that I have to clear away first."

"What's that?" he barked out in this new fashion he had picked up since he became a businessman. "What's more important than your own good, man?"

"Zintcallasappa and your son."

He turned crimson to the eyes, and a great purple vein stood out on his forehead, jagged as a lightning flash that rips across the sky. It was the danger sign in him, but in an instant he banished that mood. He stood there, looking sadly down at me.

"I thought I could talk you out of it," he sighed, "but I might as well try to talk the Rocky Mountains off their feet. Go on, Lew, say whatever you please. I'll listen."

I packed a pipe, turning the words over in my mind and making a dozen different beginnings. After I had begun to smoke, I saw the truth as the drifts of blue-brown shadows went up and flattened against the ceiling.

Words would do no good. If he had left the girl once, he would leave her again. He laid his hand on my shoulder.

"Say something, Lew," he begged. "I don't care how you damn me, it will be better than this silence. If you want to call me a dog, a heartless dog . . . a traitor, a hypocrite, I'll admit that I'm all that. I've made a mistake . . . a horrible mistake, and I want to pay for it. I want to suffer for it. Poor girl, I'll give her more than any Indian ever had since the beginning of time. I'll fix her up on a ranch in the south and see that her interests are cared for. The . . . the boy . . . I'll see that he's educated, and that he gets everything the world can give him."

"Except a father?" I said.

Whip your gentlest dog long enough in a corner and it will show its teeth at last.

Morris gave me an ugly glance, but almost at once he sighed and then leaned back against the wall.

"Don't you see, Lew?" he asked. "The whole thing is impossible. I can't bring an Indian . . . not even Zintcallasappa . . . into my life. It . . . it would wreck me."

"I don't quite see," I answered. "When I'm married, I expect my home to be nine tenths of the world to me. As long as I can keep that home happy, I won't care how the other tenth of the world shrugs its shoulders or smiles."

He looked before him fixedly, seeing the vision of such a state of things and growing red. "That would drive me mad!" he burst out at last.

I went on smoking.

Then he shouted with a new alarm in his voice: "Lew, Lew, do you mean that it will make any difference between you and me? D'you mean that it will put an end to our friendship? Lord, Lew, rather than that, I'll get her . . . I'll bring her here . . . I'll . . . I'll. . . ."

I went on smoking, watching him through the thin drifts, but, oh, how sad my heart was. His voice trailed away. He made a feeble little gesture with both hands.

"Well," he concluded, "you've seen Mary

Kearney. Can you blame me? Can you blame any man for going mad about her? Heaven put such women on earth for the special purpose of depriving men of their wits. And I have none about her. I'd despise the man who could stand in front of her for ten seconds without losing his heart." He added with a faint laugh: "Except you, old man. You have nothing but horses and rifles . . . and honor, confound you."

"Are you to be married?" I asked him, with a hand gripping me by the throat.

"I hope so. She likes me. Sometimes I think that she more than likes me. But her mind changes like a wind vane. It's all right with Mister Kearney. He's mighty rich, but he knows that I'm firmly settled as far as that goes. He approves. She doesn't hate me at least. Between you and me, I'd take heavy odds that I marry her within a year."

I could not tell why it was that the hand relaxed its grip upon my throat, but what I said made Morris gape.

"I'd like to lay that bet with you," I said.

"Damn it, Lew, what do you mean?" he cried.

"I don't know, except that the words slipped out. A man has his own ideas about some things . . . queer ideas, you may say. But I have a pretty strong conviction that you'll never be her husband."

He could only stare at me. "Lew," he said at last, frowning, "has she hit you, too?"

I broke out into laughter. "Me? A low ruffian like me? I'm not a fool, old-timer."

I told him everything that had happened. He seemed a little amused, a little serious. But at last he said: "I don't think there'll be any trouble. I know the men in this town, and they know me. They also know that you're my friend by this time. Now, Lew, it's time to think over how we're going to celebrate."

I told him that a bed was all I wanted, and, when he was convinced that I meant what I said, he made me take his own bed. I stretched out between cool sheets on a mattress for the first time in more than five years. It seemed wonderfully comfortable, and I went to sleep only to awaken in five minutes out of a dream that I was being buried alive. I took a roll of blankets out-doors and lay down under the stars. And so I slept like a stunned man until the sun shone in my face again.

Chapter Twenty-Six

ASSEMBLING AN ARMY

Everything that had been whirling through my brain when I went to sleep — whirling in confusion — was fixed and clear when I wakened. I could see the simple truth of everything. First of all, I could see that Chuck Morris would never return to Zintcallasappa. I could see, too, that it was dangerous for me to remain at the fort. Dangerous not to Morris, but dangerous to myself. When I stood up and drew a few breaths of the purity of the morning air, I felt if I saw the blue eyes and the smiling mouth of Mary Kearney once again, I should be madly, madly in love with her. So, honestly as I thought and for the sake of everyone, it seemed to me the proper thing to get back to the Sioux as fast as I could.

I went into the shack and found Chuck, snoring — not at all like the prairie days when he was always the first to rouse me. I wrote a little note and put it on the table where he was sure to find it.

Dear old Chuck:

It seems that I can't be any use. I hoped that I could straighten out the tangle and save Zintcallasappa . . . save you, too, from doing what looked like a pretty bad thing. Well, now that I've seen you and seen the other girl, I feel that I haven't a right to so much as criticize. I'm going back to Standing Bear and Sitting Wolf and the rest to say good bye to them, as you've done. You've shown me one truth, that a white man has to live his life among white people. Yesterday I came in like a wild beast and showed my teeth when people rubbed me the wrong way. I've got to learn better! I'll make one more fling at finding my father out on the prairies . . . but perhaps I've been a fool straight through. Probably he's nowhere near the prairies! Good bye, old man. The best luck in the world to you.

I jogged out that little letter and went out to White Smoke. He began to talk the moment he heard my footstep, whinnying no louder than a whisper. I led the monster out — sixteen hands and three inches of shimmering beauty and wonderful strength. Have you seen a colt frolic around its dam? That was the way White Smoke frolicked around me. At last I had to speak sternly. He stopped before me as meek as a frightened child, and I saddled and bridled him. It was broad, warm morning by this time. Instead of breakfast I drew my belt a bit tighter, as one learned to do on the prairies, and left the fort at once. I went straight up the river bank for some distance, because it took me fairly straight in the home direction, and, besides, I wanted to enjoy the trees near the water. When one has lived years on the prairies, real trees mean more than food and drink.

I went through them with my head bent back, watching the sun work through the leaves, listening to the stir of the wind, watching a squirrel working here and a blue jay watching there. The jay rose suddenly and hovered, scolding bitterly. The next moment I turned a corner of the trail and came straight upon Kearney and his daughter.

She looked at me as though a snake had writhed across her path, and cried out: "Now, Dad, be careful . . . please!"

"Damn care," said Kearney. "I have him alone, now."

He rode straight up to me, drawing himself up straighter and straighter. He was much taller than I, but White Smoke's sixteen hands and three inches gave me a shade of an advantage over him.

"Dorset," he said, "yesterday you insulted me grossly. A gentleman cannot put up with such a remark. I want your apology on the spot."

He was one of those handsome men whose jowls grow a little too fat as years increase. The rest of his face turned very red; but his lower fat cheeks were white. I saw that; I saw that he was fingering the butt of a revolver of the latest make. I also saw the frightened face of the girl in the background.

"Mister Kearney," I said, "I'm not a peace lover, but I'm trying to keep the peace now. Will you let me pass?"

He took that remark in just the wrong way. I suppose there was a bit of the bully in him as there is apt to be in pompous men. He said with a sneer: "I presume that Chuck Morris has whipped you out of the town, if you dared to meet him. Now, sir, you will either fight or be whipped again."

He leaned out as he spoke and flashed his riding whip across my face. The very end of the lash was knotted, and that knot flicked away the skin and allowed a trickle of crimson to run down. I still have the scar, like a tiny silver freckle on the skin. I look at it in the mirror and it makes my gray, wrinkled, lean face fade away and puts in its place the savage features and the wild black eyes of the Lew Dorset of those days.

He had reached a bit too far. Before he could recover, I was at him. I caught the wrist that held the whip. I caught the other wrist as it snapped the revolver out of the holster. I felt my fingers crush through the flesh to the bone, while a spasm of pain twisted his mouth. Whip and gun fell to the earth, and the girl's cry came tingling in my ears in the nick of time.

I saw what I was doing and released him instantly. "You have a daughter," I said. "That is the reason you are still alive."

Then I pressed straight past them both, with the picture of Mary Kearney's terror gathered into my mind. I let White Smoke take his own way, which was the way of the wind. A little later we were out of the trees and on the open prairie, treading softly in the three-inch buffalo grass that grew as thick as hair on a dog's back.

The red weal of the whip stroke faded before I reached the Sioux, and there was only the healing scar that flecked my temple when, ten days later, I came in view of the village. It was still a full mile away when a young brave, who was riding post, saw me and knew the flash of White Smoke. He came toward me with a shout, lifting his hand in token of friendship. By his side I rode into the camp, and he gave me the news as he went. They were gathering their forces for another attempt upon the Pawnees, for Bald Eagle, in a rage at the loss of White Smoke, had struck a recent blow that cost the lives of more than a hundred Sioux warriors. Standing Bear was to take the warpath and close with Bald Eagle if he could.

I could not have heard more welcome news. Ever since the moment when Bald Eagle had seized on me as his prisoner, instead of freeing Sitting Wolf in exchange for Two Feather, I had wanted to get back at him. Besides, I was in a frame of mind that demanded action. I dreaded to be alone, for when I was alone a thousand ugly thoughts took hold on me — and the blue eyes of Mary Kearney looked into my mind. What lay before me I did not know. I only knew that I was afraid of myself — mortally afraid that I should be untrue to Chuck Morris.

I went first to the teepee of Three Buck Elk and found Sitting Wolf with his father and mother. It was like stepping into the heart of my own family. Every soul in that teepee was mine, twice bought because I had saved the son of the family twice. Three Buck Elk seated me in his own place, gave me his own pipe, then left the place, and brought back Standing Bear, while Sitting Wolf and I were chattering. He was hugely excited about the proposed expedition. They planned to start in a day or two.

When Standing Bear came in, the old fellow went to the point at once. All the preparations had been made. Eight hundred braves, he said, were ready to take the trail today — if I thought fit. I certainly was astonished when he said this.

"Standing Bear," I said, "I am a young man, and a young man has hands, but no brains. I shall follow you where you and your brother lead me."

"The Dakotas," he answered me, "have met Bald Eagle many times, and many times he has taken their scalps, made them weeping children, and sent them running like dogs before wolves across the prairies. Only one man has met Bald Eagle and come away from him alive, and with more than he took to him. That man is Black Bear. Standing Bear has ridden many times at the head of the warriors. His name was once a terror to the Pawnees. But now he is no more to them than an old toothless woman. You, Brother, shall lead us!"

It was a compliment of such a size that I had to pause a moment before I digested it. But now that the actual power was put into my hands, I knew exactly what I wanted to do with it. Bald Eagle, in fact, had taught me.

I said: "Then we shall not ride today or tomorrow."

He nodded. "That is good. But why will my brother keep us here? The Pawnees laugh when they hear the name of the Sioux now."

"Because the Sioux have become weak and foolish. Their eyes are no longer straight, and their hands tremble."

His eyes flashed at that, and Sitting Wolf stirred in his place with a grunt.

I said: "I will prove it. Call to me the twenty braves who are surest with a rifle in their hands."

It was done. I took them with their guns out of the camp. I had a boy cut a calf from the herd of cows and send it scampering out on the plain, and then I told them to kill it. Every one of the twenty fired — and the calf still scampered away.

"It is too far," frowned Standing Bear.

"Look," I said, "when the Sioux hunt, they steal up on their game, or they ride around the stupid, slow buffalo. They come so close that a child cannot miss. But the Pawnees do not stand like fools to be killed. They are farther away than the calf, and they run faster. The Sioux must learn to shoot like men before they can fight like men." I went on: "When the prairie burns in the dry autumn, how do we fight the fire?"

"By starting other fires to burn against it," he said.

"That is true," I said, "and Bald Eagle is a fire . . . we must fight him in his own way. When he rides out with five hundred men, there is only one brain, and that is the brain of Bald Eagle. And his five hundred men are a thousand hands with which he strikes. But when we ride out, Standing Bear and Three Buck Elk are only two men among five hundred. You lead them until the Pawnees are near. Then each man rides and strikes for himself."

It was too true for them to miss my meaning. Bald Eagle had beaten them into a state of humility in which they were ready to learn a few fundamentals of the art of war. In a word, they gave themselves into my hands. It was a beautiful opportunity. I have said before that Standing Bear was followed by what was really the cream of the Sioux nation. The exploits of Rising Sun and Black Bear had been enough to attract hundreds of sterling fighters. We could put at least eight hundred men in the field. And that was as many as Bald Eagle ordinarily led. He did not care to work with half-armed thousands. He fought with a handful, armed to the teeth, and well trained. I determined to follow his example on a larger scale.

I confiscated every rifle in the town and made that possible by turning my own into the common store and having Three Buck Elk and Standing Bear follow my example. Altogether, we had eighty rifles and a fair stock of ammunition. With this I started the practice.

In the meantime I sent Three Buck Elk to the fort in charge of a huge caravan to the fort with a letter to Chuck Morris. That caravan was loaded down with beaver pelts and with buffalo robes. I told Morris in the letter that I wanted, in exchange for it, a thousand rifles and as much ammunition as he could get his hands on. I knew that the value of that caravan could never be traded out for a thousand rifles, but I suggested to Morris that new guns were not essential. Any good-working weapons would do, and I suggested that he try for them at some Army depot, for the Army discards a gun the instant it shows a bit of wear. At least it was apt to do so in those days.

While I waited for that caravan to return, I started to work on the tribe. At the time it was thought that the Indian was incapable of organization. At present there is a new idea. We have seen too many football teams turned out of Indian colleges and working like perfect machines, consummate in the art and unity of their work, and only kept from greatness by their lack of poundage. Well, the same essentials that make a football team make an army. The clue I followed was the instinctive reverence the Indians have for the heads of their families and clans. I formed the units in that way. Sometimes there were only five in a unit. Sometimes there were twenty. But each sergeant, if he could be called that, had over his men an absolute authority. Over the clans there were the natural clan heads. The smallest clan numbered fifty-two braves; the largest was two hundred and ten, which was much too large. However, I did not dare employ a regular decimal system. I worked on lines of blood throughout. Before we had been working long, more than a hundred braves from other tribes, hearing that some great thing was afoot, rode in to join us, and so we had for material, fully nine hundred and a few-odd available men, all physically strong, all brave. I divided them into two battalions.

Three Buck Elk had one battalion; Standing Bear, of course, had the other.

That was their organization. Then I started their training. The great temptation was to make them learn to drill in squads. But I knew them too well to attempt foolishly formal stuff with them. I kept the tools of war constantly in their hands. I wanted them to learn three things: to fight on foot — to obey blindly as they were commanded — and to shoot straight.

The example of Bald Eagle's successes was enough to make them realize the value of instant obedience. They did not need to be told shooting straight was an essential. But it was frightfully hard to teach them the importance of fighting on foot when they had been born to the use of horses. I demonstrated in every way I could, but the most successful lesson was by proving that one man lying on the ground could hit a distant target sooner than three men shooting from the back of even a stationary horse.

I formed the sergeants and the captains in small classes, and these I instructed in the most perfect care of a rifle. I offered a prize every day for the clan that showed rifles in the best condition. The prize system started a furious rivalry. I extended it to marksmanship. I instructed them in learning to practice, aiming empty guns, and I told them what Uncle Abner had told me, that a man should be shamed unless every spent bullet meant something dead. It was an idea they understood instantly.

The caravan arrived. Straightway every man was equipped with a rifle that in the intervening month he had learned to take perfect care of. Now I felt that my army was on a true footing.

My odd system of discipline was working out beautifully. Every clan leader could gather his men about him by a peculiar whistle or shout, and his followers learned to look to him for instructions. I kept constantly about me sixty-odd chosen braves. They served me as couriers to carry orders to the clans. They served me also as a select reserve that might deliver a telling blow in time of battle. Altogether, they were forming into an army that would have broken the heart of any army officer through its lack of uniforms, squad drill, or regular formations. But it was a little army that was shooting straighter every day, that trusted me blindly, and that was beginning to gain the greatest strength of all — a certain *esprit de corps*. They felt the power of their cohesion. I taught them it was as great a sin to charge without orders as it was to run away. Finally,

I had a compact body of dragoons who were hungry to test themselves.

Still I delayed. Marksmanship was what I wanted next to cohesion. And at marksmanship I labored valiantly. For two long months after the return of Three Buck Elk I kept putting them through their paces. It was dry autumn before I felt that they were ready for the warpath. By that time their hearts were breaking to be away, for Bald Eagle had conducted two sweeping, ruinous raids in the meantime. When all was ready, I went to say farewell to Zintcallasappa.

Chapter Twenty-Seven

SLAUGHTER

I have said nothing about my first meeting with her after I returned from Chuck Morris because I have wanted to put off recording one of the most painful memories of my life. I went to her, of course, on the first day and found her washing at the river. She looked up at me with one wild flare of hope in her eyes, but she said at once: "If he had come, he would have been here with you, or before you. He will not come, my brother! Not even for you."

Only a fool would have tried to comfort her. All I could do was make a point of seeing her every day. We used to have gay talks, for with a sort of iron strength she refused to allow her sorrow to be seen. She was always smiles when I was near her. Three Buck Elk wanted me to take her and her teepee and her son.

"Because," he said naïvely, "they will keep in your mind the memory of your lost brother, Rising Sun."

I wanted no squaw and told them so in

such a way that the topic was never brought up again. In the meantime Zintcallasappa was changing rapidly. I was almost glad that Morris did not return with me, her face had grown so pinched and her eyes so great and staring. She was always beautiful to me, because to me the beauty of a woman is not so much flesh as spirit, like a lamp shining through their flesh. So it was with Zintcallasappa, but every day she grew thinner, more silent.

When I said good bye to her, before I took the warpath with our little host, she reached up, put her hands on my shoulders, and looked into my face. "If you were the father of my son," she said, "would you be happy with him?"

I was amazed and only stared back at her.

"Ah," she continued, "perhaps one day you *will* be his father."

I thought then, bitter fool that I was, that it was sort of a leading question. I thought that she had grown tired of a single life and wanted to shift some of the burdens of existence onto the shoulders of a second husband. That thought I carried away with me like a shadow. But when I started out with our men, I forgot other troubles. I forgot Zintcallasappa and Morris and my father, and even the blue eyes of Mary Kearney shone dim and far away.

There were nine hundred and forty-six braves, all told. Each carried a rifle in excellent condition, and each man could use his gun at least as well as the average white infantryman. Each had a strong wide-bladed hatchet slung on the saddle, also some dried buffalo meat, and some parched corn. We traveled with over a thousand horses herded behind us by some of the older of the Indian boys, with Sitting Wolf in charge of the entire party. In this fashion we pressed ahead. I kept a party of thirty men on fast horses in the van a whole day's march. I had out three other parties, two far away on the flanks, and another body well to the rear. So, with four feelers far extended to take the first news of danger, we crawled across the prairies.

Standing Bear was much concerned because I had mounted the men on the worst horses and left the best to be herded behind us, but I kept my reasons for that maneuver to myself. A little mystery never does any harm when one is handling Indians. Though I was not quite twenty-two, I had learned to know the Indians as well as most men.

We crossed a vast stretch of the plains in a three weeks' march before word came in that a party of two hundred Pawnees was paralleling our advance on the right, keeping a good distance away. Standing Bear was for rushing at them at once, but I was in a quandary. I wanted to flesh my pack, so to speak, before the real shock of battle against Bald Eagle, but I did not know how to get at the Pawnees. They were out there as a strong observation party, feeding information about our movements to Bald Eagle who, somewhere on the bosom of the prairie, waited with his organized force to fall upon us. How to come near them, either by night or day, I could not tell. It is impossible for a considerable body of horsemen to move in any silence. There is always a certain amount of snorting and squealing from the horses, especially from wild Indian ponies, and one snort would be enough to alarm the Pawnee scouts.

Finally I made up my mind I must make some sort of an effort because the whole body of my Sioux was growing restless. I picked out three hundred men, took Three Buck Elk along as a second in command, and, after dark on a black, moonless night, we cut across the prairie. The Pawnees, it was said, were about twenty miles from us, keeping small bodies, of course, constantly flung in our direction. I made a forced march of five miles straight to the rear, and then we rode straight across the prairies for three hours at a stiff pace. In that time I felt that we must have covered a full twenty-five miles. Whereas the Pawnees expected us to be on the south, I hoped that we had marched around them and now lay about five miles north of them and a little more to the east.

Here I dismounted the entire body. I ordered them to wrap their rifles so that the steel might not strike against steel. We left fifty men to watch the horses. Then we started southeast. I kept two small parties of young braves scattered ahead of my main body to bring in intelligence, and at the end of two hours three messengers came back to state that they had seen the Pawnee encampment plainly under the stars.

How my heart leaped then. If God were willing, I was ready to do a thing now that would make the first black mark on the Pawnee record since Bald Eagle had taken command of their wars. If they kept many sentinels close to their camp, we had small chance of surprising them, but I felt that they would be more apt to send out their scouts to a considerable distance toward the south to guard against a surprise from that direction. And that was exactly what they had done.

When we came in view of them, we could make them out only dimly by the starlight, but here and there in the faintly silhouetted mass there were red eyes where the last embers of their small campfires were dying slowly. At least there was enough light for our purposes. I divided the men into three bodies of about eighty each. I sent them upon all three sides of the camp except the south, and I ordered them to wait until a gun was discharged. Not a man was to advance until firing was opened by that signal. My idea was that the southerly direction would be the last toward which they would flee.

With the blood thundering in my temples almost as much as though Bald Eagle himself were among those huddled shadows, I watched my men deploy. How silently they worked themselves along the ground, for here was a stroke of war they could perfectly execute. Only they would have preferred to follow their instincts and rush at once upon the sleepers.

Still, I kept them waiting while the night died and the day began to be born. I was breathless. Every moment now increased our chances of shooting straight, for the day was coming swiftly, and still not so much as a whisper from my waiting Sioux. Then a brave beside me touched my shoulder. Against the southern horizon I made out a dozen forms of horsemen swiftly approaching — scouts from the Pawnee advance parties to report what they had seen — perhaps to report that a large body of the Sioux were away and on mischief bent. There was no use waiting longer. I drew my revolver and fired it in the air.

That my lessons had not been given in vain I learned by the answering roar. Every Sioux, during the wait, had chosen a target and had been nursing his aim upon it. The answer to my shot was one instantaneous rush of fire from three sides of the circle, and the frightened shouts as the Pawnees wakened to find death in their midst were mingled with the death-scream of a score of warriors.

There was a brief interval of silence from my lines as the men, lying still, reloaded. The Pawnee camp was a scene of the wildest confusion, but, before they could surge away to their horses, the second volley crashed among them. The effect was terrible. My Sioux had before them standing targets, huddled in a thick mass and at point-blank range. I was too excited to handle my own gun. I merely stood up and watched the shock of the second volley sweep down what seemed to me half of the Pawnees.

Now they were at their horses, but right into the face of my line they stormed off to the north. It was a trying moment to me. I knew that my Sioux were by no means sure of themselves on foot. I had sworn to them a thousand times that no cavalry could ride down fast-firing infantry, but I could not tell how my assurances would weigh with them. So, holding my breath with a groan, I watched and waited. On went those rushing Pawnees, screaming like frightened demons, but the Dakotas lay still and finished the rapid reloading. Then up went their guns into a flashing line. The fire spurted in jets and broad masses. The Pawnee charge staggered, swayed, and then rushed away to the south. Ah, to have had only fifty horsemen to throw on their flank on the rear at that moment. How I cursed the stupidity that had kept me from bringing up even a handful of mounted men and keeping them in the distance until the moment when the fighting began. However, enough was done. Out of that deathtrap some four score Pawnees rushed away to the south. When we poured through the camp, we found and counted a hundred and sixty-five dead. It was frightful work for such a short combat. I say dead advisedly. Not all died under the rifle, but the rest were finished by the knives of the scalpers. I could not check them. I turned away from the horrible business and went off to a little distance, for I knew that there would be no holding back the Dakotas. It had been too long since they had really fleshed themselves thoroughly in a slaughter. Now their yells of victory were more terrible than the shouts of the Pawnees as the remnant fled over the horizon of the dawn. Horses and rifles and bows and arrows were the booty we carried back with us. As for trinkets, I ordered them piled in one heap and set fire to the lot. I did not want my army encumbered with useless baggage.

Considering that we had every advantage of surprise and discipline, training and weapons on our side, it was not a battle at all. It was simply a massacre that might as well have been of women and children. Even the rush of the Pawnees toward our lines had been the flight of desperate fugitives rather than a charge. I was glad of one thing, at least — that my men had seen how rifle fire will blow a cavalry charge to nothingness. As for the Sioux themselves, they rejoined their comrades of the main body as though they came back from conquering the world, and they were received like so many heroes. It does not take a great deal to depress Indian warriors, neither does it take a great deal to raise them to the skies. They started that campaign fairly confident they were a formidable lot, but pretty certain, in their hearts of hearts, that Bald Eagle and the Pawnees would be too much for them. That single surprise attack was enough to convince them they were invincible. From that moment my thousand were willing to attack ten thousand, if I gave the word for it. This was all very well. I was glad to have their courage redoubled, but I was wondering how long it would take Bald Eagle to sweat the confidence out of them.

Every day I kept them at their books. In the morning they practiced their maneuvers and handled their guns. In the afternoon they proceeded with the march. On the twelfth day after the surprise of the Pawnees, I received word for which I had been waiting. It did not come in the way of a prisoner's confession. It was a Pawnee herald who took his life in his hands by risking himself among my cutthroats. He was a battered elder with a face that would have served in the worst nightmare that ever frightened a child. He came up to me and looked me over haughtily. Then he informed me that Bald Eagle was weary of seeing fish hawks in his lands and had come to take scalps. However, he was a gentle and a kindly chief. If we would abandon all our horses and half of our rifles, he would allow us to retreat safely from his presence. Otherwise he would fall upon us and cut us to bits.

It was the plainest sort of bluff, delivered in a loud voice for the purpose of overawing my men. But I was not raw enough to let such stuff pass. I pulled myself straight on the back of White Smoke, who was sniffing noses with the Pawnee's stallion and telling him in the very plainest sort of horse talk that he was aching to get at him and knock him to bits.

I said: "Go back to your chief and tell him that a carrion crow may hide in a cloud and make the Pawnees think that he is an eagle, but the Sioux are men, not children. They have come to show the Pawnees they are children and fools."

This was rather strong, and the Pawnee glared at me like an incarnate devil for a moment. Then he wheeled his horse and darted away.

Chapter Twenty-Eight

ON BALD EAGLE'S TRAIL

I knew Bald Eagle was no gullible young fool who would fly into a blind rage. But I felt that my message might make his gorge rise a bit. I had talked like a boaster, but I was also determined to act like a coward to lead him on. Frankly I felt that in a real campaign I should never have a chance to win against this Napoleon of the prairies. I wanted to encourage him to a headlong attack. So that very hour I ordered my little host to wheel about and start a retreat. I had them dismount from the tired and worn ponies that had carried them up to this time and mount, instead, the fresh animals that had been herded at our heels by the boys. I sent the horse herd toward home as fast as they could jump. I followed with the army at a brisk gait.

It was a hard thing to do. The Sioux glared at me as though I had turned into a mangy dog, and Standing Bear came to me almost trembling with impatience. I explained to him the real truth. We were out to take vengeance on Bald Eagle. The minute he felt that we were shaking cowards, he would swarm after us as fast as he could. Otherwise we might have to attack him behind entrenchments. The Sioux could recall what had happened the last time they besieged that warrior. This was enough for Standing Bear. He spread the word along the line — it was only a ruse — this was a false flight and was conducted merely to lure the great Bald Eagle toward us. Then we would turn and strike him down.

That was enough. They marched on again as happily as children bound for a picnic ground. For me it was a fearfully anxious week that followed until, at length, the scouts to the rear announced they had sighted the van of the Pawnees, swarming hotly over the prairie. There might still be other stratagems working in the cunning brain of Bald Eagle, but it seemed that he was at least preparing to close with me at once, and this was all that I could ask. While my men felt the invincibility, and before a bit of maneuvering had revealed me as the very foolish young general that I was, I wanted to come to grips with the warrior. To this extent he was playing into my hands.

When I asked my scouts how many Pawnees were following me, they said they thought about six hundred and fifty men. Again my heart jumped with relief. This being a true history, and not a foolish story, I have to admit that I was not at all anxious to meet Bald Eagle on even terms. I had a slight advantage over him, and I felt that this was just about what I should need. He had thrashed five times his number of Sioux in the open field, for that matter. Now he prepared to swallow me alive. There was no faltering, no pausing to skirmish or to recruit his tired men. He brought them straight on at me while I drew up my Dakotas. He was dismounting his fellows almost as soon as I was dismounting mine.

It was the same sort of tactics on both sides. The Indians were off horseback and ready to engage on foot — by preference. While their horses were herded to the rear, I arranged my fine fellows in two lines — exactly as my enemy did. In the first line was Three Buck Elk, a wild and headlong fighter, as I well knew. In the second line was Standing Bear, far brainier and more apt to act with caution, though every whit as well qualified to maintain a resolutely fierce front against the enemy. Where was the chief who commanded the army, whose almost legendary duty it was to stand in the forefront of the host? Well, I should like to say that I was in the very van, standing like a hero, or riding along the line to encourage the men, but as a matter of fact the post I chose for myself was in the rear with a guard of fifty men around me. There were a hundred more, but they were stationed among the horses and directed to keep themselves out of sight until they heard from me. Then they were to come, and come mounted. My idea was partly, I confess, to keep away from death, and partly I wanted to be where I could overlook the whole battlefield and see the point where I might be most needed. To that point I intended to march and strike with my hundred and fifty men of the reserve as hard as we might, with the greater ease because we would be mounted and, though our fighting might be less effective, our shock would be the greater. In the two main battle lines I had eight hundred men that I thought ample to hold in check the six hundred and fifty of Bald Eagle — or at least throw their attack into confusion until I could strike the decisive blow with my horsemen.

It seemed to me a neat plan. It still seems a clever one to me as I look back from a distance. Still, I was not at ease. I knew that I had no ordinary man opposed to me. Yet the attack started exactly as though Bald

Eagle were a bloodthirsty madman. I still feel that his many successes had turned his head a little. He knew that the Sioux dreaded him like an incarnate devil, and that they felt he was more than half invincible. What he could not estimate was the value of the lessons we had recently been learning and, above all, the moral effect of that night stroke at the Pawnees.

At any rate, he dismounted his men the instant they were at long range. A select number fell back with the horses, which they brought up close and kept in good order — a measure I envied at once. The Pawnees then came steadily on at a jog trot, and many men in motion seem to have thrice the velocity of a few. Though each man was only jogging easily, the whole mass of the Pawnees seemed to be rushing upon us at great speed. I had ordered the Sioux to hold their fire and to remain lying down. But, when they saw their enemies coming at them, it was too much for their control. A rifle exploded at the right of the first line. A scattering fire then ran along, and every man discharged his piece. I groaned when I saw the effect of that random volley. The Pawnees were still too far away, and the skill I had drilled into the Sioux seemed to have been wiped away from them. Only a very few of Bald Eagle's men dropped from the line, not enough by any means to answer the number of bullets that had gone whirring toward them. I saw Bald Eagle wave a hand above his head and laugh.

He was instantly conspicuous. While I remained to the rear, that bold chieftain advanced to the very head of his men, brandishing a long rifle like a feather in his hands. He looked more than human in his stature. His hair was not trimmed to form the scalp lock but blew about his shoulders in long black streams. His height was made greater by a cluster of feathers plaited into his hair, and it waved above his head.

After our first fire he set his men the example of rushing forward at full speed. They swept suddenly upon us, yet I was not afraid of the consequences, for I knew that the Sioux had time to load before they received the charge. What maddened me was to see them rise almost *en masse* to meet the rush of the Pawnees. But no headlong charge was in the mind of the great chief. Some thirty paces from our line a thundering shout left his lips, and his men dropped instantly to the ground. How marvelously he had brought those wild Pawnees into the hollow hand of his discipline. They fell flat, couched their rifles, and at another word from him they loosed a solid volley.

I have heard men talk of the days of wooden ships and the effect of the first close-delivered broadside — how it keeled the vessel over and filled it with the thunder of crashing, splintering, falling timbers. Like a broadside was that volley of the Pawnees. The imbecile Sioux, who had stood up almost to a man, were perfect targets. And I saw my first line literally blown to pieces. As a fighting machine that section of my army was broken to bits. They ran here and there, yelling, lamenting. Some started for the rear. Others stood still and screamed an hysterical defiance at the Pawnees. And the Pawnees were still lying flat on the ground!

Vastly tempting as that confusion in our ranks must have been to those savages, they obeyed the discipline they had learned and remained in their places, loading their rifles as rapidly as they could. The instant that was done, they lunged to their feet and leaped in at us.

We were in a frightful condition. Our first line, as I have said, was hopelessly disintegrated. Our second line could hardly fire effectively because of the confusion of the first. Only the onrush of the Pawnees forced the broken first line to squeeze through the second. Standing Bear, in the meantime, had forced that second line to kneel, and from that kneeling position, with the Pawnees straight before them, they poured in their fire. The effect was ghastly, of course. But Bald Eagle's men were already very close. Some, in their death agonies, leaped in to deliver their dying strokes. The others, with the immense voice of Bald Eagle flooding their ears, halted for a single instant and then poured in from their recharged guns a fire almost as effective as that of my kneeling second line. Then they closed.

I had not the slightest doubt what the outcome would be. I had, altogether, about eight hundred men in those two lines, and there were a few less than seven hundred Pawnees, but the impact of their charge was irresistible. I saw them drop their rifles and begin to swing their hatchets. Here, there, and again they burst through the line. I saw Bald Eagle, transformed into a giant fiend, catch up a Sioux warrior and swing him before him like a club. I have never seen such a show of sheer might of hand and arm. He himself scorned to use a hatchet. He was armed, a moment later, with a heavy clubbed rifle, which was a toy in his hand, and every blow crushed a skull like an eggshell.

The Sioux were beaten, but still they did

not fly. I cannot say how my heart rose as I saw, at last, the magic result of my patient work. Their line was shattered, but, as their leaders yelled the gathering signal, group by group and clan by clan gathered to itself, and, forming in rough circles, kinsman at the side of kinsman, they kept a formidable face to the raging wolves of Bald Eagle.

Where were the horsemen of my reserve? All of this had occurred in a single rush, but, as I saw the Pawnees break through the line, I felt that I could not wait to gather the hundred men who were now extricating themselves from the mass of the horses and beginning to form behind me. I took the fifty who were immediately at my side and headed straight for Bald Eagle. To this moment it seems incredible. He had around him only wild savages, who were on the point of gaining a great victory, who were maddened by the lust for blood and scalps. Yet at the thunder of his call a full hundred of the braves banded together and faced my charge — faced it, loading their rifles with a wonderful rapidity.

Even before we were on them, I knew what would happen — exactly what I had proved to my own men — that cavalry cannot withstand a calmly delivered infantry fire. And these Pawnees were calm. Their faith in Bald Eagle was like the faith of the prophet in the Lord. Here he stood among them, thundering forth his commands. With the greatest coolness they loaded, took aim, and, as we dashed at them, they met us with a sheet of flame. Half the saddles were instantly emptied, and the rest of us were thrown into confusion. The charge lost impetus, but still I had to strike home if I could — I had to strike, even if I were almost despairing.

I stood up in the stirrups and shouted my own cry. It was fiercely answered by my men, and I knew that, few as they were, they had the heart to follow me. Then we struck the Pawnees. Bald Eagle was my goal. I drove straight at him, for I knew that, if he fell, the field was ours. White Smoke needed no reins. The grip of my knees and the sway of my body were enough to drive him forward or stop him at my pleasure. I had a revolver in each hand, and, as they spoke, the Pawnees fell. Between me and my target was a writhing mass of those devoted Indians. The bullets I intended for Bald Eagle struck their bodies. I emptied my guns, and still the thunder of that great voice held the Pawnees firm. I clubbed a rifle and made play with that in a frenzy, but I saw that all was lost. The Pawnees were at us like tigers

307

now. The impetus of the charge had been crushed against that human mass. Now they surged in, screaming like veritable demons, and my poor Sioux went down on every side.

Two brawny villains made at me with hatchets. I dropped one with the butt of the rifle. But my blow missed the second and merely knocked the weapon from his hands. Then, with a leap, he grappled with me. I had him by the throat in a trice, but others of his friends were at his heels, grinning with a thirsty joy as they saw Black Bear already in their hands. Then it was that I heard the sweetest sound that ever met my ears — the battle yell of a band of Sioux, rushing to the fight. I looked aside and saw a wild and joyous picture, indeed. Yonder came the last hundred of my mounted men, sweeping in on the flank of the Pawnees. At their head, the organizer of this final stroke, rode none other than young Sitting Wolf, naked to the waist, painted hideously and swinging a club.

When they struck, the shock sent the entire battle reeling. My throttled Pawnee dropped senseless to the ground. Around me there was only a terrible confusion. They no longer thought of butchering me. They were intent on meeting the new danger. But they turned too late. That hidden reserve had dropped upon them like a bolt from the blue. In an instant the Pawnees were torn from the bleeding remnants of my footmen and dashed into hopeless confusion. Now each unit of my clansmen turned from defense to aggression. In that mêlée they retained an efficient order. They still fought shoulder to shoulder while the Pawnees struck at random, hardly knowing friend from foe. And still the horsemen were lunging among them, making every blow tell.

A shout that was deep with groans rose from that throng. It was the despairing cry of the Pawnees as they saw themselves lost. Numbers, order, everything was now against them, and they dropped like deer before a forest fire. They strove to draw clear and get to their horses, but the Dakota cavalry swept in before them, spattered with blood, and still hungry for more, insatiable for slaughter. Victory made them double in strength. Defeat weakened the Pawnees.

For my part, seeing that the end was here, I reined out of the press and looked about for Bald Eagle. There was no real or complete victory until he was down, and I wanted that death for myself. Then, to my bewilderment, I saw a horseman rushing far away across the prairie with two or three rushing behind him. It was Bald Eagle, who knew that the cause was lost on this day and had made a wise decision to save himself. It was as though nine tenths of the victory were slipping from my hands. I gave White Smoke the reins and shot after him.

Chapter Twenty-Nine

FACING CERTAIN DEATH

Behind me I could hear the Sioux, finishing the feast and relishing every morsel they tasted. There would be a scalp for every survivor, that I knew. Many a trophy would dry hideously over the teepee fires of the Dakotas. This day would pass into song and story. I had other work before me, and that work consisted in running down the men before me. I loaded my rifle and my revolver while White Smoke was at a brisk gallop. Then I straightened him out on the trail and flew after them. They came back toward me as though they were standing still.

There were three Pawnees besides Bald Eagle. What they must have done, at the instigation of their great chief, was to take the horses of some of the fallen Sioux in the midst of the battle and so ride out to freedom. But I was hard at their heels. They turned back, one by one. Doubtless they could have escaped if they had spread out and scattered to either side, but that was not their intention. They only had the thought to cover the retreat of their leader. Each whirled, as I came up, and charged, sending a rifle bullet at me. But bullets fired from a running horse I laughed at. I brought White Smoke to a halt, faced each charge, and sent that Pawnee to his last accounting. Three men whirled at me; three men died. Now there remained before me only the strong roan horse that carried Bald Eagle away. I had felt some pity for him in his defeat, but what seemed his consummate selfishness in allowing his braves to sacrifice themselves for him made me as cold as steel for the work to come. I swept closer, with White Smoke running swiftly and easily as the wind. It was a stanch animal, that roan, but even on equal terms it could not have lived at the pace of my stallion — and weighed down with the bulk of the Pawnee chief, it seemed anchored in one place.

He unlimbered his rifle and fired back at me. I heard the whir of the shot close to my head, and I saw the rascal, who had slackened the speed of the roan, look back and start with surprise — so confident was he in his marksmanship. My own rifle I left in its case. A revolver was enough for me, and already he was in range, but still I pressed in to make assurance doubly sure. I even drew White Smoke back to the roan's own pace, to let Bald Eagle taste his death before it came to him. I could see him work like lightning to load his gun.

It was done before I dreamed it could have been finished. The roan was brought to a sharp halt, and the big man twisted in the saddle with the rifle at his shoulder. I snatched out my own revolver and fired what should have been the bullet that clove through the heart of the chief, but, at that moment, the roan, whirling, threw up its head and through its brain my bullet crashed. It dropped instantly, but, as it dropped, Bald Eagle fired. All I knew was that a stroke of darkness flicked across my brain.

When I wakened, I was bound hand and foot. Bald Eagle sat cross-legged beside me, smoking a pipe. I saw that the end had come for me and sat up to face it. There was no doubt in me now that this was an Indian and not a white. The deep copper of his skin seemed too true for dye to have made it, and his shaggy hair fell partly across his face.

"My young brother," said the chief, speaking excellent Siouan, and his heavy voice rolling the words like soft thunder, "my young brother has frightened Bald Eagle from his nest, but at last my talons are in his flesh."

I nodded, and, as I moved my head, a trickle of crimson from the glancing scalp wound that had felled me slipped over my face. "The scream of Bald Eagle," I said, "has frightened many a Dakota, but now they know him at last. The young men have forgotten their fear. Even now they are riding to take the Pawnee women and children as their slaves. They are riding with scalps at their belts and with many rifles, and, when they come home, fifty thousand Pawnee horses shall run before them."

He looked at me and frowned. "I have only to stretch out my hand," he said. "Black Bear was cunning. He made men of the Sioux. I shall turn them into children again."

If I was to die, there was no reason why I should not sting the heart of this villain if I could. I said, smiling: "The claws of Bald Eagle are blunt and dull. The Sioux have seen the Great Spirit is not fighting on his side. They have made him run away like a whipped boy."

He stared at me savagely for a moment. Then he said: "Black Bear is young. He does not know that great things grow from small beginnings. One small cloud is the beginning of the storm. When Black Bear is dead, there are left to the Sioux only fools. They will forget his lessons. It is for that reason that he must die. Is he ready?"

I closed my eyes, and nodded, and then looked up at him, still smiling. "Luck and the head of your horse saved you," I said. "It is your turn, Bald Eagle."

"Luck is the wise man's friend. As for my horse . . . White Smoke will content me."

"You can never ride him," I said, looking sadly at the great stallion. "He will throw you and tear you to pieces, as the buffalo wolf tears the calf."

"If I do not ride him today, I may ride him tomorrow. And after tomorrow there are many tens of days. He shall come to know me, little by little. As the Pawnees came to know me . . . and as they will come to know me again. Great things grow from small." He added sharply, rising to his feet, "What word shall Bald Eagle take from the dead lips of Black Bear to the Sioux so that they may pierce their flesh and weep for him?"

I saw in that moment no face in all the world except the blue eyes of Mary Kearney. And what would a message from me mean to her? "I have no message, except to one who lives in a place that I do not know, but he will hear of my death in time. And when he hears, he will come for Bald Eagle."

The chief smiled. "It is well," he said. "I

shall welcome Rising Sun, as I have welcomed you, Black Bear."

I smiled in turn. "It is not Rising Sun," I said. "Though even he may take the trail to find you. But the man of whom I speak is such a one that, if Bald Eagle were to see his face, he would be filled with fear. He would become a woman. He would hide in the grass like an antelope."

The chief lifted his lion-like head. "This is well," he said. "I have lived a man's life and seen men, but only one worthy of the name . . . and that is Black Bear. Therefore, I am glad there is another to meet. Is his skin red, my young brother?"

"My father is white as I am white. I have hunted for him, and I have not found him. But somewhere between the East and West he lives on the prairies. Of that I am sure. And in some way he shall learn of my death, and then Bald Eagle shall die. Let every day now be a happy day, Bald Eagle, for it may be your last! He is coming. He shall take you in his hand and break you as I break this stalk of dead grass."

At this he strode to me and leaned. I felt the blow was coming and made my glance steel to meet his eye. He put his great hard hand beneath my chin and raised my face. The words he spoke were the purest English.

"Have you a father, boy?" he asked.

"I have."

"Tell me his name," he commanded.

"I shall tell you," I said, "so that you may know when he is coming. For when he comes, ten thousand Pawnees and the speed of White Smoke cannot save you from him. His name is Dorset."

I felt the grip of his great hand grow sterner while he scowled down into my face. As I watched his face and as I remembered his last words, I was now finally convinced that my first suspicion had been right. This man was white.

He released me and stepped back. "Are you that man's son?"

"Yes. In the name of God, Bald Eagle, do you know him? Then, when he faces you, tell him before you die that his son. . . ."

He raised his hand to silence me. "That man," he said, "is dead!" And he spoke with a certain solemnity that made me feel this was the truth, indeed. It seemed to me then it was time for me to die in turn since he was gone before me, and so the last Dorset should pass from the face of the world.

I simply said: "I am also ready to die."

"Young man," he said, "you are safe from my hand. I have killed the father. I cannot also kill the son."

"If I live, I shall find you. And, when I find you the second time, you will die. If you love life, man, put an end to me while you can."

"I do not love life," he said. "If I meet you again, I shall crush you again, as I have crushed you today. But, as for your father, boy, he was unworthy to live."

"That is a lie and a black one!" I cried.

He asked me with a sort of wonder: "Did you love him? A murderer?"

"I know you now," I said. "You are one of the Connells, and you have followed him from Virginia like a ferret. You followed him, found him, and shot him in the back, because no one Connell ever dared to meet him face to face. Murderer? You know, as I know, that he fought with six men fairly and killed three in open fight. Is that murder? No, by the heavens, and I love him three times more for the three men he killed."

It seemed to me that his breast rose high and fell as he heard me say it. He turned sharply away and walked up and down for a moment. Then he came back to me and stood, scowling down upon me.

"You know his life, then?" he said.

"I know that he broke from prison and came West."

"Do you know the things that he has done since he left prison? Boy, boy, I tell you that his hands were redder with blood than mine."

"They drove him like a hunted wolf. If he turned on them, it was his nature and his right."

He shook his head.

"You damnable hypocrite!" I shouted at him. "You with your Pawnee throat-cutters to talk of murder . . . you with your white skin under that cursed painted face!"

He merely smiled down at me in ineffable contempt.

I cried at him: "I tell you, he was worthy of coming back among men and living as honestly and as freely as any man who ever drew breath!"

He shook his head again, talking down to me from a sort of calm height. "His own crimes drove him out," he said.

Then he turned his back upon me and set about kindling a small fire. I tried to draw him out. I begged him to tell me when and where my father had died. I begged him to tell me how the death fight came to be. I entreated him for his name. But, though I raved at him, cursed him, and swore to have his blood if I lived, he answered not a word until the brush was gathered and the fire rose high. Then he came and stood behind me where I sat, bound and helpless on the ground.

I felt the shadow of his raised hand behind me, and I hardened myself to meet the final blow. But instead of the death stroke, I felt his voice, deep, and strong — and now that his painted face was turned away from me, it seemed to me that there was a familiar sound in it, something I had heard before, as if in a dream.

"Child," he said, "go back among your own people. Be one among them. Your father is dead. If there was good in him, I tell you this from my heart . . . I should have known it, because I knew him as no other could have known him. But he was black, black! He deserved to die. And I have killed him. You will never know how he died, except that it was for his sins. You will never know where he fell, except that his bones are on the prairie. As for me, you will never see my face again."

I heard him through a daze for, as the deep, powerful voice swelled around me, there was such a note of agony in it that it went to my heart and opened the shut doors of my brain to the truth. Yet, what I saw was so blinding and great a light that I was choked by it. I was mute while I saw him turn away westward over the prairie into the dusk of the day, for the sun had set some time before. I saw him go, his huge shoulders swinging with his stride, until he became a dwindling form.

Then my voice came back to me. I shouted: "Come back! For the sake of God and my sake, Father, come back!" He turned as though a bullet had struck him, and I cried: "We will go together, if we must. But not you alone."

At that I saw him throw out his arms toward me, but it seemed as though the gathering darkness behind him had a power that drew him irresistibly away. He turned, rushed down a dip in the prairie, and was lost to me.

In a frenzy I worked my way to the fire. The flames burned the wrists I held into them as they burned the ropes that bound them until at last, after a long agony, the strands parted with a snap.

White Smoke had drawn near me and was touching my shoulder with an inquisitive muzzle. With the smoke of my own burned flesh thick in my nostrils I turned to him and snatched a revolver from the saddle holster and with it blew in two the rope that fastened my feet. Then I was in the saddle and plunging through the night after him.

Chapter Thirty

BACK AMONG THE SIOUX

I rode like a madman, bending low from the saddle, searching the plains with my eyes. In five minutes I reached a river whose smooth surface was speckled with the silver of the stars. Up the bank I raced, then turned, and fled down it. On the farther side were low, jumbled rocks in which he could hide from me, if he wished, or where his trail would disappear. I swam White Smoke across the stream, and all that night I kept the horse wandering, to and fro. In the dawn I saw a saddled and bridled horse, feeding on the prairie not far from the stretch of rocks, a refugee from the battlefield. My heart sank, for perhaps my father had found another and ridden west upon its back.

I cut for his trail. There were tracks of other horses — yes, and some of them led westward. Which should I follow? I took them one by one that day, and the next, and the next, following each until it ended by swerving east again, a direction in which I was sure he would not go. At last I found one that went west, indeed, and that I followed with a heart hot with hope — except that priceless days had now passed.

It ended, at last, in a herd of wild horses. Still I would not surrender. Those bitter long weeks that followed were an endless torment, a ceaseless agony, until finally I knew that I was beaten. Perhaps he had chosen death in the river, for all I knew. I felt that his ways could never be fathomed by me. So I turned back wearily to find the Sioux.

I hardly cared if I found them or not. A dulled sense of duty drove me on. There was Zintcallasappa. I must see her. After that, I hoped to turn my back on the prairies and never see them again. That was the first bitterness. As I rode back along the endless gray sea of the plains, I grew calmer, wiser. He who had gone to his death in the river, or to another life in the Western lands beyond it, knew better than I what was fitting in a man. No matter how my heart might ache for him, perhaps he was right. If he returned to live among his fellows, the law might find him out and damn the end of his days. He had made himself a war chief in one wild tribe; perhaps, if he lived, he would be a war chief again. And if we love the beauty of a hawk on the wing, should we, therefore, try to capture it and imprison it in a close cage?

I was in that humor when I found the tribe of Standing Bear at last. But they were now in the bosom of their nation. Two great bands under famous chiefs, hearing of the end of Bald Eagle, had joined Standing Bear's men to participate in the celebrations. The feasting and the firewater filled the day with sleep and the night with hideous riot.

They greeted me like the God-sent deliverer of their race. Had there been a less deep melancholy resting on me, I should have been a happy man, indeed. But, as it was, I hated their noise. The entire lot of them, drunk and sober, lined the way with yelling as they led me to a great teepee and made me look inside. It was stacked with rifles, ammunition, meat, with furs and beadwork by the hundred weight. Here was more Indian wealth than I had ever seen before at a stroke of the eye. It was all mine. It was my share of the loot they had swept in during the raid of the Pawnee village that had followed, as a most natural course of events, the destruction of Bald Eagle's chosen men. But this was only a part. Hundreds of the best horses were mine. And, if I were not contented with what I had, I should have more — as much more as I could ask and they could give. This was told me by Standing Bear while Three Buck Elk stood by, grinning and nodding like a happy child, and Sitting Wolf watched me with a trembling delight.

I had to make them a speech, of course. I told them that I was happy to have led them into success, that fortune had helped me, that Sitting Wolf had really delivered the decisive blow, but now I was going back to my own people. I had spent my last day among them. As for this heap of wealth, it should go to Zintcallasappa.

Sitting Wolf touched my arm almost timidly. "Brother," he said in the deep silence that followed this announcement, "Zintcallasappa has fallen asleep, and she will waken no more."

I remembered her thin face, her great dark eyes when I last saw her, and a new stab of sorrow reached my heart. It is strange, these things that unnerve us. I had borne the loss of my father — with an aching heart, God knows — but without a trace of unmanliness. This second and smaller blow brought tears to my eyes. I pressed my hand across them. The salt tears worked a way through.

Sitting Wolf cast his blanket over my head and led me away through that host of warriors, all silent with shame because so famous a warrior should have proved such a woman at the end. He led me to his own teepee, for since the battle he had led an independent life, had been voted a brave, and had been made worthy of a brave's privileges by the entire tribe. There he sat down beside me, with his head turned a little away lest he should see my shameful grief. If there had been any working of pride in me, I suppose I should have controlled myself well enough. But there was no pride left in me. I was broken completely.

The sixteen-year-old warrior laid a hand on my arm. He said with a voice as gentle as a woman's: "Dear brother, if the Dakotas wonder when they see Black Bear weep, I, Sitting Wolf, do not wonder. I understand, and my heart is sad. But all the Sioux are stricken with grief, for they have heard Black Bear say that he is turning back to his own people. Now I see the shadow of my father and my uncle in front of my teepee, and I know what they have come to say. Shall they enter, my brother?"

I made shift to dry my eyes, damning my weakness heartily. Then I motioned to Sitting Wolf, and he opened the flap of the teepee. In strode the two chiefs, wrapped formally in their blankets, staring at me with a sort of fear, as though they could not understand the sickness that had taken hold upon me. Standing Bear was the first to break the silence.

"Friend," he said, "the Dakotas have heard Black Bear speak, and they have seen that he is angry. Therefore, they are sad. But they know why he is unhappy. Twice he has saved my brother's son from death, and at last he has raised his paw and struck out of the air the great Bald Eagle who slew us like little lambs in the coming of spring. He has done all this, and last of all he has ridden alone onto the prairie. No man could follow him. The wind stopped and watched him dart across the prairie faster than an arrow, like a bullet that never grows weary. At last he found Bald Eagle. Three great warriors were with that mighty chief. They turned back, one by one, to stop Black Bear, and each fell and was left to make a scalp for the Dakotas and a prey for the wolves."

He made a little pause here. The rascals had trailed me to the spot where I had disappeared across the river. So they had seen the dead Pawnees whom I had met. Standing Bear went on.

"Bald Eagle flew fast, but faster flew Black Bear. At last Bald Eagle turned. First they fought with rifles, and the bullets turned aside, fearing to strike such mighty chiefs. They stood closer and fought with their revolvers that speak many times, but still the bullets dared not strike. They leaped upon one another with their knives, but the steel would not bite. And then they closed on one another. Dreadful was the grip of Bald Eagle. Where his talons held the arms of Black Bear, the skin and the flesh were torn away."

He pointed in proof to the big, ugly red fire scars upon my wrists. Three Buck Elk could not prevent a shudder of wonder and of admiration, but the orator went on: "Though Bald Eagle was mighty, still mightier was Black Bear, for he fought for the glory of the Dakotas. He took Bald Eagle by the throat. He strangled the wicked chief. He carried him to the smooth-sliding black river and gave his body to the water.

"Then Black Bear lay for a long time in the hills, resting, weak and sick, for his wounds were great . . . very great. But at last he was healed, and he came back to the Dakotas. He found them singing and drinking and feasting. The wealth of the Pawnees was their wealth. They had all that the heart could wish, and each brave was rich. But they took Black Bear to a single little teepee and told him that what was in it was his. Yet he had given them everything that gladdened their hearts. His own heart was broken, and he went to the teepee of his brother, Sitting Wolf, and he covered his head, saying that the Sioux are dogs and the sons of dogs."

Here I interrupted. I wanted to tell him that I had not beaten Bald Eagle, but I knew that there was no use in saying such a thing. I would have to give proofs, and they already were sure of their knowledge, for they were aware that he was not among the Pawnees any longer. I could not speak of that subject, however, it made me too sick at heart. I told Standing Bear that they had given me more than my heart could have asked. But I must go back to my own kind. I wished to take with me the son of Zintcallasappa and one old squaw to take care of the child. Also, I would take with me the wealth the Dakotas had awarded me, not for my own sake so much as the sake of the child of Rising Sun.

It was a bitter stroke to both of the chiefs. I had brought them prosperity before, and they wanted more of it. They pointed out to me that we had barely made a beginning — that there were many, many more Pawnees — all villains, all horse thieves. When we had wiped out the Pawnees, there were other great tribes worthy of our wars. We would become sole lords of the prairies. How very little he tempted me. I simply shook my head and asked that the boy be brought to me. Sitting Wolf made a sign to them, and they ceased all persuasion at once.

The boy was brought and an old squaw with him who was to be his nurse and declared that she would gladly go with Black Bear and be a mother to the orphan. I hardly had a word for her; my eyes were so entirely filled with the face of the boy. I have said that he had blue eyes and golden hair. There was white blood in his mother, and in the boy all the Indian traces disappeared except, perhaps, that his skin was a trifle dark for such brilliant hair and eyes. In a word, he was the bright image of what Chuck Morris himself must have been at that age. He was a gay little mite, already toddling around, falling down every step or two, and then pulling himself up again. I took him on my knee and made a silent vow that if Morris disowned him — and how could he help doing that if he wished to marry Mary Kearney? — I myself should be a father to him.

Chapter Thirty-One

THE HEIR OF RISING SUN

The next morning the preparations were made quickly. A hundred willing hands packed my belongings which doubled or trebled in amount before the packing was ended, for I think that every woman, child, and man in the tribe made some sort of a donation when it was known that I was fixed in my intention to leave them. Then a number of young braves volunteered to help me drive the herd of horses toward the fort. An old, abandoned trader's wagon was repaired for the use of the squaw and the boy. Then we started out.

The whole tribe came out and accompanied us for a few miles. Then they said farewell. Sitting Wolf was very much broken up. At the last moment he wanted to accompany me, but I told him that we were parting for the moment only, and that he and I would see much of one another from time to time. If it had not been for this promise, the whole lot of them would have insisted on all sorts of formal ceremonies before they let me go. By noon the last of them had disappeared across the horizon, and my caravan hurried on toward the fort. We were twenty-five days in reaching it, the last five days through a very steady fall of snow, so that we were glad enough when, one evening, we made out the dim lights of the fort in front of us. We camped in the snow that night. The next morning I pitched my camp on the edge of the scattered town. The Indians who had accompanied me started home, each with a man-size present under his belt. Before I went to find Chuck Morris, first of all I visited the store and bought a good suit of clothes, from boots to hat, a complete equipment. I purchased a new saddle for White Smoke. I visited a barber and had my long, shaggy hair cut properly short for the first time in many years. When I looked at my new self in the mirror, the wild man of the prairies had disappeared. In his place was a sober-looking young man with a touch of gray at his temples. In this fashion I went to Chuck.

It was as easy to find him at Fort Kempton as it was to find a full moon in a clear sky. Everyone knew him. He was more important there than the commandant of the fort himself. In the few months since I last saw him, his little storeroom had grown into a big emporium. He conducted a double business. On the one hand, he supplied the traders who sent long caravans over the prairies. On the other hand, he traded directly with the Indians who chose to come into the fort itself. I was told that he was busy when I asked to see him. He was talking important business; he could not be disturbed. I wrote down my name and told the clerk to take it in.

"He'll cut my head off," said the boy.

"I'll put it back on again, then," I said and grinned at him so confidently that he carried the bit of paper into the office.

Morris came lunging out at once, a brand new Morris. His trousers were so fashionably tight that one could see the big double bulge of the thigh muscles in front of his leg. His boots shone like polished ebony. His coat was like a glove upon his back, and his throat was wrapped in a snowy stock. Altogether, he might have stood for the portrait of a duke. But, though I was quite overawed, he was as hearty as ever. He took me into his office, got rid of two weather-bitten traders in a word or two, and sat me down for a talk. I could hardly hear him at first, I was too busy staring at the thick, rich carpeting on the floor, the shining desk, and the numerous pictures on the wall.

"Good Lord, Chuck," I broke out. "This cost a fortune!"

"It did," he admitted, "but I like it. Besides, it's a good investment. I found that I could put my prices up after I had a room like this. It looks like success . . . it *is* success . . . and the traders are impressed. That's what counts. Not what a man is, but what he seems to be. That's business. We'll talk about that afterward. Thank the Lord you've come back to me. And I see by your clothes that you've come to stay."

"I'm no longer a Sioux," I admitted.

"We'll talk about your business future in a moment. First I want to know the truth of all these stories that have been rolling into the fort. The colonel was about to take out an expedition against those thieving Pawnees when he heard a great war chief had sprung up among the Sioux and smashed the cream of the Pawnees to smithereens and killed the great Bald Eagle himself. The name of that chief, as we have heard it, is Black Bear. Lew, the game went through, then? You *did* beat them?"

I told him the whole story in ten seconds. I simply said: "Bald Eagle turned out to be my father. I tried to get him to come back to civilization with me or let me go on with him. He did neither. He simply disappeared.

And that's part of the reason I'm here."

He was always quick to respond to another man's sorrow. I saw the tears spring up in his eyes. He even had to get up and walk about the room for a moment. Then he put a hand on my shoulder and said: "Old fellow, all I can do is to try to help you forget. Now the next thing is to know the other reason that brought you here."

No matter how cruel he had been to her, it was hard to face him with the truth. I managed to say: "Chuck, I brought your boy in with me."

He turned the gray of ashes. "Zintcallasappa is dead?" he blurted out at me.

"She is dead."

"May heaven forgive me," he said.

"Amen," I said with such solemnity that he started.

"After all," said Chuck, "what else could I do? I couldn't be an Indian the rest of my life. I . . . I took care of her after I left."

I made no effort to answer him. It was his business, not mine, and I have never had any sympathy with people who fight the battles that ought to be left to the conscience of other men. Morris began to frown.

"And I'll handle the boy, too," he said.

Here I broke in with: "If you want the boy, take him. If you don't want him around

. . . I'll be glad to have him."

The frown left him. He looked at me with the happiest smile in the world.

"Would you do that, Lew?"

"Gladly."

"If I had him . . . even in the background . . . there would have to be explanations. And. . . ."

"Your wife might not care to know about it?" I asked, looking fixedly at him.

He shook his head. "I haven't married her yet," he said. "And, between you and me, if the truth about this leaked out, I'd be ruined with them. They're an old New England family. Proud as Satan. Well, you've seen Kearney, and you ought to know. He hasn't stopped talking about his last meeting with you. He says you took hold of him as a man might take hold of a child. He's a rare good old fellow, under that high-handed manner of his, and he swears by you. I told him a few things that were not against you, of course. But this Pawnee war of yours has been the finishing touch. He says you're a man in a million.

" 'But his manners, Father,' Mary says and turns up her pretty nose. God bless her.

" 'Manners be damned,' says John Kearney. 'A hero doesn't have to have manners.'

"He will treat you like a son when you meet him again, Lew. As a matter of fact, what made him like me was because I beat him in a business deal. He despises the weak . . . that's all. But now about the boy . . . Lew, you will be my savior if you can manage to get him out of my way. One hint, one whisper about such a thing in my past, would be the end of me with Mary. The absolute end. You see, I'm none too strong with her. She likes me. With her father egging her on to the match, she's become engaged to me. But she keeps putting off the wedding date most damnably. I'm constantly worried for fear something may happen. Every day I have to handle her with gloves."

I said to him slowly: "Why, Chuck, if she doesn't really love you, of course you don't want to marry her."

"Don't want to marry her?" he cried. "Are you mad? But you've only had a glimpse of her. Oh, I tell you that she's rare. Marry her. I'd steal her with a band of Indians, if I thought that there were no other way. I'd do ten murders, if I thought it would help me to get her."

He did not say this in a rage of emotion but in a cold and settled way that sent a chill through my blood, because I knew that he had not overstated things a whit.

He went on: "Now the very first thing, dear old man, is to get the youngster out of the way. Don't look at me as if I were a ghost. I mean . . . take the boy away. I'll supply all the money, of course. We'll take him East, say, and put him in some school. He'll be supported like a prince. But I'll have to trust to you to arrange matters."

I nodded.

"When can you start?"

"At once, I suppose."

"Will you do it?"

"Yes."

"God bless you, Lew. When you told me that you had brought the boy to the fort, you turned me to ice. Because something was apt to leak out. You can say that it's the son of a trader who was murdered by the Indians. Say anything. But start soon . . . soon! Go anywhere you want with him. Place him well. Send me the bill. No, take cash enough with you . . . here."

He tore open a safe that stood in the corner of his office and thrust two heavy bags of gold into my hands.

"You'll want to see him, I suppose?" I asked.

"See him! Damnation, man, why should I want to see him? And be connected with

338

him through gossip in that way? No, no, no! I wish him all the happiness in the world, and I hope that I never lay eyes on him again."

It was rather hard talk, no matter how I tried to look at it. I stood up, very thoughtful, and Chuck followed me to the door. He had his hand on my shoulder all the way, muttering, "You'll be back in a month, at the most. Leave everything with me. I'll sell your horses and the rest of your stuff for twice what you could get for it. I'll have it all cleaned up for you. In the meantime don't let old Kearney see you. He's sure to try it when he knows you've come. Don't let him see you, and don't let him see the boy. Lew, if you love me, get that boy out of the fort within the hour. Ride White Smoke to death. Every minute is precious. Now, hurry, hurry."

I hurried, of course. I did not even say good bye but simply waved to him, because I was hot with anger. A man who disowns his past is to me a man who disowns himself. Yet, I knew that Chuck was not master of himself. Behind all of this emotion there were the blue eyes, there was the smiling mouth of Mary Kearney.

At any rate, I rode straight for my camp, leaped out of the saddle, then strode into the teepee and found, seated upon the floor with the bright-haired little boy between them, Mary Kearney herself and her father at her side.

Chapter Thirty-Two

CHUCK'S ULTIMATUM

It was as pat as any scene in a melodrama. It took me back like a loaded gun, pointed at my head. Here they were, standing up, she with the boy in her arms and the tumbled golden head on her shoulder.

"We came to call on you, sir," said Mr. Kearney. "I owe you an apology, Mister Dorset. My daughter owes you another. By the Lord, I'll make mine first with all my heart. Dorset, I treated you like a dog. I want your pardon and your hand."

"Sir," I said, "I have no unkind memory, but I thank you." And we shook hands.

"Now, Mary," commanded her father.

She was a little flushed. Her eyes were a little wide, but she cried back at him: "You don't have to command me, Dad. I'm here because I want to be here, Mister Dorset, because of the atrocious things I've said before you. Of course, William has told us a great deal about you . . . and the beautiful things you've meant to one another . . . and I trust that you'll forgive me, Mister Dorset."

It was only by an effort of the mind that I made out that *William* referred to Chuck Morris.

I said: "I'm the happiest man in the world that Chuck has made my peace with you."

"Chuck? Not a bit of it," broke out Kearney. "Tush, man, we know everything. We have heard of what Black Bear has done. Well, well!" He seemed as happy as a child because he had identified me. "We know it all . . . we know it all," he went on. "A trapper came in last week and told us that the Pawnees swear you are not a man but a devil, and that they will never fight with you again because it has been proved that bullets will not pierce you and that steel will not harm you. But is this your boy, Dorset?"

"No," I said. "It is the son of a friend of mine." I stammered a little. "The son of a trader . . . killed by Indians."

"How terrible," murmured the girl, but her keen eyes rested upon me for a cold instant, and I knew that she had detected the presence of a lie. She began to stiffen a little as she put down the youngster hastily. "We will have to go, Father," she said.

"Not at all. Not at all," said John Kearney. "Not until you have promised to come to my house. . . ."

342

"I am leaving within an hour," was my reply.

"What? What? Why, man, I have been promising myself that I should hear the wildest story of Indian fighting that ever. . . ."

Here he was interrupted by a startled cry from Mary as she stepped out of the teepee. I sprang after her and found that the cause of her fright was two stalwart Dakotas with Sitting Wolf standing before them. Their impassive faces lighted when they saw me.

"They are Sioux . . . they are my friends," I hastened to explain to Mary Kearney. "Is there trouble, Sitting Wolf?"

He had learned to speak excellent English, though he simply translated his Siouan dialect into the nearest English words.

He said: "Oh, my brother, Black Bear, there is no trouble except sadness among my people since you have left us. You departed in haste and left behind you . . . this. We followed to bring it."

With that he held out to me the first Colt I had ever owned — the old gift of Chris Hudson that I had prized so much. In my haste I had left the gun behind me. I was as glad to see it as I would have been to see a friend's face.

"Brother," I said, speaking the Indian tongue, because I shrewdly feared what the

Kearneys might overhear if the conversation were in English, "this is more to me than the hand of a dear friend beside me in a fight. This has taken the lives of my enemies. I thank you with all my heart."

Sitting Wolf was as quick as a lightning flash to take a hint. He knew that I wanted the talk to be in Siouan, but the temptation to show off his English before strangers was too great for him. He took a little suit made of the softest deerskin and handed it to me next.

"And this," he said, "belongs to the child of Rising Sun. We have brought it also that. . . ."

Here he was stopped by a startled cry from Mary Kearney. My own heart had leaped into my throat.

"Dad," she said. "Did you hear?"

I looked at Kearney. He was very pale, very grave. That one word had damned Chuck Morris. For my part, I only wondered that the golden hair of the boy had not made them do some shrewd guessing long before. But, oh, what a consummate dolt I had been to bring the boy near the fort in the first place.

"I heard," snapped out Kearney. "I am not deaf, my dear. Dorset, I think this needs a little explaining."

Where was the tongue, then, that had learned to tell fluent lies even in the presence of so keen a judge as my Uncle Abner? Where was the stony presence of mind I had learned among my Sioux brothers? All was gone. I could only stare like a fool, while the wind came cold against the perspiration on my forehead.

"Damn it, man!" exclaimed Kearney. "It's too horrible! Can you say nothing? Are you dumb? By the eternal, you have been hand in hand with the villain while he was attempting to take my daughter. . . ."

Rage and shame stifled him. He forgot his dignity enough to shake his fist in my face, and that gesture was almost his last on earth. The hand of Sitting Wolf moved just a trifle faster than the paw of a panther when it strikes. I managed to knock up his hand and the knife it gripped, with the scream of the girl, tingling in my ears. The two braves behind Sitting Wolf had been slower, and my shout made them stand back.

John Kearney and his daughter made for their horses and swept away toward the town. I remained behind, a very sick man, indeed.

"What is wrong, brother?" asked Sitting Wolf. "The dog deserved to feel this tooth between his ribs. What is wrong?"

I could only say: "This is a sad day, Sitting

Wolf. You have done me a great harm. You have done a great harm to Rising Sun. Oh, lad, remember what I say to you. Words spoken among white men are dried powder with sparks always near it. Now forget what has happened. Come into the teepee. We must smoke the pipe. We must eat. And you must tell me of the people."

They went gloomily into the tent, and there the squaw hurried about to feed them. They had barely begun to eat, it seemed to me, with Sitting Wolf watching me in a nervous anxiety, when I heard the rush of a horse's hoofs outside and then the voice of Chuck Morris.

By the mere tone of it I knew that Kearney had gone straight to my friend to hear an explanation, gone straight to him while Morris was unprepared with any manner of lie whatever to explain away the child. I hurried out to meet him and found him like a man in a frenzy. He leaped off his horse and came raging at me. He caught me by the shoulders with such a grip that the tips of his fingers bit against the bone, and he groaned: "I warned you, Lew! I warned you! Now you've ruined my life!"

"I couldn't help it," I said. "Listen to me, Chuck. They were in the teepee when I arrived. They. . . ."

"Why did you ever bring the boy to the fort?" he snarled. "What right had you? Did I ask you to do it? Did you have my permission?"

When a man asks such questions as these, he doesn't want an answer. He has established the answer long before in his own mind. I said nothing and waited in the hope that he would grow calmer. But he went about striking his heavy fist against his forehead, saying: "He looked at me as if I had been a leper. He called me a sneaking hypocrite. I tried to make some explanation. He wouldn't listen. He told me that he never wanted me in his door again. But I'll go there in spite of him. I'll hear the last word from the girl, not from that stodgy old fool. If he stands between me and her, I'll wring his neck . . . I'll break him to bits! I've lived this sleepy town life long enough, and now I want action . . . I want action! I'll find something to do."

He was utterly beside himself, and I tried to stop his talk, but he went on savagely, clutching me by the shoulder again: "What is she that they should hide her behind a hedge? Does she know anything worth knowing? Has she done anything in her life that's worth boasting of? Bah! She's only a pretty piece of flesh, and yet they act as though she were carved out of one entire diamond. By heavens, it maddens me, and mad I'll go, in fact, if I don't have her. Lew, will you help me to her? Will you help me, Lew?"

"Do you want any man's help?" I asked him.

"No," said Morris with a huge oath. "I'm enough by myself. I'll have her . . . or no other man shall have her. So be it."

With that, he flung away and left me in a deadly fear. Not a fear of him or for myself, but a terror lest he should actually lay hands on Mary Kearney and force her to marry him. He was capable of it. I could see that clearly enough, and, looking back through his life, I could see also that he had never been able to deny to himself anything that he really wanted. Only to me he had been the soul of honor and of generosity. For the rest of the world he had a use only insofar as it was a help to Chuck Morris.

When I went back into the teepee, I found that the three Indians had stopped eating and sat with their blankets folded around them, stiff as statues. The face of Sitting Wolf was as stony as the faces of the others. I tried to urge them to eat and be merry, but Sitting Wolf, as the spokesman, told me that he saw now that he had done me a great harm, indeed, and that he and his friends would leave me. It was quite useless to attempt persuasion, and they stalked off, one behind the other. Their horses galloped away. I was left with the greatest problem of my life.

To leave Kearney unwarned seemed to me the worst crime I could imagine. Still, to warn him was an act of treason to Chuck. I sat with that problem spinning through my mind for an hour. At last I saw the first honorable step before me. I went back to Chuck and found him, lying in his room at the back of the big store, face downward on his bed, with his great hands sunk in the pillow as though they were buried in a man's throat. He did not stir when he heard me come in. I stood over him in a yellow shaft of sunshine and said: "Chuck, have you changed your mind?"

"About what?" he groaned.

"About the girl. Have you changed your mind about forcing yourself on her?"

He thrust himself erect and glared at me. "I have not," he said. "I intend to see her again."

"You're wrong. You're mightily wrong, Chuck. It will make trouble if you start that sort of work. If you weren't half insane just now, you'd never think of such a thing.

They'll be warned, and they'll be ready to defend her."

"Who'll warn them?" he asked.

"I shall."

An old rifle hung on the wall beside him. His hand darted out to it instinctively, and then relaxed its grip again.

"Why, Lew, I haven't heard you say that. I haven't heard you say that you'd turn against me."

"Not against you, heaven knows. But not *for* you, if you try to do this thing."

He ran his hand over his forehead, throwing his hair into the wildest confusion. "Lew," he groaned, "don't tell me that you're in love with her, too?"

"You'll hate me if I confess it, but I *have* to confess it. I love her."

"Don't say it!" cried Chuck Morris, and, as I remember his face now, I think there was more horror on it than there was anger. "Because if you're crooked, there's no honest men in this cursed world."

"I'm coming to you to tell you the truth," I said sadly. "Chuck, you've missed her. Not that I'll ever have her. Heaven knows she's far beyond any wild hope of mine. But you've missed her. And if you try to steal her away. . . ."

"Wait," broke in Chuck. "If you talk like

that, I *shall* go mad . . . murderous mad. I want to go over this thing with you, bit by bit, as if we were back in school, studying a lesson. If I'm wrong in anything, stop me and tell me so. Lew, when I met you, we fought. I beat you fairly and squarely."

"Yes."

"But, when I saw what a wild young tiger you were, my heart went out to you. I'll never forget how you came staggering in at me, when your face was just a blur of blood, not knowing where you hit, but still fighting. I swore, even while I was fighting you, I'd beat you that day and make you my friend afterward. While I lay on my back, getting over that fight, I turned the same idea in my mind a hundred times. A good friend is worth millions. I decided to make you my friend. After that, we lived together for years. We were never apart. I taught you what I knew of the prairies. I gave you a horse. I gave you everything that I had to give . . . freely. I would have laid down my life for you."

"I know it," I said.

"At this moment, ask whatever you can dream of, and I would do it for you. I would put my last dollar in your pocket. Do you doubt that?"

"No."

"If ten men came through that door to

take your life, I'd stand before you. Do you doubt that?"

"Heaven knows it's true."

"But, if you turn against me in this thing, Lew, the love I have for you will turn to the blackest hate that any man ever felt. Mark that. I'm a hard man, Lew. I'm determined to get out of my life what I can. But I've made one exception. I've kept you apart. I've never had a thought about you that wouldn't have been worthy of your brother. I've never envied you, never scorned you, never used you. But, if you strike at me now, God help me to grind the life out of your heart. Now, when I need a friend and you turn on me, I call you a hypocrite, a sneaking traitor, worse than a dog. Do you hear me? Do you know that I mean it?"

I started to speak, but he stopped me.

"Don't answer me now," he commanded. "Go by yourself and think of what I've said. Oh, you may think that you love her. But what do you love? Her pretty face? That will change. She'll be wrinkled in another ten years or so. The blossom will leave her. Will she be worth giving up what you'll give up in me? Go away and think it over."

And he turned his back on me and went to the window where he leaned out, breathing heavily.

Chapter Thirty-Three

BLACK BEAR TALKS

I knew that thinking and time for thought would not change me, but I wanted to be alone to weigh in my mind all the dangers in the thing that was before me. I knew that he was not shamming. All that he had said had been spoken very seriously. He would do what he threatened, and, if I turned against him, he would put a bullet in me with as little compunction as any Dakota ever showed when he held a Pawnee at his mercy.

It was not the physical fear that moved me most. It was the fear of losing that friendship which now, it seemed to me, was all that I owned of any value in the world. I had closed the Indian chapter of my life. I had left my father dead or living, somewhere lost upon the prairies. And now, as I came to meet the conditions of a new life, I needed more help from big Chuck Morris than I had needed even when I first went onto the prairies.

I went to the river's edge and sent White Smoke slowly through the woods. Most of the trees were naked. There was no touch of color, but here and there were a few patches of brown leaves, trembling miserably in the wind. All the ground was thick with crusted snow. I rode until the voices from the fort died away, only some occasional shouting coming, small and thin, out of the distance. Never in my life have more melancholy thoughts passed through my mind.

I had gone some distance, following the winding of the river's bank, watching vaguely the flash of the water in the sun and the shining, metal black of the standing pools nearer to the bank. Then I heard the rapid thudding of hoofs to the rear. I had a tingling premonition, after all, that it might be Chuck Morris come after me to retract some of the stern things he had spoken. For he always rode like that — at a headlong pace. I turned about, and then I saw break into the clearing, where I was, none other than Mary Kearney herself.

When she saw that I had stopped for her, she drew rein so suddenly that her horse slid up on stiffened legs and cast a shining cloud of snow dust into the air. It would have dismounted an ordinary girl, but she rode like a wild Indian — a part and parcel of her horse. She sat the saddle very flushed, with her eyes sparkling at me.

"I was afraid that I'd never overtake you!" she exclaimed. "I thought that White Smoke would be whisking you away like the wind upriver."

Most men, I suppose, have on the tip of their tongue a thousand pleasant little things to say on such occasions. They make a girl perfectly at home and put small bridges from one bit of conversation to the next. But I have never had that talent, and, besides, I was too astonished to use my wits very effectively. She went on at once, as though she had hardly expected an answer from me.

"Of course, I want to talk with you, Mister Dorset. Dad was too excited and too angry. He's still excited when he remembers how near that knife came to his heart. But he's forgotten a good deal of his anger. How have you managed to live happily among such wild wolves as those Dakotas?"

So dexterously had she brought the conversation around to my viewpoint that she started me talking about myself. And I suppose, after all, that those famous conversationalists who held forth in the great French salons were not talkers at all, but simply cunning creatures able to make any man talk freely — about himself and his ideas. Why is it, then, that we are so hungry to speak of ourselves? Why is it that I have written all this tale of my past with such a warmth of happiness, unless we feel, when what is in us is exposed to the eye of the world, that the world will wonder and applaud? It is very foolish. But I was as happy to have Mary Kearney ask me that question, as though she had put a treasure in my hand.

"They are kind people very often," I said.

"To everyone?" she asked me.

"No, of course not. But the son of a chief took a fancy to me. After that they adopted us into the tribe."

"But why did he take a fancy?" she insisted.

"Well," I said, "Indians are like us and form likings as quickly, and for reasons just as obscure."

At this, all at once, she began shaking her head and smiling at me in a quiet way as though she saw straight through me and found within me nothing at least to hate. There was never such kind mockery.

"You are a modest man," she said. "But Mister Morris told me how you saved the life of Sitting Wolf. Was that the beautiful young savage who tried to sink a knife in my father . . . when Dad grew angry with you?"

"You see," I explained to her, "the Indians very often do their thinking with their hands, and an Indian's hand is apt to have a knife in it. But, when one grows accustomed. . . ."

"To being stabbed while one talks?" she finished for me. "But, of course, they were afraid of . . . Black Bear."

She brought out my Indian name with a soft little laugh, as much as to say: The others may fear you, but I not a whit. To this moment I close my eyes and remember how that flutter of music went sadly and sweetly through me.

"You may not answer a single question I wish to know," she said gravely after that. "And if you won't, tell me so. But I've come to ask you to tell me about the mother of the son of William Morris."

I thought then, by the manner in which she uttered his mere name, that he was further from her than if he had been the man in the moon. I turned her question slowly through my mind. To answer it might seem a betrayal of Morris. And yet, now that they knew the first facts, they had only to ask among some of the Sioux, and they would learn all of the story and learn it in a naked brutality that would be far worse than the truth as I could tell it.

I said at last: "I am Chuck's friend, and he has been more to me than any man in the world. We were together a good many

357

years. We've bunked together when we didn't know whether or not our scalps would belong to a Cheyenne before the morning came. I've owed him my life, you see."

"And he has owed his to you," she exclaimed. "He has confessed that. That evens the score, I imagine."

I shook my head. "There's no way to repay some things."

At this she stared a little in a high-headed way that reminded me of her father's haughtiness, but she changed almost at once and was smiling at me as she had done before. I could almost have prayed her not to smile in that way. There was something as hard and as strong as ice in me — I suppose I may call it my manhood. When she smiled, I felt that strength melting away under her shining eyes, and a great yearning, that was half fierce and half sad, came over me. Ah, but she was a lovely thing on that day, like a bright bit of spring flowers come among those naked brown trees.

"What an honest man you are," she said. "I felt it before, and I know it now. He is your friend. I can't ask you to talk against him."

"The truth has to come out. And, if I am his friend, I should like to be . . . your friend also."

It was quite possible to say such a thing in the most genuine manner, just casually enough to make it seem no more than a rather intimate tribute. But as I have said before, I had no conversational training and no tact. I wanted to talk to her not in English, but in the Sioux tongue with all its strength and all its wildness. Because its strangeness would have made it possible for me to say things that I could not put into bald English, with the matter-of-fact sun of common sense shining on it. And now I brought out this speech to her as if it were a thunderbolt, escaping my lips. It left me trembling. It left me hot and crimson, too, as I realized that I was making an ass of myself. God bless her for the manner in which she took it. If she stiffened a little at the first, and if she lifted her head in her father's overbearing way, she abandoned that attitude at once. She merely looked down to the ground, and I felt that she was casting about for some withering phrase to blast my forwardness.

"I wish I had not said that," I broke out.

Up flashed her eyes at that, and, to my bewilderment, there was no more danger in them than a light of laughter.

"Oh, Black Bear," she said, "you may be a great warrior, but you are a great boy also.

I'm glad you said it . . . because I *want* you to be my friend. And you will be, if you tell me all that lies behind that poor little bright-haired boy in your teepee. After all, haven't I a right to know?"

I could not help saying: "Yes." Then I told her the story. "You see," I began, "Chuck was always so big and so strong, so quick with his hands and so quick with his brains, that other boys had no chance with him. When he grew up, other men had no chance with him. He got into the habit of doing what he wanted to do, because he was free, and no one could stop him. He still was like that when he joined the Sioux with me. After we had been with them a while, Standing Bear wanted us to take squaws."

"How horrible," she said.

"It isn't like marriage exactly," I tried to explain. "An Indian divorce comes very easily. A chief may have half a dozen wives, you know. A squaw . . . is just property, perhaps . . . like a horse."

"Ah?" she said with a cold little lift to her voice.

"We had been years with them. We thought we might spend more years with them, because I was still hunting for my father."

"Yes, William has told me about that,"

she said, and, oh, her voice slid into my very soul, as gently as the sound of the running river beside us. "And did you never find a trace of him?"

I remembered, and the memory brought the old agony fresh on me.

"Forgive me. I have no right to ask!"

"I want you to know," I insisted. "Because I want you to know me . . . and my father is a part of me, and what he is, I am also . . . partly. He had gone among the Indians because . . . there was a crime behind him."

"What crime?" she asked me.

The word stuck in my throat, and, when it came, it was a hoarse whisper. "Murder," I said and watched the shock of it make her shudder.

She said: "They may have called it murder, but it must have been a fair fight."

"God bless you for thinking that!" I cried. "Yes, it was one man against six. All I knew was that he had gone west. Well, while I was with the Sioux, we met and defeated Bald Eagle, their great chief."

"It was you who did it. I've heard that story."

"I saw him leave the fight when it was hopelessly lost, and I rode after him. . . ."

"And killed his three men, one by one, and then killed Bald Eagle himself!" she cried. "That was a glorious day for you."

"I found Bald Eagle at last. My bullet went through the head of his horse . . . his bullet grazed my scalp and knocked me senseless."

I took off my hat and touched the white scar. She was mightily excited now, letting her horse come on until it was touching noses with White Smoke, for her hands were off the reins and clasped together.

"He tied me with ropes. I woke up and found him sitting beside me. He was waiting for me so that I could see my death come when he was ready. I told him, at last, that if he killed me, he himself would not have long to live, for Will Dorset, my father, would find him and crush him to bits. When I said that, he stood over me and looked down in my face, and I thought he would strike then. But, instead, he built a fire. Then he stood beside me and told me to go back to my own kind, because I should never see my father. He, Bald Eagle, had killed him, and I should never see his face again.

"Then he left me. As he went away, through the dusk, the truth came over me and choked me. At last I called out: 'Father.' "

"Dear God," cried Mary Kearney, "it was he?"

"He turned and threw out his arms to me, but he would not come. He went stumbling off through the evening. I burned my ropes away and rode after him. I hunted for weeks. But I found no trace. He may have drowned himself in the next river. I know that I shall never see his face again."

I could not speak again for a moment, but I looked down, fighting hard as the grief took me by the throat and turned my blood to water. When I could look up again, the tears were running down her face.

"Poor boy," she said. "But you *will* find him."

I shook my head. "I've slipped away from Chuck Morris," I said. "I was saying that he and I expected to be more years among them, and, when the chief urged us to take squaws, it seemed only natural and right to Chuck. He didn't look on it as a sin. It was just something new to do. There was a pretty girl in that tribe with a dash of white blood in her. She was called Blackbird, which is Zintcallasappa in Sioux. Chuck took her. Afterward this child was born. And, after that, Chuck came to the fort and saw you and knew that he could never go back among the Indians."

"And she?" said Mary Kearney.

"It broke her heart. I came back from trailing my father and found that she was dead. I brought the boy in to see what Chuck wanted me to do with him. Perhaps I've made a bad story of it. I want to explain how Chuck was simply headstrong . . . it didn't seem a crime to him. It was only an adventure, you see? And, after he left her, he took care of her well. She lacked nothing. An Indian would have thought he was a fool to be so good to a squaw he no longer wanted."

"But he was not an Indian."

It was a sharp blow. I saw that I had done poor Chuck more harm than I dreamed. "If I could make you see . . . ," I began desperately.

"They wanted you both to take squaws. Did *you* take one?"

"I was younger than Chuck. I couldn't bring myself to it."

What a warmth and what a brightness came up in her face. "I knew that you had not," she said. "Ah, Mister Dorset, I'm glad I've met you, if only to know what a difference there can be between two men who have lived the same lives."

"If I have hurt him," I told her, "I shall never forgive myself. But I wanted to tell you the truth, rather than let you hear some story. . . ."

"Hurt him?" she said coldly. "I tell you, he was dead in my mind the moment I heard the Indian say the name of the father of that poor little boy. And what will become of the child?"

"Of him? Oh, I'll take care of him, of course. For the sake of Zintcallasappa, poor girl."

She said hotly: "If all the rest of his life were given to good work, when he came to the gate of heaven, the face of that Indian girl would stop him and send him back."

She was so close, now, that she could reach out her hand and rest it on my arm.

"But I thank you for everything you've told me. Mostly for what you've told me about yourself. For we *shall* be friends. Will you promise me that?"

What could I do but take her hand and wonder at the tears of very kindness in her eyes and call myself the happiest man who saw the setting of the sun that night?

Chapter Thirty-Four

CHUCK AND LEW — ENEMIES

When she went back, I could not go with her. I wanted to be alone and turn over in my mind again all the strange wonders that had come to me in my talk with Mary Kearney. I felt as though I had drawn a star down out of heaven, and now it was so close that I could almost hope, some day, to hold it in my hand. I let White Smoke wander over the snow until it was red with the sunset. Then I turned back to the town. It was still twilight when I came to the edge of it. There was a great, bald-faced, golden moon, hanging in the east, but the day was still bright enough to shut the moonlight away. Out of the shadows of some trees near the road a horseman came out and hailed me.

"Lew Dorset?"

"I'm Dorset."

He came up to me and held out an envelope.

"Miss Kearney sent me out with this," he said. "She told me that I'd find you on this side of town. I've hunted, but you seemed to have disappeared."

I ripped the contents out hungrily, and this is what I read:

Mr. Dorset:
This is to warn you that you are in great danger, and danger from the man you call your friend, William Morris. I met him on my way to the fort, and, when he talked to me, I told him what I knew. He guessed at once that I had been talking with you, and, when I confessed that I had, he went into a terrible passion and swore that I should never see your face again.

Mr. Dorset, he means murder, if ever a man meant it. When I told him that, if I had ever meant to marry him, the story you told me would have changed my mind, he went literally mad.

If I have broken a friendship which you prize, may God and you forgive me, but on my honor he is not worthy to call himself your friend!

Come to my father's house. There are armed men here. They will protect you, and my father is eager to have you. I am eager, too. If any harm comes to you from this, I shall

never have a happy moment from this to the hour of my death.

In most dreadful anxiety, your friend,

Mary Kearney

It is before me now, this letter time has yellowed and worn the creases until the light shines through them. The ink is pale and brown, but it brings back to me now freshly the wretched sorrow that came over me when I first held it, unfolded, in my hand. For I knew, then, that he would find me, and, when he found me, one of us must die.

Oh, time that has put this wrinkled mask over my face, you have no power to change or mask the soul of a man. Mine turns cold and hot, as it turned cold and hot while I rode on into Fort Kempton, watching the shadows on either side of the way, waiting for the glint of the increasing moonshine on the steel barrel of a gun.

He was not lurking there. I reached my teepee on the farther edge of the town and dismounted from White Smoke. As my foot touched the ground, it slipped on a round pebble and made me stoop suddenly forward. That stooping saved my life, for the gun that barked behind me sent a bullet whistling a scant inch above my head.

It was not Chuck Morris who fired that shot, for the man with whom I roved the prairies, in whose hands my life had lain a thousand times, could never have met any enemy and taken him from behind. It was not Chuck Morris. It was the devil into which he had turned on that day and which has not left him even to this present moment, as I sit here writing. How I dread and hate him for all the evil he has done me and all the evil he has hoped to do.

I had wit enough to keep on, lunging down as I heard the gun. I fell flat upon the ground, but with Hudson's old Colt in my hand, as I fell. Then I whirled over and fired at the shadow that was rushing upon me. I fired and heard him snarl like a wounded tiger. At the same moment a bullet went through my thigh from his flashing revolver. He could have finished me with another shot, but in his madness it was not a killing with his gun that he wanted. He wanted to use his hands. He wanted to feel me die beneath them.

"Traitor and devil!" Morris cried and drove upon me with all his weight.

I could not have risen to meet him, but, as he fell upon me, reaching for my throat, I met him with my hands. The instant they were on him, I knew that I was his master. Yonder lies the iron bar that I bent in my youth. My feeble hands now lift it and wonder over it, for God had given me a strange and marvelous power in those dead days.

I caught him by the wrist, and with the turning of my hand the muscles were bruised against the bone, and the gun dropped to the ground. With that he seemed to know that he was overpowered, for he flung back from me with a shout of fear. His free hand caught up the fallen gun — not by the butt, or that would have been my last second of life, but by the barrel, and he struck the heavy handle against my head. It glanced, cutting the scalp like a knife and loosing a hot flood of blood that poured constantly down during the rest of our battle.

Out of the distance I could hear the squaw in my teepee, screaming for help. But that meant nothing. What can bare-handed men do for one assailed by a tiger?

Before he could strike again, I flung myself close to him and got him in the grip of both arms. I scooped up my own gun and beat it into his face and with three strokes turned all that beauty of his into the hideous mask that men knew afterward and that I, alas, was to see many times more. And he, responding to those crushing blows, screamed with rage like a great panther that feels an arrow in his flank.

I had weakened fast under the double drain of blood. He managed to tear his hands loose and get them at my throat. Both of them I could not budge, but one I did, and, while my head swam and darkness poured through my brain, I took his bulky left arm in one hand and across a crooked elbow and broke it like a rotten stick. Like a bulldog his other hand kept its pressure. I fumbled for it in utter blackness. But my hands were too weak to budge it. I reached for his own throat, found it, and fixed my grip on it as I sank into unconsciousness.

Afterward, as they told me, they had to tear us apart. Each was more than half dead. Each, lying in a half trance, was surely killing the other. What Morris awakened to, I cannot tell. What I wakened to was the soft arms of Mary Kearney about me. The pressure of a bandage was around my head and the loud voice of John Kearney was exclaiming: "If he does *not* live, Doctor, this country west of the Mississippi is too small for you."

Not live, when I had this to live for? By the crooking of one finger she could have called me back from within the very gates of hell. Not live when she was weeping over me, praying over me?

Oh, my dear, pray for me still in that other life that you have inherited. Pray for me still and lean closer out of heaven to read what I write now: That I loved you no more then as you drew me back to life than I love you now.

Here, then, is a proper place to write: The End. Though why books should end with love and marriage, I cannot say, when love and marriage may be only the gate through which man passes to a new and greater life. As death, in turn, shall bear me with the mercy of God to a newer and to a stranger life where my happiness has gone before me. How will that death come upon me? Not in my bed, I think, after the life I have lived. Perhaps some unknown enemy will come upon me. Perhaps the endless malice of Chuck Morris will yet contrive a trap for me. Yes, that is most likely of all.

About the Author

Max Brand is the best-known pen name of Frederick Faust, creator of Dr. Kildare, Destry, and many other fictional characters popular with readers and viewers worldwide. Faust wrote for a variety of audiences in many genres. His enormous output, totaling approximately thirty million words or the equivalent of 530 ordinary books, covered nearly every field: crime, fantasy, historical romance, espionage, Westerns, science fiction, adventure, animal stories, love, war, and fashionable society, big business and big medicine. Eighty motion pictures have been based on his work along with many radio and television programs. For good measure he also published four volumes of poetry. Perhaps no other author has reached more people in more different ways.

Born in Seattle in 1892, orphaned early, Faust grew up in the rural San Joaquin Valley of California. At Berkeley he became a student rebel and one-man literary movement, contributing prodigiously to all campus publications. Denied a degree because of unconventional conduct, he embarked on a series of adventures culminating in New York City where, after a period of near starvation, he received simultaneous recognition as a serious poet and successful author of fiction. Later, he traveled widely, making his home in New York, then in Florence, and finally in Los Angeles.

Once the United States entered the Second World War, Faust abandoned his lucrative writing career and his work as a screenwriter to serve as a war correspondent with the infantry in Italy, despite his fifty-one years and a bad heart. He was killed during a night attack on a hilltop village held by the German army. New books based on magazine serials or unpublished manuscripts or restored versions continue to appear so that, alive or dead, he has averaged a new book every four months for seventy-five years. In the United States alone nine publishers now issue his work. Beyond this, some work by him is newly reprinted every week of every year in one or another format somewhere in the world. Yet, only recently have the full dimensions of this extraordinarily versatile and prolific writer come to be recognized and his stature as a protean literary figure in the 20th Century acknowledged.